UNKINDNESS
OF
CRIMSON
RAVENS

ARYA SLOANE

Table of Contents

Content Warning

This book contains content that might be triggering to some readers, included, but not limited to, mentions of sexual assault (does not happen on the page), murder and death, explicit language, sexual content, alcohol usage, blood play, violence, panic attacks, grief.

Viewer discretion advised. Your mental health matters.

Chapter 1
Nocturnal Animal

Crimson bouquets surrounded my presence, overwhelming my senses on this sorrowful day. Celebrating seemed foolish, if you would've asked me, but no one valued my judgment. Perhaps they didn't lose as much as I did: didn't experience the suffering and grief.

Today was not a celebration day, it was a memorial. At least it was for me.

Seven years should have been enough time to overcome my distress—my disgust—for today's festivity, yet I was still all the same. Disgusted. No matter my feelings, I must play by the rules of our twisted ways. Putting differences aside, I would be a good daughter, a good princess. That was what I'd promised.

"I suppose I needn't remind you to behave?" A familiar voice came from behind me, making the air in the room grow colder as though the winter herself walked through the front door and settled down near my heart.

Masking my discomfort, I slowly turned to face the woman standing in the threshold of my bedchamber. The woman looked like me, yet foreign all the same. Her long face, fair skin, and dark hair were all I saw when looking in the mirror; though her features felt sharper, as if even her appearance had to announce the importance of her presence. "Your Majesty," I bowed.

"I expect your punctuality, Cordelia." The Queen exclaimed, turning on one heel towards the door without sparing me a glance.

If it hadn't been for the restless night I'd had, I would have laughed at the absurdity of this situation. My mother came here to remind me to behave as though I was a child that knew no manners. Ridiculous.

I shook my head in disbelief as I took my seat at the dressing table, preparing for the most uncomfortable evening awaiting.

Mories' studying eyes bored into my skin, yet I ignored it altogether. I did not need her pity. Not today.

Her fingers brushed over the ends of my old braid. "Would you like your hair down for the celeb—"

"No." My heart dropped just at the idea of it. Mories sent me a nod of understanding, reminding me of the horrors I had endured.

No matter Mories' soft touches, the moment my hair fell down my shoulders my muscles tensed, as though my hair grew thorns that punctured my flesh. I fidgeted and shivered, though it did not seem to bother Mories: she kept quiet.

Her dull eyes were full of exhaustion, or maybe it was just her age that made everything about her look weary. Her wrinkled and scarred skin revealed a long life of battle and hard work.

"Thank you," I mumbled, avoiding her gaze.

In complete silence Mories skillfully worked through my long raven hair while I stared at my reflection in the mirror: something I'd tried to avoid doing at all cost in the past month.

My red dress revealed my shoulders, stopping right above the scar that marked my heart. I stared and stared, not recognizing the person I saw: as though in a dream, when meeting a stranger you'd known your whole life.

"You look lovely, dear." Mories tucked the stem of a bright red flower into my braid.

A small smile of reassurance tugged on my lips despite the anxiety and anger deep in my stomach that threatened to sabotage all the promises I'd made.

"It is time," she whispered, squeezing my shoulders. "Everything will be well."

I nodded, heading towards the door, leaving my last moment of peacefulness behind.

My heart banged against my rib cage with every step I took. My stomach turned upside down the closer I got to the reason for my restless sleep.

The ballroom doors at the end of the hall entered my vision moments later. Red flowers made the door look as though it was covered in blood. I supposed that was the intention.

The guards stood at their designated spots adjacent to the entrance, ignoring two small figures leaning on the wooden door.

"It is my turn, Frederick!" Eleanor tugged on her brother's tunic when I reached the door. "Let me see!"

"You two should not be here and you know it." My voice froze my young siblings in place.

"But we want to dance too!" my little sister whined. "Please convince Mother to let us attend."

"Come now, we both know I cannot do that; besides, these balls look far more fun than they truly are." A small smile spread across my face as my fingers brushed along Eleanor's blonde hair. "I'd much rather stay out here with you." I let out a small chuckle, acutely aware of the truth in my words.

"We just want to dance." Frederick sighed.

"Please, Cordelia!" they whined in unison.

"Take them back to their rooms before they find trouble." I whispered to one of the guards before returning my gaze back to my siblings. "I promise we will dance all day tomorrow if you go back to your rooms right this moment."

"You swear?" Frederick narrowed his eyes on me.

"I swear to the Moon." I said, ushering them towards the guard.

My words seemed to convince my brother and sister as they took the guard's hands, dancing down the hall.

Soon enough they would have to learn manners and enter a very boring—proper—Royal life. Just like me and Sandra. A life full of expectations. A life that took your freedom away.

My eyes traveled back towards the ballroom as I waited for my announcement.

The red doors opened before I had a chance to prepare myself; although I was unsure I would ever be ready to face the nightmares that had been haunting me the last month.

The ballroom's stone walls were fully decorated as well. Red flowers represented the blood of our enemies after a deadly battle: celebrating the day our kingdom became free of vampires. I wanted to laugh at the absurdity.

Candles rested on every single table, illuminating the faces of those gathered. All eyes were on me.

My chin rose high as I put on a mask of indifference. The mask I was required to wear when in public as the first in line to the throne. The mask I hated so much for stealing my identity. The mask that couldn't protect me from the horrors of gruesome people.

I had to play a role I did not choose, but on which my reputation and the reputation of our entire family depended. *For the good of the family* as Mother would say.

I put my trembling hands behind my back and headed for the Royal table.

Mother sighed with relief, clearly worried I wouldn't come—as though I actually had a choice. I bowed, greeting the Queen just like etiquette required; my sister sat to her right. Sandra offered me one of her happy smiles unaware of what the night had in store.

I waited for Mother's dismissal before taking a seat beside my sister who wouldn't stop grinning. The hairpin I gifted Sandra for her eighteenth birthday decorated her golden waves. Her hair and deep green eyes reminded me so much of Father.

"I heard the Barrens were coming," she whispered to me. "Perhaps Timothy will ask you to dance."

"Perhaps he will," I replied with more disgust than I intended to show and I scolded myself for not playing my role well already. "Maybe someone will ask you for a dance." I pinched her side.

"Maybe." She grinned, scanning the ballroom.

Using Sandra's distraction, I glanced around before my hands stretched out towards the meat. Covering it with a napkin, I hid it in my sleeve.

"There!" Sandra whispered to me, making me jump in my seat; though she didn't seem to notice my reaction nor did she notice the food I'd stolen. Sandra carefully pointed at a man in red attire. "Hm... He might be a noble from the North, came here to find a bride!" she fantasized. "Me, perhaps."

"Sandra," I laughed, "he is too old and not nearly as handsome." Sometimes it seemed Sandra just wanted to leave no matter the groom. I couldn't say I judged her for it, but Moon forbid she'd end up like me.

How could I ensure her future husband would treat her right? How could I trust another soul to keep my Sandra safe?

"What about that one?" Sandra crooked her head, peeking from behind me. I attempted to turn in that direction, but she quickly stopped me. "Cordelia!" Sandra hissed at me. "You will give us away!" Her adorable reaction made me crack a smile—a genuine one—at her terrified face.

"I will be careful." I promised my sister, turning towards the two men engaged in—what seemed to be—a serious conversation.

"The one on the left," Sandra whispered into my ear.

The man she *chose* was handsome indeed, yet my gaze traveled past him.

In the corner of the ballroom stood a man in a black and gold vest. *Odd*, I thought to myself. Today's dress code was red only. At the end of the day we were celebrating the end of the *Crimson War*. Him dressing like this was at the very least disrespectful.

I studied the man, trying to figure out who he was. Of course I couldn't remember every single member of the court, but him I had never seen—that I knew for a fact.

The stranger held wine in one hand and a pipe in the other. He didn't seem to care about his appearance whatsoever. Arrogant, indeed.

The man looked young, in his twenties perhaps. He had dark brown hair that fell on his face in a perfect mess. His curls barely touched his shoulders. His sharp features contrasted with his smooth bronze skin.

"Well, what do you think?" Sandra leaned in.

"Arrogant."

The stranger smirked. Our gazes locked as he sent me a curt nod.

I'd been openly staring at the man this whole time.

Straightening my back, I tried to mask my embarrassment. How unroyal of me: I'd been scolding a stranger for his outfit when I myself had forgotten any manners. I couldn't just stare at strangers. People would talk.

"Cordelia?" Sandra nudged my shoulder; judging by the tone in her voice, she'd been calling my name for a while.

"He's fine," I finally spoke not even remembering who she had pointed at.

How dared he smirk at me? The audacity behind such a gesture! The arrogance! Was he mocking me? I'm sure he was; that smirk on his face was full of pure amusement.

"Timothy is here," Sandra whispered.

My lungs expanded in an attempt to calm my unresting mind. *I will not show fear.* I told myself, hoping I would act on this promise. Yet it was anger that consumed me.

Don't do anything foolish, Cordelia.

"My lady." Timothy tried to reach for my hand; a disgusting smile decorated his face.

A Royal should never put anyone down. I ignored the screaming voice as I swallowed the lump in my throat.

"It is *Your Highness.*" I raised my chin despite the trembling in my body. "You shall respect my status, *Lord Barren.*" I put emphasis on the last two words in a clear reminder of his own: the only way to truly hurt Timothy was to remind him I was the one with the power here—even if it was not true.

I'd told Mother I would behave for the sake of the family, yet Timothy's presence made it impossible to commit to such a promise. The memory of the pain he'd caused overpowered any common sense. My spilled tears demanded revenge.

A low murmur went around me, though my eyes didn't leave Timothy's. He was visibly struggling to maintain his features. Perhaps I just worsened my already deplorable situation.

My stomach turned upside down at the idea of what awaited me when we were forced alone, but it was too late.

Timothy nodded once and took his leave without apologizing—not that I'd expected him to.

My lips trembled as I turned to face the disaster I was the creator of. The Queen involved herself in the conversation with some nobles when her withering gaze swept over me. Sandra squeezed my hand tight.

No one had asked me for a dance that night.

"I will take my leave now." I aligned my silverware neatly before getting up from the table.

"Mother will notice." Sandra caught my sleeve.

"Please," my voice was barely a whisper.

Her lips turned into a thin line. "Fine." She sighed, "I will come up with an excuse." Sandra let go of my dress. "You owe me!" She gestured me towards the door.

"Thank you." I quickly smiled at her, fleeing out.

My trembling legs stumbled towards the garden before I even realized. I clung to every breath as though it was my last.

Royals are collected. Royals know how to control their emotions. You are to be a queen—act like it. My mothers's voice echoed in my mind as I threw myself past the arc of the palace, hoping for privacy.

Privacy? I almost laughed at myself. I had always been short on privacy, but after my oldest brother's death made me first in line, privacy became nonexistent.

I slid down a cherry tree that often served as my refuge from prying eyes when the orchestra of nature finally eased my mind. The cold air enveloped me in its embrace; the owls and ravens sang me their lullaby.

A pair of golden eyes studied me from the darkness.

"Hello, friend." I whispered, unwrapping the meat I'd stolen. "I brought you dinner."

The gray cat took a careful step forward, assessing his surroundings.

For a while, we sat behind the cherry tree enveloped in the darkness of this cold night. Silver—what I'd named the cat when we first met—settled in my lap after he quickly devoured his dinner.

The trees dropped their beautiful red and orange dresses, letting the wind carry them away, abandoning them before my feet. I picked up a leaf from the ground, studying its fire-like colors.

How could something so glorious exist in such a dark place?

My mind wandered, listening carefully to the tale of the garden—

"What do you savages want from me?" a painfully familiar voice grumbled.

Gods, no! Someone is here. I scrambled to my feet, preparing to face whoever decided that a walk in the garden was a good idea at midnight.

The *voices* seemed to stop just a few feet away from me, behind the arc of the garden.

Please leave! I begged my intruders, yet they didn't follow my request. Apparently, whoever it was preferred my garden to the foolish ball in the palace and I could not even blame them.

Dozens of needles prickled my skin when the stranger's voice came in reply. His voice was as soft as velvet and as sharp as briar.

I could barely make out the conversation, as though my intruders spoke a different language. That would be impossible: there were only three languages used in our Kingdom, and I knew all of them to perfection—thanks to my tutors. Perhaps, I was too far.

I peeked out from behind the tree to see who was wandering this late at night. Despite the darkness, the gold patterns of the vest shone bright under the moonlight.

My heart threatened to leave my chest as my head flew back from *their* view. It was the same arrogant man from the ball, and he was not alone.

Their hushed voices filled me with an odd feeling of paranoia I couldn't make sense of.

Mother wouldn't allow me into the council meetings anymore, but I was no fool. I knew people had gone missing in the last month; I knew about the *Vanishing List* she kept.

I needed to get closer, I needed to know why the Royal garden—my garden—was the place they chose to meet in the dead of night.

Careful not to disturb the dry leaves underneath my steps, I took a step forward: just close enough to see their faces without abandoning the sanctuary of my tree. They both—the arrogant man and a woman I'd never seen before—seemed on edge. The frustration in his eyes shone bright.

His eyes... I'd never seen such abnormality in nature. His amber eyes reflected the moon light in this darkness like a nocturnal animal. My eyes traveled past him.

The woman by his side was the most beautiful woman I'd ever seen. Her youthful eyes were not quite right either: light brown and glowing just like his. Her copper hair shimmered in different shades of red; she—just like the man—neglected the dress code: her dark blue gown looked as though she'd walked out from the depths of the ocean.

"Roxanne." The man snapped at the ocean woman. His hand touched hers in a kind of comfort I could not quite understand. "You're making a mistake not believing our words." He faced the dark silhouette: the figure wore a hood that completely covered their face.

I'd never heard such an accent before. The accent was quite beautiful: harsh but gentle all the same. The words flew in charming waves, as though they were delicate touches of piano and violin. The sound brought satisfaction to my ears, and I consumed every word with joy, despite my inability to fully understand them.

Focus! I chided myself for such an easy distraction.

The arrogant man spoke again. He talked so fast and quiet I could only catch a few words out of everything he'd said. Army, attacks, winter.

Army? My brows furrowed. *Attacks?* I shook my head, waiting for more when the mysterious silhouette's voice reached my ears once again. "That won't be necessary." they bit out.

Where have I heard this voice before?

"Then we have nothing to talk about." Roxanne drew out every word. Her tone left no room for an argument. She shared the accent of the arrogant man, though hers was softer.

The mysterious figure just hummed in reply, heading back towards the palace.

The strangers waited for a few moments before speaking: just staring at each other, as though they needn't words to communicate. "You should go, Rox." The arrogant man broke their silence.

The ocean woman looked as though she was about to protest, glaring at the man. After a long pause Roxanne shrugged—apparently she'd lost their silent argument—before turning to leave.

"Don't forget your manners, Francis." The woman called over her shoulder. "She is a royal." Roxanne smiled as she disappeared into the darkness.

Chapter 2
Royal Cage

Royal? My stomach dropped. Suddenly I had the urge to run. Something told me I did not want to stay long enough to find out what the ocean woman meant.

Filling up my lungs, I readied to fight my way out, but the man had left as well. *Odd.* Maybe I'd misunderstood them: they hadn't been talking about me. Either way, I took this as an opportunity to flee and started the opposite direction—just a precaution.

As much as I wanted to avoid the front gate, that was my best option given the circumstances. I would've rather dealt with the consequences of slipping away from the ball than be the next name on the *Vanished List*. I just needed to reach the gate, the guards would've been on their night watch—I'd be safe.

The fog spread on the ground like a blanket, enveloping the naked trees, keeping them safe on that gloomy night. I walked for a long time, going all the way around the perimeter of the palace. The sounds of nature were my only companions, keeping me calm on my way home.

I regretted not stopping by my room to grab my cloak, though the cold air seemed to welcome me with open arms, distracting me from the misery of my spirit. My mind soothed as I got closer to the main gate.

Turning the final corner to the front gates, I froze. My heart dropped to my stomach as I retreated a step, disturbing the dried leaves settled down on the ground.

"Your Highness." The arrogant man bowed graciously in front of me, looking completely harmless: as though he was indeed bowing before his ruler.

I raised my chin and straightened my shoulders in an attempt to seem intimidating. I could only hope he did not notice my body tense. Maybe I could talk my way to safety.

I hated to use my status, but today it seemed as if it would save my life—if I played my role well. Threatening a Royal life would turn out bad for him, and I wanted him to remember that.

He took a step forward looking at me with interest, as though I was a painting in the gallery room. *Is he going to kill me?* Yet, Francis didn't seem to move a muscle, just stared at me, studying.

Nature became silent, depriving my mind of the only sign of peace, as if hiding from whatever danger this person possessed.

How dared he stare at me like I was his to stare at?

"Weren't you taught that eavesdropping is bad manners, Your Highness?" His accent finally broke our silence when he crooked his head as if talking to a child. The arrogance!

"How dare you speak to me in such a manner?" I replied to his arrogance with my own. "How dare you even look at me?" Perhaps it was the adrenaline speaking for me, provoking this man where no one would even hear my scream. Perhaps I'd completely lost my mind in this disaster.

Should I run? Where will I run? He was directly in my way and if I were to turn around I would be trapped. *Perhaps, I can make it to one of the hidden passages if I am quick enough.*

A big smile spread across his face, amused by my reply. "Well, well..." Francis' brows furrowed, without dropping his smirk. "If my memory serves me right, *you* were the one gawking at me in the ballroom."

We were dangerously close—he wouldn't have even needed to put in any effort to end me right now.

Not again.

Fear overwhelmed me, sending my mind into a hurricane of my memories as I took a step backward, putting myself out of his reach.

"You definitely have the nerve to talk to a woman this way, mister," I said at last. "Your arrogance will do you no good. Now, let me pass, before this will end badly for you," I bit out.

Hoping he was not foolish enough to cause me harm on the palace grounds I started walking past him, pretending nothing was out of ordinary, but Francis sidestepped the moment I thought I could make it, putting him directly in front of me.

Our bodies didn't touch, although I could feel the whiff of cold coming from him, as if he was winter himself. The strong smell of tobacco and jasmine overwhelmed my senses, making my head spin.

"Of course, Your Highness," Francis said sweetly as if he didn't just stop me from doing so. "I wouldn't want to keep you from your royal duties," he murmured, leaning close to me.

Not caring if I showed any fear, I moved away, putting the distance back between us. "I just want to make sure our princess knows how to keep secrets first." The grin on his face was so wide, it made my body shudder.

The adrenaline from the danger I put myself into ran through my veins, settling deep in my stomach.

It was challenging to be intimidating when he was taller, so I raised my chin even higher, paying attention to every move he made.

"Did I hear you correctly, sir? You are threatening a Royal?" My heart finally won the battle, and escaped my chest for good. Goosebumps covered my skin head to toe in dozens of needles.

"Unfortunately, I'm afraid I am," he replied with theatrical hurt on his face. I despised this man. "What do you say, Your Highness? Do we have an agreement?"

"And what do *I* get in return?" I found the nerve to ask him. I should have just taken my opportunity and left as quickly as possible, but my mouth was my biggest enemy.

He stared seriously at me for a moment before replying. "Well, your life, of course." Francis looked confused as if I'd asked the most obvious question ever.

My lungs froze, unable to take the next breath.

"It was nice talking to you, Your Highness, but I fear I must be on my way." Francis grinned again. "Have a great evening." He bowed, with such grace, as if the whole conversation did not happen, and we just had a nice chat about the weather. "I hope you could forgive any rudeness on my part."

Francis said, walking past me, leaving me alone in the darkness.

Still stunned, I was not sure what to do. *Some stranger just threatened my life and I just stared at him.* Next time I decide to walk at night, I better bring a weapon.

Shaking my head in disbelief, I turned around back on my pathway. The guards paid me no attention as I passed through the main gates.

I was halfway to my room, feeling relieved I didn't meet anyone else on my way here, yet my relief was short-lived. The Queen patiently waited for me by the door to my bedchambers. *Moon help me.*

Mother did not look pleased when her eyes finally found mine from across the hallway.

"Your Majesty," I bowed, preparing myself for the absolute worst. Mother didn't reply to me, just turned around on one heel, walking into my rooms.

I followed her like the obedient daughter that I was, closing the door behind me.

My mother stopped in the middle of my bedchambers, looking at me with so much anger that I would rather face Francis again than her. She was still in her ball gown, with hair still down in beautiful dark waves.

"I am deeply disappointed in you, Cordelia." I flinched at the sound of my name. Mother only called me by my name when she was angry. Unable to hold her gaze for any longer, I lowered my head and asked the Gods for one more favor. *Please help me stay quiet.*

Know your place! With a tongue like yours you will find trouble, Cordelia. Disrespectful child, how dare you talk back?

The memory of my mother scolding me flashed in my mind, and I felt a helpless child again.

"Using your status like this with *me* present in the room," she continued in a calm voice. "And with whom?" She paused for a second as if actually expecting my reply. "Your future husband," Mother finally answered for me.

The word *husband* set my blood aflame as my attempt at self control went to shreds.

Her calm anger terrified me, but my own wouldn't let me stay quiet. "Betrothed," closing my eyes, I corrected her in a whisper. I shouldn't have, but I couldn't seem to help it.

"Come again?" My mother's voice sucked the air from the room. She stared at me for a long while, before continuing. "Listen to me, child—"

"I am—" I swallowed the lump in my throat. "Not a child." My eyes finally met her gaze. This was not the way to talk to the Queen, even if you were one's daughter.

"Then how come you act like one?" She snapped at me. "You *will* marry him!" Mother took a step towards me. "Do you hear me?" She grabbed my chin, making me look her straight in the eyes. "Cry all you want. You will marry whomever *I* order you to marry."

"But, Mother!" My voice grew a few octaves. I could not afford to raise my voice at the Queen, especially not now, not when my future was held hostage in her firm grasp.

My hands shook at the memories of my birthday ball. My lungs ached, unable to expand, at the realization of what my future held for me if I didn't convince her to reconsider. I blinked fast, refusing to let tears drop in her presence; I would not give her the satisfaction of witnessing my pain.

Sometimes I wondered if it brought her joy, knowing I was hurt. Or perhaps she simply did not care. Nevertheless, I intended to do whatever it took to not let my nightmare come true. "You know what he has done to me." I whispered, afraid if I were to speak any louder, my voice would break the delicate wall I built in my mind for all the unwelcome memories I possessed.

The queen did not seem to care for my words, looking bored as though my words carried no meaning. I battled with my temper, trying to keep it in check, yet my emotions were fighting for freedom, refusing me any clarity or logic.

I could not let this happen, I refused! I refused to be defeated on this matter, I would do what it took to change the outcome of this tragedy. Anything at all.

My pride be damned. Falling down on my knees I begged her, despite my haterade for such dramatics. "Please, Mother, please. Anyone but him... Ple—"

"Enough." She extended her hand out, stopping me from saying another word. "Begging won't help you. You are smart enough to know why we need this marriage." She gestured for me to get up on my feet. "Stop being the selfish brat that you are. You are to be the Queen. Act like it." She bit out, staring down at me in disgust. "If it's good for the Kingdom, you are to do it." Her harsh words forced my lips into a thin line. "Next week we are to attend a dinner at the Barrens' Duchy. You will apologize to their heir, and excuse your horrible behavior."

My mouth opened wide in horror; I could not force the air into my lungs. "Please! Don't make me do this! You cannot!"

"I beg your pardon!" The back of her palm landed on my cheek, sending my face on fire, forcing my eyes to see stars. "How dare you talk to your Queen this way?"

A silent tear fell down my abused cheek, and I didn't bother hiding it.

Mother did not speak anymore, just stared at me with an indifference I could only envy. *How can you allow this?* I wanted to scream at her. *Why would you hurt me this way? You are a disgrace to my father's honor.* I stared at her, wishing she could hear my thoughts, wishing she would always walk beside the shadow of my pain for she was the creator of it.

"Father would never approve of this alliance." My words were barely a whisper.

My eyes studied hers, trying to find the mother who loved, mother who protected and cherished her children. The Queen's eyes were full of exhaustion, boredom, and... sadness.

My palms turned into fists, nails digging into my skin, distracting me from the pain I felt in my heart.

Would she change her mind? Would she stop the marriage? I stared at her with a plea in my eyes, begging for salvation, and for a second every part of me believed she would put this nonsense to a stop. She would protect me, as she swore she would.

I didn't dare to make a sound—my whole world came down to whatever my mother would say next.

Taking a deep breath, she finally broke our silent conversation. "We will be discussing your wedding then," she said. "I want you wed two weeks from now, so if you have any preference for your celebration, don't delay your requests."

"No," I whispered in disbelief.

"Goodnight, daughter," the Queen said, gracefully leaving the room, leaving me to this disarray.

"No!" I shouted after her from the top of my lungs, not caring that the guards by my door would hear me.

As if there was a huge invisible hole in my stomach, I placed my palms in an attempt to make my entrails stay in place.

"No! No! No!" I fell to my knees once again, hitting the marble floor with all the strength I had left in me, until my voice became hoarse.

My heart ached, as though someone stuck a dull dagger in it: slowly twisting and squeezing the blade into my wound, waiting for my heart to bleed out and to still forever.

My soul had finally escaped my body, floating to freedom. My hands kept hitting the marble, until they started to bleed, painting my skin bright red; my hands hit the marble, until soft, gentle hands held me tight.

"You will be all right, dear," Mories' soft voice whispered through my sobs. "You will be all right."

No, I won't! I wanted to argue, but I could not take my next breath to let the words out. I could not take the next breath to scream, even though that was what my soul demanded.

There was no air left in the room. I was under water. Deep down in the ocean, where only darkness accompanied me. I tried to fight my way out with all the remaining energy, trying to fight my way to the surface, but Mories' hands held me firmly in place.

I'm dying! I wanted to shout at her. *I am dying, let me go!*

"I will not let this marriage happen, my dear, I promise." Mories said gently, moving the hair from my face.

How can you lie to me? I wanted to confront her. *How can you promise something you cannot do?* I wanted to scream.

"Once, a little girl befriended the moon.

The moon sang her songs in a beautiful tune.

The moon sent the girl beautiful stars,

The stars were protecting the girl from dark charms."

Any attempts at speaking fell short as Mories' soft voice reached my ears: an old lullaby that put my mind to rest.

"Once, a little girl befriended the moon,

The moon sang her songs in a beautiful tune.

The moon sent the girl a beautiful pearl,

The pearl was so precious, as was the girl."

My lungs finally expanded, allowing the air in.

"That's right, dear. Breathe." Mories whispered, rubbing my back.

For a while we just sat on the floor, surrounded by my own blood. Silent tears fell on my gown, but my mind was empty of any thoughts, and I treasured that moment while it lasted.

This is a dream! Wake up, Cordelia.

I tried to move my muscles, but my body failed me. I tried to force my eyes open, tried to scream: all in vain.

Wake up!

Jumping from the bed with such force, I knocked my violin from its stand, making the room thunder in a dull ring of my instrument.

Just a dream. I kept repeating my mantra, hugging myself tightly, trying to force the images of the nightmare out of my head.

I woke up from Timothy forcefully kissing me in a hallway, trying to rip my gown to shreds.

Stop being so prude, Cordelia. He had told me before making himself the main character of my nightmares. I woke up from his disgusting words that had haunted me for the last month. The words that were still loud and clear in my head.

I woke up from the knife in his hand.

I woke up from the blood on my gown.

I woke up from his hands, holding me by my hair.

It was a dream. Just a dream.

Just a dream for now. Soon enough my nightmare would become my reality once again. After the wedding there would be no salvation, no rescue. My life would be over the moment the vows were said at the altar.

No one could save me, no one could change the Queen's decision. Brian was not here to protect me, Father was not here to put this nonsense to a stop.

You stole them from me. I told the Moon. *You didn't even let me say my goodbyes.*

The walls of my bedchamber were narrowing, trapping me in, crashing my body.

My hands stretched out toward the dagger underneath my bed as I put my cloak on. My mind was deprived of any thought, the instincts in me took control over my body when my legs carried me across my room.

The wardrobe door creaked when I sneaked through it, straight to the secret passage hidden within. My secret passage that led just outside the garden, just outside the perimeter of our land, right to the cemetery.

Chapter 3
Peacefulness of the Dead

Walking outside at night was dangerous enough, walking outside the perimeter of the palace was terrifying. Walking among the dead of the night was straight insanity. An insanity my heart greatly allowed to take over my mind, for it was my heart that craved the comfort of the only people that had slayed every enemy for my well being. The only people who had understood my worries, who had known every curve of my long shattered heart.

Fresh air reached my face, calming me down. Now, when I was no longer an emotional disaster and could think clearly, fear took over my mind. I should get back, yet something was pulling me to keep going.

I was not eager to go to a cemetery on a sunny day, accompanied by my guards, and here I was walking down the rows of the stones all by myself way past midnight. My impulsiveness would do me no good.

Still in my nightgown, underneath my cloak, I wrapped my arms around myself to keep warm. It was not yet winter, but the weather suggested it might as well be. The trees dropped their garments, readying for the repose.

Some explained this drastic temperature as the Gods sending us a warning: something was coming. I did not believe Gods would do such kindness, but something indeed was coming. Mother spent more and more time in her study with her most trusted counselors, but whenever I had asked about it I was left with *It is not your concern, Cordelia. You should spend this time studying, not wandering around.*

Walking down the Royal cemetery where my father and brother rested alongside Royal warriors, I faced twin stones: Father's and Brian's. *Brian was a great warrior, brother, and heir.* The engraving on the stone suggested.

Brian was my age when he had fought in the last battle of Crimson War. He protected our kind at twenty four, when all I did was argue with the Queen.

Would I ever fulfill the expectations of an heir? Would I ever fulfill the expectation of my mother? I wasn't born to rule and lead, Brian was. People had adored him. People tolerated me.

What would Father say if he saw what became of me? What became of all of us? What would Brian do if he was in my place? Would they have been disappointed in me like Mother was? Would they have seen rationale in my words, unlike our Queen?

For a long time I sat by the stones, staring at the names. My mind imagining what life would be like were my loved ones still here when the realization of an abnormal silence shocked my senses. The wind had quieted down, the crickets went silent. The cold sweat broke through my skin.

A shiver went through me when I felt a pair of eyes watching me from afar. Slowly, my head turned in the direction of my company when a loud croak interrupted the peacefulness of the dead.

The raven studied me with its hypnotizing eyes as it let out another loud croak. Stretching out its powerful wings, it made its way across the cemetery, flying past me, settling down onto my brother's stone.

The raven's feathers were the color of the night ocean, shimmering under the moonlight. The raven crooked its head, its eyes did not leave mine for even a moment. I swallowed a lump in my throat, careful not to move.

Why does it look at me as though I am its next meal? I wondered, when something made its way across my neck. My hands flew towards the sensation, brushing my exposed skin of any unwelcome creatures. My body shuddered.

Slowly, I got to my feet, retreating a step back from the bird when my eyes found dozens of ravens surrounding me in a tight circle. Goosebumps covered my skin from head to toe.

Come now, Cordelia, they are just birds. Ravens do not attack humans. My breathing quickened.

They all stared at me when they started singing in unison, making the cemetery into their own orchestra. My eyes traveled through the unkindness of ravens when I saw bright crimson blood that colored some of their feathers. "What in the Kingdom..." A whisper escaped my lips.

Gods. Dear Gods! My palm covered my mouth.

Refusing to think of where the birds got their crimson ornaments, I forced my legs to carry me away from the horrors of feathered creatures who kept croaking after me.

The sound rang in my ears as I made my way back towards the palace's grounds. It did not stop until I was out of the raven's view, far enough to not hear their cries.

The bright moon that lit my way here was now hiding behind the clouds. *Alas, I didn't even bring a candle with me.*

When the entrance of the passage entered my view, a branch broke behind me.

Gods, Cordelia, it's just a squirrel, you need to calm down. I shook my head, holding my heart, as if that would stop it from jumping out of my chest.

The image of the ravens did not leave my mind as I kept walking. I forced my lungs to take deep breaths when the sound of crackle reached my ears once again. *Just a squirrel! When I get back to my rooms I will be laughing at my own imagination.* Nevertheless, I squeezed the handle of my dagger, pulling it out of my pocket.

I tried to see the source of the sound that scared me but saw nothing. I saw nothing, but had an unsettling feeling as if I was being watched. I knew the feeling well. When you would think you were alone, but a Royal was almost never alone—that I had learned early in life.

Breathe. I commanded myself, but couldn't seem to do even that, my body froze like a statue.

There was a part of me that was convinced that one of the knights saw my departure, and decided to follow for safety. Perhaps, they decided to hide, allowing me privacy. There was a part of me that was curious to see what might be behind the tree line, but I was not foolish enough to act on such a twisted idea.

The fog had become denser, covering my vision. The hair on my arms and neck rose and suddenly the air felt even colder—if that was even possible.

When my legs finally listened to me, I turned around back on my pathway. Thankfully, I was not far, but the cold air slowed down my moves: even the adrenaline rush did not help my muscles work. Perhaps I'd used up all of my resources on the previous day.

The crackling grew louder and I was not convinced it was a squirrel anymore. My walk broke into a run. I tried to look back at the cemetery, but my feet stumbled the moment I did that. *Watch your feet!* The last thing I needed was to fall straight on my face.

Air rushed past me in strong waves of a hurricane that almost knocked me to the ground. A wave was so strong it spun me around; I could barely see anything past my extended hand. Whatever or whoever this might be, most definitely was not here to protect me.

My stomach dropped.

Horror washed over me, my mind was stuck in the storm of my unresting imagination. *Help!* I wanted to scream, yet the sound did not come out. My lungs were empty.

Something grabbed my wrist, squeezing tightly, making the dagger fall with a terrifying clang—the only sound in this abnormal silence.

Its nails dug into my skin, breaking through my veins. My mind became rigid; my heartbeat ripped through my chest, smashing into my ribs. Every muscle in me was paralyzed, despite my best attempts to break free of my attacker.

The sharp pain in my wrist made my body shake; my wrist felt warm and cold at the same time. The force came so fast, faster than a wingbeat of a hummingbird. Though, it left just a second later, leaving me to the mercy of this unbearable torture.

The loud croak broke through the invisible wall around me. My head flew towards the sound. The unkindness of ravens circled above me. Their wings broke through the air, slicing it into two. The blood from their feathers fell down on me, the crimson drops hitting my face in a rainfall.

My instincts took over and I ran like never before. The moon was hidden behind the thick clouds now, as though it did not want to witness the horror either, leaving the night pitch black.

I only hoped I was running towards the palace—not away from it. Either way it didn't matter at that moment, I just needed to get away as far as I could.

Unsure how long I ran for, I didn't stop, nor did I look back. I did not stop until the pain in my wrist got impossible to handle, that even the adrenaline in my veins failed to mask it.

In half an hour—perhaps less, perhaps more—I was far enough from the cemetery, far enough from the birds, in the depths of the night forest. Unfortunately, far enough from the palace as well, but I would deal with that later; right now I had to find the strength to examine my wrist, which only got worse with every passing moment.

Leaning on the nearest tree, I searched my surroundings for any sign of life. The woods were vacant and for the first time in my life I was grateful to be alone in the night forest.

Yet my relief was short-lived; the pain in my wrist cut through my bones, icicles grew inside of my veins.

I rolled up the sleeve of my wounded arm through the agony, using the inside of my cloak as a cloth to clean up my injury.

Excruciating pain erupted the moment the cloth made contact with the skin, as if fire itself wrapped my wrist, holding it hostage. A suppressed cry escaped me without permission. The ground started to move upside down, moving me with it.

I had to find my way back to the palace before I lost consciousness; I had to find a healer. I prayed to all the Gods and the Moon, I did not just catch rabies. *Breathe.*

When the wound felt clean enough, I put my hand towards the moonlight, forcing the air into my lungs. *I cannot afford to faint right now.*

Feeling steady enough, I took a glance at my injury.

A terrified gasp escaped my lips.

"No," I whispered, examining my wrist.

No.

It was no animal that had bitten me, the mark was of a human.

No.

I failed to keep my breathing steady, and cared not if I lost consciousness right this moment. In fact, I wished that would have been the case. I wished it was all a twisted jest of my imagination.

My mind wandered trying to find *any* possible explanation, beside the obvious one.

Perhaps I was wrong, it was some sort of a wild animal that had bitten me. Perhaps the events of the ball and the news of the upcoming marriage had been too much to handle—it must have made me paranoid; perhaps it had made me see things that weren't actually there. I just needed rest. I barely had any sleep, and this night had a lot on its plate. I must have gone mad.

Sleep. I just needed sleep, before I completely lost my mind.

I wrapped my wrist in a cloth to stop the bleeding, and to cover it from my own eyes, because in the back of my mind—even if I wouldn't ever admit it—I knew. I knew what this was.

A death sentence.

A horrified scream—my own horrified scream—disturbed the sounds of nature around me. Sharp pain came in a new wave, even more powerful than before, making my legs give up.

My whole body was on fire, consumed by it. The scream didn't stop, growing louder than ever, until my head spun so much my vision went bright white, then completely disappeared.

My consciousness was leaving my body, leaving the pain to take its place, and I was ready to accept my fate, ready to welcome death—begging it to take me away.

Chapter 4
Crimson Wine

My fingers brushed through the soft covers of my bedding, enjoying the sensation; the fur felt as though it was made of fine silk. I covered my head with the blanket, sighing. Oh, how I wished I could stay in bed for the rest of the day.

Soon enough, Mories would come into my rooms to help me prepare for the day. Of course, I was no longer in need of her help, but in the last month I'd been grateful for her company.

She seemed to not let me out of her sight after my birthday ball. After all, she had been the one to calm my tears.

If it weren't for her status, I was sure she would have strangled Timothy with her bare hands after she saved me that night.

Timothy. I had humiliated him in front of everyone last night, and—regardless of how much my mother punished me for such an outburst—it felt incredible. My lips spread into a grin as I remembered his face falling the moment he had realized what I had done.

My grin fell flat as the rest of the memories about last night caught up to me. The fine silk covers I was clinging onto were suddenly replaced by briar.

My eyes stumbled around not recognizing the room I was in. The walls were made of dark stone, the ceiling held a black metal chandelier with long extinguished candles on it. A painting of a woman with a black widow instead of a mouth stared at me from the opposite wall. My head was spinning as I realized the whole room was black and certainly not mine.

"You shouldn't have brought her here." A quiet voice came from behind the black wooden door.

Dear Gods! Dear Gods, help me. My lungs squeezed all the air out; icy sweat broke through my palms.

"What else was I supposed to do?"

No.

Gods, please, no!

My body shivered at the familiar accent coming in reply. "Leave her alone in the woods?" the voice continued. "Besides, she is his last creation, she might be of use."

Run! Hide! My mind screamed at me. As though my soul left my body, I looked at the room through someone else's eyes. My body did not belong to me any longer.

My body moved away from the door without my command. Slowly, my shaky legs carried me through the room towards the farthest corner.

"She is a royal!" The stranger did not bother keeping his voice quiet anymore. "They will come for all of us, brother."

I spun around in hopes of finding something heavy or sharp, but saw nothing handy. *I will die here.*

The door creaked and I staggered backwards, hitting the big windows hidden behind the black curtains. The light from the hallway lit up the room as the silhouette of a man showed up at the threshold. The man was holding a goblet in his hand, as he smirked down at me.

"You must be hungry, Your Highness," Francis said sweetly, taking a step forward.

A thundering howl broke through me, ringing in my ears. That nightmare corrupted my soul, making its slow way towards my heart. *This is not real.*

Wake up, Cordelia! Wake up!

My voice snapped like a tree during a hurricane. My throat was cut by dozens of needles and was left to bleed dry.

"Bloody hell." Francis groaned, rolling his eyes. "No wonder I could hear you miles away in the woods." He smirked. "And sorry to disappoint, I am quite real."

His voice cut through the ringing in my ears, echoing off the back of my head. *Not real, this is not real.* I kept telling myself, yet I lost confidence in my own words by the moment.

"Well?" He crooked one eyebrow. "Would you like to join me for supper?"

Everything stopped. My mind wandered through every possible solution, finding none that would allow me salvation. Surrender knocked on the door of my sanity, but I held the entry firmly closed. I would not surrender and accept my grave without resistance. I would find my way out.

My gaze slipped towards a candelabra standing nearby. It looked heavy enough to serve as a weapon. Taking a slow side step, I watched Francis carefully.

He seemed to forget about my presence as though I became another ghost in this eerie room. Francis carefully studied the color of the wine in his hand before taking a small sip.

He chuckled when I grabbed the candelabra, gripping it in front of me.

"Stay the fuck away from me!" I yelled, arcing the candelabra towards my foe.

He only laughed at me with amusement, leaning on the doorframe. "Such language for a royal."

Ignoring him, I repeated myself, hoping I did not sound as scared as I truly was. "Stay. Away. From me!" I screamed out every word.

"Would it be best if I returned when you're done whining?" Francis stared at me more annoyed than ever, though he did not take a step forward. "I brought you dinner." He shrugged, holding out a goblet of wine towards me.

Dinner? Is he jesting?

His eyebrows flew high, expecting my answer, but all I could focus on was the candelabra in my hand and the open door behind him.

"Let me go. My mother will give you gold." I blurted out, hoping I sounded confident.

"Go if you wish." Francis shrugged, gesturing me out. "I am not one to keep such a liability as a prisoner." He rolled his eyes at me. "Do you know they can be rather expensive to support?" He smiled at me sweetly. "I prefer slaying my enemies. It's quicker and far less costly."

What in the Kingdom is he implying?

Dizziness' sharp knife clefted through my insides, tying my stomach into a knot. Every cell in my body threatened to explode. The illness rushed through my veins, begging my body to surrender.

He intends to end me. Right here, in this black room, where no one will hear my last words, where no one will come to my rescue.

My jaw clenched. Anger and terror rushed through me in a powerful wave. The vulnerability I was forced into made my blood boil as though it was fresh lava. My vision had become little more than a red blur. I struggled to recognize myself.

Will he be merciful to end my suffering quickly? Will he prolong the torture for his own pleasure?

Francis sighed, taking a sip of the *dinner* that he had brought me. He caught my unresting gaze, holding out the goblet towards me.

"I did not tell anyone about your meeting." My voice shook no matter my best efforts at sounding brave. "I will not say a word, just let me leave peacefully."

His bright laugh traveled through the room. "Why, I appreciate your loyalty, Your Highness." He bowed, still laughing. "But as I already said, you are free to go. Though, I would suggest staying away from the royal grounds. Humans tend to be rather dramatic in our presence, naturally." Francis smiled, revealing his teeth that were now covered in wine.

What in the Kingdom?

The realization consumed my senses. *Oh, Gods.* My screams were interrupted by the sound of the candelabra colliding with Francis' head.

"For god's sake." The man gripped onto his injury, cringing, as I took my opportunity to flee.

I ran out the door to the hallway, bumping into a man and a woman I had never seen before, taking them off guard.

Desperately looking for the exit, I sprinted, turning left-right-right-left down the endless sets of stairs. My lungs were on fire, but I did not stop even for a moment, nor did I look back.

Which way was the palace? Where in the Kingdom was I? By now someone would've noticed my absence, my mother would've sent a search group into the woods. I could only hope I had left tracks behind me.

I ran through the endless labyrinth of stone hallways, praying that luck was on my side today.

The hallways had no windows, the only source of light were the candles on each side of the wall. I grabbed one, just in case.

As panic started to settle deep in my stomach, I finally saw a light that didn't look like fire—a window perhaps, maybe even a door; though, I didn't want to get my hopes up.

The shaking in my legs just increased, nausea hitting me with a terrible wave. *Breathe.* So close, I was so close.

A door. *Thank the Gods.*

I forced the heavy door open, falling flat on my stomach. I was outside, I had to keep going!

Pushing through the pain in my body that threatened to destroy me right there, I gathered to my feet, when a terrifying scream escaped me. My wrist felt as if it was set on fire, corrupted and abused by it. Staring at my injury, I didn't stop screaming. *I have to keep going!*

"You are going to give me a headache, and I haven't had one in ten years." Francis shook his head, leaning against the door that I just fled out.

I gasped, moving away from him as much as possible while still on the ground.

He was going to drag me back inside, back to the black room if I didn't get up right this moment.

"Did you enjoy your run?" He flashed his crimson teeth.

Watching him, I slowly crawled backwards.

Francis put his hands up in defeat, "I am *staying the fuck away*." He rolled his eyes, repeating my words from earlier. "Just *please* stop screaming, would you?" Francis said calmly as he took another sip before returning his hands above his head.

Excruciating pain made me want to cut my hand off.

The bite was now bright pink, looking freshly healed. Healed! *The bite.*

A scary realization paralyzed me, taking away my ability to inhale. *The bite.*

"What did you do to me?" I roared, desperately trying not to succumb to the injury Francis created.

"I wouldn't recommend staying out for this long. The sunlight can still hurt you, even on a rainy day." Francis took a long sip of his wine. Blood.

I wished I had another candelabra to wipe the arrogance from Francis' face, but the pain radiating from my wrist made it clear that it would need to wait.

"Why did you bring me here?" my voice thundered.

"You're welcome, Your Highness," Francis bowed. "I am sure you meant to say 'thank you' for saving your life before humans found you and set you on fire. Or worse, you would be stupid enough to go back to the palace yourself and get killed."

My entire body shook as thunder traveled through every inch of my flesh. "What is happening to me?" My voice didn't sound like my own.

"You know what is happening, Your Highness," Francis scoffed.

I saw a glimpse of sorry in his eyes. Sorry? How dared he. None of this would've happened if it weren't for him. "You did this to me!" I shouted. "You can go straight to hell!"

He ignored my outburst as though I was the woman from the painting with nothing but a black widow for my mouth.

"I can help you, Your Highness." Francis smiled at me again, no trace of the sorry in his eyes from a moment ago.

I wanted to tell him to stay away from me, but the pain—the fire—in my body made it so all I was capable of was wailing, until my throat was on fire too.

It didn't take long for this torture to reach my head, forcing my consciousness to give in.

I fell back on the ground as my vision blurred and darkened.

Francis picked me up, walking back inside the castle, and I was too weak to fight back.

The last thing I heard was Francis' exhausted sigh, right before the world went completely black and disappeared. Again.

Chapter 5
Gruesome Beasts

The next few days—perhaps even a week—I was in and out of the oblivion, unable to sit up on the bed, most certainly unable to escape. When I did wake up, I was greeted with the darkness of that eerie room that gave me chills.

The dark green sheets on the bed were cold and sticky from my sweat. My skin prickled with an uncomfortable ache all over my body. My muscles felt weak, as if someone pulled and stretched them for hours without stopping.

Every time I woke I tried to think of an escape plan, but all I was left with was pain all over my body that drowned me into nothingness again and again.

Until one day the pain was finally gone, as though it was no more than a twisted jest of my imagination—a dream even.

For the first time in longer than I could remember everything seemed peaceful.

"Oh, good, you are awake!" An overly enthusiastic voice exclaimed, which caused me to jolt up on the bed. A strange woman stood in the center of the room, smiling excitedly. Was she here to finally kill me? "Sorry! I didn't mean to startle you," she said, lighting a candle in her hand.

Moving away from her until my back touched the bed frame, I eyed her expectedly. The woman was grinning at me without saying a word. What in the Kingdom did she want from me?

The woman looked to be around twenty years of age, though I could not be certain. She marveled at me with her warm brown eyes that reflected the candlelight in her hands; the bright smile did not leave her face for even a second. Her golden dark skin shone even in that lightless room, as if she was sunshine herself. She moved her black curls away from her face, taking a step towards me.

"How are you feeling? I brought you some blood, it should make you feel better." She stretched out her hand with a goblet of wine. *Blood. Not wine.* A shiver went through my body at the realization of what she expected me to do. "I am so excited to have you in our family! Here. Drink it."

A family? Was she mad? I moved farther away, not wishing to believe all of this was actually happening. It was all a jest, a prank. I had gone mad.

"All right..." the sunshine woman said, stretching out the first syllable. She placed the glass on the nightstand before sitting down on the bed. "Gods, it is so dark in this room, no wonder you looked like a scared animal." She laughed, looking around. "I told them I should have gone to meet you first, but they never listen." She mumbled more to herself than to me.

My eyes grew wide. I wished to scream at her to leave me alone for good, but I seemed to have lost my voice. Perhaps *I was* like a wild animal: unable to scream, unable to move. It was a wonder I did not forget how to breathe as well, for my body seemed to completely give up on following any of my commands.

I sat on the bed, watching the stranger's every move, clutching at every word that left her mouth. She did not seem to care for my reaction; in fact, I was not even sure she remembered I was here. Her fingers brushed over her sleeves, playing with the golden material. It did not appear she was here to hurt me, though I did not allow myself to even blink. I could not trust a soul here and I would never forget that.

After a few moments, the woman's eyes found mine once again, and the bright smile returned to her face. "I will bring you more candles, or we could go find something for your room together." She looked at me expectedly, as though it was my turn to speak, but I merely glared at her. "Lord, where are my manners?" The woman laughed, shaking her head. "I am Florence! You are—Cordelia, correct?" Her hand stretched out in an attempt to meet mine. My eyes tried to catch a glimpse of dishonesty in her features, something to prove her true nature, something to show me the danger I found myself in.

"I understand." Florence dropped her hand and gave me the kindest smile I've seen in my life. "You surely hate me right now," she laughed again. "That's okay. I just want to let you know that no one here wishes you harm," she added quietly.

My breathing deepened as a new wave of panic washed over me, though there was part of me that was relieved by her presence. I was glad it was her sitting here, and not the man I have seen earlier, or worse—Francis. Though, I could not help but to feel anger towards her all the same. Telling me the sweet lies—that I desperately wanted to believe—of me being safe here, and I hated her for it, regardless of how nice she seemed. I could not trust anyone here: Florence was no different.

Florence played with the sleeves of her yellow dress, while I waited patiently for whatever irritatingly joyful thing she would say next: but she didn't say anything.

After a few very awkward moments of silence, Florence finally took a deep breath, getting up from the bed. "Well, all right then. I shall take my leave now. Let me know if you need anything, my room is at the end of the hallway," she said smiling, as she started towards the door. "Rest."

This might be my only chance.

I had to know.

"Wait." I said, surprising myself at my own bravery.

Florence turned, her smile even brighter than before—if that was even possible. Fear overwhelmed me, but I had to ask; even if I knew the answer already.

"What am I doing here? When can I leave?"

Florence's lips turned into a thin line. "Francis is trying to help you." She said, "You need rest."

"No." I shook my head, squeezing the blanket in my hands. "I need to go home!" My voice broke on the last word. "My siblings need me—"

"I'm sorry." Florence whispered. If I didn't know better, I would have assumed it was pity in her soft voice. "You cannot go back to your human family, Cordelia. They will kill you the moment they figure out what you are."

As if the ground broke into two, capturing me, trapping me in its depths, depriving me of light and freedom, I was falling. "No. I—"

"I am very sorry, Cordelia."

I swallowed the lump in my throat, putting all of my remaining strength towards holding back my tears. I would not cry in front of her. I closed my eyes tightly, as if I could disappear from reality by doing so.

The sound of the door creaking shut reached my ears, and I slid back under the covers when quiet tears fell hard from my eyes.

It had been foolish to give myself false hope, but I did all the same. I'd known what had happened to me the moment I'd been bitten. I'd known, yet still had believed, still had hoped for a different outcome.

A fool. I was just a fool.

A princess knows to keep her emotions to herself. A fool! I'd gone to the cemetery at night, at night and all by myself. What had I been thinking? A fool! I'd ran to the woods like a chi—

A fool!

I should've known better. I did know better!

My chest rose and fell, though I could not feel the air inside of me. My throat closed off, as though an invisible rope was tied around my neck; I could not breath. My hands flew towards the rope, trying to free myself, but they were met with nothingness.

I didn't bother keeping my sobs quiet anymore. I cared not how weak and uncollected I seemed. How very Royal of me. *A princess controls her emotions.*

My sobs grew louder and louder, echoing through the stone walls. My hands turned into fists, my nails dug into my skin deeper and deeper with each tear that fell. The pain in my heart and stomach had nothing to do with my physical condition anymore, this was what heartbreak felt like. I knew it, I remembered it.

I watched my palms go red, blood slowly dripped onto the bed. My breathing labored as the memories of the pain Timothy inflicted on me flashed through my mind.

My jaw clenched at the memory of my mother ignoring my pleas, still forcing me into marrying him.

My eyes saw red at the idea of my dearest sister, Sandra, suffering the same fate and I would not be able to be there to stop it, to save her.

My breathing became rapid when I stared at the barely visible bite through the tears. I was no longer myself, if *myself* even ever existed. Everything I knew was gone, and so was everyone I loved. I was gone. There was no turning back from it, I knew that. I'd studied plenty, there was no cure, no salvation, just death.

Brian and Father had lost their lives, protecting us from these horrible creatures, protecting me. They had been brutally killed by one of them, and I'd sworn that day I would not let their sacrifice go to waste. I'd sworn to hate these gruesome beasts. I'd sworn and became one of them.

I had failed them.

I had failed them all.

The tears didn't stop for a long time, until my consciousness fell into blackness.

I was not sure how long it had been, but every moment drained me more and more. Every time I tried to move, my body screamed in protest. Would this ever stop? Part of me wished to cease existing altogether.

I turned in the bed and somehow the dark room became even darker, or maybe it was my imagination.

The room smelled delightful despite my hatred towards it. The smell was so pleasant, but hurtful at the same time, it prickled my throat as if I had swallowed a dozen needles.

My eyes followed the smell until they spotted the goblet Florence had brought earlier. The realization of the source of this delicious smell washed over me, and my whole body shook in anticipation.

My breathing quickened, every instinct challenged me to dry out its content. Only my will stopped me from doing so. I was not sure I could resist the urge for much longer, my treasonous mind would lose this battle—I knew it.

My lips trembled as I slowly sat up on the bed, not taking my eyes away from the goblet, wishing I could destroy it with my gaze alone. I swallowed the pain in my throat that had only doubled with every passing moment.

My cheeks turned wet as I extended my hand towards the hostile goblet—would the tears ever stop? I peered at the contents of the cup not believing what I was about to do. Did I even have a choice?

Vampires—the word alone made me shudder—could not die of... well, hunger, I believed. At least I'd never heard of such a case, but no matter the haterade towards my new being, my instincts refused to let me find out.

My treasonous hands slowly brought the glass to my lips.

The drink was thick and soft, melting into my tongue like honey. It didn't taste like anything in particular, nevertheless it was the most delicious flavor I'd known in my entire life. Like a person who grew up in a dungeon, seeing the sun for the first time, I devoured the drink. Suddenly, I was not sure how I could live for twenty four years without it.

The drink warmed up my throat, making it prickle with sweetness, soothing my thirst. My mind spun in euphoria, craving more of this delightful salvation.

Once my mind calmed and clear thoughts returned to me, regret clawed into my chest, crushing my heart into small pieces.

How could I? What have I become? Disgusting. *A princess knows self-control.* Disgusting. My fingers squeezed the stem of the goblet until they hurt, my knuckles whitened. What was I capable of? How easily did I give in to the temptation? My body shook with rage. Disgusting!

I threw the goblet with all the strength I had. The sound of glass shattering traveled through the room, but the sound was suppressed by my own roar.

"Cordelia?" The voice behind me whispered.

I didn't bother looking who that was, nor did I stop screaming. Falling to my knees, the glass pieces on the floor cut through my uncovered skin, I didn't feel the pain. This pain could not compete with the pain I felt in my chest. I studied the blood under my nails, imagining my own hands ripping through my skin, freeing my injured heart.

Florence picked up the remnants of the goblet from the floor and sighed. She didn't say anything, just left me be. Left me alone, staring into the nothingness of this dark room.

Chapter 6
A Deal is a Deal

Time crawled by. Florence came, brought the disgusting drink, and left. She spoke less to me as the days passed, but her overbearing glee held strong nevertheless.

Eventually I'd stopped throwing the goblets against the wall.

Was this my eternity now? Awaking in darkness, drinking crimson liquid, losing my sanity.

Eternity. I had an eternity, and no purpose.

The knock on the door distracted me from my own misery. Florence. She was the only one who came to visit me. I hadn't seen Francis since he'd dragged me back to this nightmare; it wasn't as though I wanted to see the arrogant man anyway. He did this to me.

"Cordelia? Are you awake?" Florence whispered, making it through the room. She left the door open—the only source of light in this darkness.

"Yes," I replied, surprised hearing my own voice.

It was the first word I'd said to her in weeks and it made her grin. How could one be so happy all the time? Smiling so much... She smiled more in a day than I had in my entire life.

"There is a ball happening tonight, but of course you don't have to attend," she said after a long pause, clearly being taken off guard that I'd finally replied.

"Aye, she does," a voice came from the doorway. I turned my head towards the sound as a chill of fear ran down my spine. Francis stood there, with a smirk on his face, looking amused as always. My pulse quickened at the mere sight of him.

"Leave her be, Francis!" Florence sidestepped to hide me from his view. "She needs rest."

"And she's had plenty," Francis countered. "She can't stay in this room forever. It's been months, for god's sake."

"She shall stay for as long as she wishes," Florence hissed in reply.

Months? How many exactly? I'd lost any track of time. Had it really been that long? *Months.* Oh Gods, it could not be. My family had not found me. Were they even looking for me? *Of course they were, Cordelia. Don't be foolish.*

Not that I could have gone back—I could never go back—it was not safe for them nor was it safe for me.

I can't go back.

If I did, they would kill me immediately: I was now a threat to humans; and if they wouldn't, I might act on my instincts and take someone's life myself. The thought of hurting the twins, hurting Sandra or Mories, turned my stomach upside down: yet I still had hope of seeing them again.

Perhaps, I'd lost all ability to control my emotions, jumping from one to another in mere seconds. As Francis grinned down on me, I knew the horror I felt was shown on my face.

"I will do as I wish," I argued. I'd had enough of people deciding for me. I would not let Francis dictate me as well. I was not ready to leave this room, and perhaps I never would.

"The princess found her claws! Finally! I wondered how much time you were going to spend weeping." He smirked at me and I had a sudden urge to throw another candelabra at his head. "All the same, you are going to attend." The man shrugged. "I would suggest changing, though." He pointed at me, wrinkling his nose as if smelling spoiled milk.

Only then I realized I was still in my nightgown covered in blood and dirt. My arms instinctively wrapped the covers around my body trying to hide my exposed skin—I was practically naked.

Francis snickered, finding my reaction amusing when he turned to leave.

"Don't listen to him." Florence took my hand in hers. "He's a fool!" she proclaimed towards the ajar doorway. Her hands were cold as ice, but the gesture was still comforting despite me refusing to admit it.

"I heard that!" Francis shouted from the hallway.

The ball. The last two balls I'd attended didn't turn out the way I had wished. Perhaps, I should never attend another.

"Here," Florence passed me a goblet of blood. "You should have some."

I glanced at the glass in disgust, but still took it. As much as I hated my new state, I didn't ever want to experience pain like that again. If I ever did, I might as well set myself on fire—the only way to kill a vampire for good.

Without thinking of the taste and texture of the drink, trying to get it over with as fast as I could, I emptied the glass in a single gulp. I passed the glass back to Florence, cringing at my own actions when a knock on the door distracted me from any unwelcome thoughts.

"Your Highness," the sound of his voice covered my skin in goosebumps. Francis bowed at the threshold.

The words he addressed me with made my blood boil; my hands balled into fists. My eyes narrowed in anticipation for whatever nonsense he was about to drop.

Francis held out his hands offering me a velvet dress I had no intention to wear. "I brought you something for our small gathering tonight. I hope you won't be too disappointed, since our balls could never hold a candle to a royal event," he smirked. Would this man ever stop smirking?

"I'm not going," I replied, dismissing him.

"If you won't come voluntarily, I wouldn't mind dragging you down there myself," he replied calmly.

My jaw dropped at his audacity. "I dare you." The disturbing urge to set him on fire truly worried me. I'd never wished anyone harm, but it wouldn't have gone past me if the opportunity arose.

"I guess it's a deal." Francis walked towards the bed, carefully putting the dress on top. "*Highness*," the man bowed at me once again before taking his leave.

I faced Florence who held an odd expression on her face that I could not make sense of. She quickly masked it, putting on her bright smile. "I have some errands to run, you are more than welcome to join." Her eyes lightened.

"I would prefer staying here." Perhaps I would never leave this room: now that I truly had nowhere else to go, nowhere to be.

Florence nodded in understanding. "I will see you later then." She shrugged, sending me a smile of sunshine.

I returned the nod, getting comfortable on the bed—the only place that felt safe as of recently.

Waking up from an unsettling feeling of someone watching me, I gasped as a dark silhouette stood above me.

"I am here to deliver you to the ball as promised, Your Highness." Francis' accent broke through the darkness.

"Leave this room immediately!" I hissed at him, covering myself with a blanket—not that he hadn't seen my night-gown already.

Francis sighed, pure annoyance written on his face as he took a step towards me, effortlessly picking me up from the bed. I had no time to react.

"You wouldn't dare!" I pushed him away, trying to free myself. "Put me down right this moment!"

"A deal is a deal." He shrugged, crossing the room in mere seconds. He walked as though I weighed no more than a bag of feathers.

I kicked and punched, yet it didn't seem to hurt him at all. "Put me down!" I shouted again, but all my efforts were in vain. The amount of arrogance this man had in his possession was ridiculous.

Francis didn't acknowledge my demands as we left the room, even after my attempt at grabbing onto the door frame.

All the insults I came up with in the last few months flew out of my mouth, yet he didn't bother sparing me a glance: reigniting the urge to set him on fire.

Music in the hall grew louder with each step. The laughter and orchestra playing impregnated the stone walls: we must have been close.

This was humiliating! Perhaps, that had been his plan all along: to humiliate me in a room full of strangers while covered in dirt head to toe. He must have been jesting. He wouldn't have dared! Would he have?

"Fine! Fine!" I surrendered. That seemed to catch his attention as he slowly put me down, still not letting me out of his grasp; his eyebrows shot upwards. "Fine!" I hissed at him again. "I will go! Just let me change."

Francis gave me a half smile clearly feeling triumphant. A long sigh accompanied my defeat. Surrender left a sour taste in my mouth.

"Don't take long, or we will be forced to repeat our fun adventure." Francis smirked as I slammed the door in front of his nose.

Groaning, I made my way to the bathing chambers attached to the room.

Who did he think he was? Why was he so adamant over my attendance? He had already ruined my life. Was that not enough? Clearly not. But what choice did I have?

Even if I managed to lock myself in this room I was confident he would still find a way to drag me to the ball as I was. He seemed just as stubborn as me, but I was not about to show up barely dressed just to win an argument. I was a princess after all. Or at least I used to be. Still! Just because these people knew no manners, didn't mean I could forget my own.

Undoing my old braid, I glanced at the mirror in front of me preparing for the worst. A gasp escaped my lips: I looked... beautiful. Covered in dirt, of course, but still beautiful. It had been a while since I looked this healthy. How was this possible? I looked alive. Ironically, more alive than when I—well—was actually alive.

My fingers traced down my face as I studied the person in the reflection.

Still the same features but sharper or softer I was not quite sure. My eyes reflected the light from the candle, shining so bright. Inhumanly bright. My lips were as crimson as blood. Because it was indeed blood on my lips, I quickly realized.

Not wishing to look at it for longer than I had to, I quickly wiped my lips with the back of my hand. A constant reminder of my new being.

Disgusting. I turned to the bath and let the water run.

After the bath that—conveniently—took a while. I stared at the dress still displayed on my bed. The dress was gorgeous: bright red, with some gold appliqués running down the skirt.

The dress reminded me of autumn... and blood. Hating that Francis had brought it for me, I sat on the bed contemplating my options.

I didn't need anything from him. He and his constant smirk disgusted me to my core. Although, I didn't seem to have much of a choice: it was either his dress or my old nightgown.

My hands stretched out toward the nightgown, brushing over the familiar fabric. Dried blood painted the gown dark—almost black—red. Small cuts covered every inch of the material rendering the gown unwearable. Francis' dress it was.

The dress sat perfectly on my skin as if it had been made by my measurements. I refused to think how Francis had known my size.

Putting my hair in a simple braid, I tied it around itself in a low bun. The action immediately calmed my breathing. Even being alone in a room with my hair down was unbearable.

A loud knock made me jolt in place. "Are you trying to flood the castle there, Princess?" The smirk in Francis' voice was unmistakable.

Rolling my eyes, I slowly made my way back to the mirror: just a quick glance. The dress was even more gorgeous than before, embracing my light skin and dark features.

Staring at my smooth skin, my eyes widened. The small scar on my cheek had disappeared. It had been there ever since I was little, it became a part of me. If that scar had disappeared perhaps—

My trembling hands moved the fabric from my chest as disappointment washed over me. No. The scar Timothy had left me was still in its place. The memory of the knife flashed through my mind, making me shudder.

The knock on the door distracted me from my disarray. "Princess! My patience is running out. If you don't come out in a minute I will be forced to—" I didn't let him finish the sentence as I swung the door open. "You look—" Francis trailed off.

"Let's be on our way." I cut him off, annoyed. Annoyed at him, at myself, at this stupid ball. Annoyance and anger were my new companions.

"Of course," Francis said without the arrogance I'd grown accustomed to.

I started towards the music, not wishing to look at him for a second longer. I was not eager to attend the ball, although there was a small part of me that was curious to see what all the fuss was about. Or maybe it was the isolation I'd lived in the last couple of months. Either way, I was never going to admit I wanted company, even to myself.

We made our way through the labyrinth of endless hallways until I could finally recognize the music that was being played. It was a waltz. One of my favorites, actually.

I remembered learning it on my violin a few years back. I remembered my tutor, Master Waldrey, telling me to feel it rather than play the notes. The memory faded as though it had been in another life. Perhaps, it had been.

I quit thinking about it, afraid I would break down in tears. *I will not cry today!* Especially not in front of Francis.

Putting on the mask of indifference that I'd mastered in my years of being a future queen, I prepared for the worst.

Francis opened the door to the ballroom.

Chapter 7
"Moonshine, sweetheart."

For a few moments, all I could do was gawp at the view of this gigantic room. I could hardly call it a room, it must have been at least five times bigger than the ballroom at home.

I hope you won't be too disappointed, since our balls could never hold a standard of a royal event. Francis' words flashed in my mind. Arrogant man. Of course, this *gathering*—as he'd called it—was more luxurious than any I'd ever attended before. I should not have been surprised, but I was all the same.

The room—more like a hall—was truly glorious. Stained glass decorated every window, depriving the sun of the ability to intrude the space, wherever I looked. Every single one was different: from beautiful landscapes to mythical creatures. On the sides of each window sat many different sculptures, some of them made me feel uneasy.

Looking towards the ceiling, I gasped. A luxurious mosaic depicted several Gods—some I saw for the first time. Some were holding glasses of wine and I couldn't help myself but to wonder if it was indeed wine.

The whole room was glorious and I couldn't even begin to imagine what the rest of the castle was like.

I faced Francis who had been staring at me this whole time. He smiled, clearly feeling proud as though he'd made all of this art himself.

I shouldn't like this place, even if it was truly a work of art.

Evidently, Francis saw my inner battle as he winked at me. Winked! Moon, help me.

"Can we go eat?" The annoyance in his tone was unmistakable. "Now that you have appreciated my house for long enough." Francis rolled his eyes.

How dared he act like I was a burden on him? I'd never asked for any of this. If anything I was the one who had the right to be mad. I shook my head, my hands turned to fists.

We walked across the room, swaying around dancing pairs. I tried my best to stay invisible, though it didn't seem to matter: everyone here was too busy with their partners, not bothered by my presence. Not being used to that, I was unsure what my expectations were. I'd never liked big crowds, but at least at home, I'd been taught exactly how to act in one's presence.

Engaging conversations and laughter occupied the room—something I had not been expecting to hear. At home the balls were solely about alliances, even when the occasion had been someone's birthday, or marriage. There had never been any fun at such events, the fun that Sandra had craved so much.

By the time we had made our way across Francis had already found himself a drink. He passed me an identical glass, freezing me in place.

"'Tis wine, Princess." Francis laughed at me. "Drink."

A princess should keep her head clear. Mother's voice exclaimed in my mind as my hands stretched out towards the glass. Maybe being drunk wasn't the worst idea given the circumstances.

My eyes didn't leave the drink, studying it as though it was poison. A sigh escaped my lips before I finished the wine—it was indeed wine—in one gulp.

Francis' eyebrows shot up, he stared at me like he'd never seen me before. Francis passed me another glass which I finished in mere seconds as well. In pure surprise he was finally silent. Studying me, as though I'd grown horns in the past minute.

"Cordelia!" Florence called from behind me. "I'm so glad you decided to join!" she exclaimed as she hugged me.

Decided? I wasn't aware I had a choice, but before I could say anything her hands wrapped around me excitedly. She hugged me tight, as if we'd known each other for a while. My hands barely touched her back in an attempt to return the gesture, yet my mind just wished for all of this to be over.

For the next few hours I sat in the corner, pouring myself wine, watching people dance. I watched Florence in Roxanne's embrace as they danced beautifully through the hall. I hadn't seen Roxanne since that secret meeting in my garden, but her bright copper hair was unforgettable.

Occasionally Florence laughed at something Roxanne said.

In the garden Roxanne seemed very cold minded and mean, perhaps I'd been wrong. Or perhaps she was indeed mean to anyone but Florence.

I looked away when they started kissing. In the Royal court kissing so publicly would be considered rude, but here no one seemed to mind such gestures.

My eyes traveled through the hall until they landed on a couple in the corner. A woman in a dark green dress sat atop a man's lap. His lips were on her neck, kissing it ruthlessly.

My brows furrowed in disgust, though I could not seem to move my eyes away from the pair. A low moan escaped the woman's lips when the man's hand brushed along her cheek.

These people knew no manners. I poured myself another glass of wine.

"If you are trying to get drunk, this won't work," a voice behind me whispered. I jolted in surprise, meeting the eyes of the man who pointed his finger at my cup. "Sorry! Didn't mean to startle you," the man smiled at me.

His hair was bright ginger like the fire itself, and he wore green attire with gold ornaments on it.

"Simon." He extended his hand in greeting.

"Cordelia." I mumbled, ignoring the man's hand.

Perhaps my dismissive tone would make the man leave. Though, Simon seemed to have different plans as he moved a chair next to me, taking a seat.

"You should try moonshine, wine will not get you drunk," Simon said.

I poured myself another glass, ignoring the man altogether.

"I see, no one explained anything to you, did they?" Simon chuckled. "Your body heals too fast, wine is not strong enough to have much of an effect. It would be the same as drinking grape juice as a human." He shrugged. "Moonshine, on the other hand..."

"Moonshine it is then. Where do I get it?" I asked him with an enthusiasm that made him laugh even more. He didn't seem to mock me though, his laugh was kind, as though he, for some odd reason, found me funny.

"Definitely not here. Eager to get drunk?" Simon grabbed the pitcher from my hand, pouring himself a drink.

"Very."

"Then you should visit my tavern. I have plenty of moonshine there." He winked, taking a sip of his drink.

Despite my best attempts at dismissing this strange man, he managed to keep our conversation alive, throwing at me all kinds of questions about my life.

My short answers didn't seem to bother him as he kept talking and I couldn't help but wonder if he knew who I was. Simon talked to me as his equal. Something I'd never been allowed to do.

"Shall we dance?" He asked me eventually.

"I don't dance," I shook my head lightly. The last thing I wanted was to attract attention to myself.

"Liar." He laughed and for a second I didn't know what to say. No one ever called me a liar. They wouldn't have dared. "There is no way a princess cannot dance." Simon continued before I could find an answer.

So he did know, I see. My mood darkened at the reminder of my reality. Would he have even spoken to me had I not been Royal?

"Yes, I know who you are," Simon said, reading my face. "I'm afraid everyone here knows. The crown made a big deal about a princess who went missing."

The crown? My brow furrowed. They had been looking for me. *Of course they have, silly.* My mind traveled. Were they well? Were my siblings well?

"Are they still looking for me?" My gaze met Simon's, dreading his answer.

He quieted for a moment, choosing his words carefully. "They had a funeral a few nights ago," Simon said softly.

My eyes widened. A funeral? Everything in my body stilled. They thought I was dead, well, I suppose a part of me was dead, but the thought still made me nauseous.

"On second thought, here. You need it more than me." Simon interrupted my hurricane of thoughts, taking out the canteen from the inside pocket of his cloak. He opened it, offering it to me.

"What is it?" I asked, taking the bottle from his cold hands. I didn't wait for his answer, drinking the contents.

Whatever this was, it made my eyes water. The drink tasted absolutely disgusting, but I made sure to finish half, wishing it was poison that would end me right here.

"All right, all right. That's enough," Simon chuckled, taking the bottle from me.

A cough broke through me, as my eyes and nose watered. What in the Kingdom had I drunk? The tears fell from my eyes as if I poured salt water into them.

"Here," Simon handed me a napkin from the table and I gratefully took it from him: still coughing my throat out.

"It does get better, you know." He looked me straight in the eyes, as if making sure I listened carefully. "I know you don't believe it yet, but I've been there. It does get better, Cordelia." He sighed. "At least your family had a funeral." He slightly shoved my shoulder, laughing. Though his laughter fell short when his eyes met my glare.

For a while we were completely silent. My mind quieted when I returned to the people dancing, though I couldn't help but only to criticize the dancers. No one seemed to care for the proper technique here, or even count—for that matter—though at least they appeared to enjoy themselves.

The pair in front of our table doubled, so did everyone else. My head spun. I felt dizzy and suddenly... unnaturally calm.

"What was in the drink?" I said, mumbling over my words.

"Moonshine, sweetheart," Simon smiled. "Have you drunk before?" His brows flew up.

"No," I replied looking at the now two headed Simon. I blinked, trying to figure out which head was truly his.

He studied me carefully and for some reason his facial expression made me giggle.

"Are you—" Simon crooked his head. "All right?"

The question put me into a stupor. Was I all right? I had no way of knowing. The dreading feeling of my body shattering into small pieces was now dull. I could finally breathe without constantly battling my lungs to obey me. I supposed I was indeed all right.

"Yes!" I said, surprised at my own discovery. My head spun again, not in a nervous, terrifying way, but in a way that made me feel as if I was in a dream: flawless, weightless. "Are you?" I said, giggling. My tongue felt like it was in a knot. It was so hard to make the words out, but for some reason, there was no panic, the opposite: I found it funny. A little.

"You will feel better in a few minutes," Simon patted me on my shoulder, giving me a half smile.

"I'm fine." A small smile spread across my face as my eyes traveled toward the dance floor once again. Everyone danced so graciously, flawlessly. I was almost jealous. Almost. "Shall we dance?" I asked Simon, not believing my own words.

"You shouldn't dance right now. You will fall on your pretty face." He said, smirking.

Was he doubting my skill? Surely I could dance, I was not nearly drunk enough to fall. Or was I? How would I have known, I'd never danced drunk before. His mocking tone made me want to prove him wrong.

"Is that a challenge?" I replied, clearly not being myself. Was I really asking him to dance with me? What was I thinking? I barely knew this man. "Well?"

"All right, let's dance," Simon said at last. Getting up from his chair, he offered me a hand.

I took his hand in mine, as he led me to the dance floor.

Chapter 8
Devil's Creatures

Standing before Simon, I curtseyed, readying for our dance. He bowed for me, taking my right hand into his. The music played by the orchestra set the slow motion into our steps. One, two, three—one, two, three.

I had a strange feeling I was being evaluated, just like I'd been when dancing in front of court at home. I locked the feeling behind the wall in my mind, not wanting to think about it too much.

I followed Simon through the dance floor, keeping up with his movements with absolute perfection—as I said I would. Had he thought he could actually win this challenge? I'd been dancing since I was four, it would've been a great disappointment if in the last twenty years I hadn't perfected my performance.

Simon nodded approvingly when the music started playing faster, more intensely. Listening to the rhythm of this piece, I adapted to the new tempo with less confidence than I had had a moment ago. I had never danced to a waltz that fast, though I couldn't help but admire; the music was glorious.

I was used to slow dancing, loving the tension in each note, though this music made me feel something else: not romantic per se, but powerful, even free.

We passed dancing pairs graciously, moving to the cadence of the piece when my eyes spotted the orchestra for the first time. They all wore scarlet suits, playing their instruments with such elegance, such skill, they would've put any human orchestra to shame.

Mesmerized by their mastery, I watched them, thinking about my own violin. My fingers itched with desire to play my beloved instrument that was still at home. Would I be able to retrieve my goods one day? Would I take another step on the palace grounds?

Simon spun us to the center of the floor, letting go of my hands, allowing them to move freely in their own dance.

Lightning traveled through my body all the way down to my fingers. The pulse of the instruments reached my skin, reached my heart, making it beat with the same frequency. My breathing quickened, my body ached in exhaustion, but I cared not to stop. Addicted to the rush of excitement, my mind quieted.

Despite my years of firm training that deprived me of the ability to do the same, I now understood why no one paid much attention to the technique in this place. The music was too passionate, too intense to think about the strict rules. No matter my struggles, I still managed to make zero mistakes, though Simon didn't seem to care if I did.

The music reached its climax, slowing toward the end of the piece. Simon spun me for the last time, graciously moving me to his side for the ending sequence. One, two, three. The music quieted, slowly transitioning into the next piece.

I looked up at Simon, enjoying my victory. "Someone told me, I will fall on my face..." My brows flew up.

"That someone must be a fool, then," he replied with a smile on his face.

"Looks like it's my turn." Francis' voice carried from behind me as he graciously stretched out his hand toward mine, his other slowly moved to my waist. He gently turned me away from Simon. "Come now, Princess, I am a better dancer than your previous partner." He glanced at Simon, effortlessly spinning me around.

"I've danced plenty tonight." I bestowed him with the most annoyed look I could possibly manage. "Besides, I don't dance with amateurs."

"I promise, I won't outshine you, Your Highness." Francis purred into my ear, sending dozens of needles down my skin. "Just one dance, and you won't ever have to attend another ball if you don't wish to."

"Bargaining feels desperate even for you, don't you think?" I raised my brows, but did not move from his embrace.

"Is that a yes?"

I needn't his permission to not attend another ball, though something told me he took great pleasure carrying me through the halls. "One dance and no more balls?" My eyes narrowed.

A triumphant smile spread across his face, as he led us into the dance.

The back of my neck prickled when Francis' cold hand caught my waist. As though his skin grew thorns, it pierced the fabric of my dress, burning my flesh.

It's just a dance, Cordelia. I repeated in my head every-time his fingers moved so slightly. *Just one dance.* My knees shook with every step I took, my stomach turned in disgust.

I turned away from him, focusing on the musicians, praying they shorten their piece despite its beauty.

"You are doing the wrong steps, Your Highness," Francis pulled me closer, whispering into my ear.

A shiver went down my spine when I met his gaze. His amber eyes bored into mine, the corner of his lips turned up-wards. I swallowed the growing lump in my throat, adjust-ing my steps to his. "Perhaps I wouldn't make mistakes were I given a competent partner," I countered.

Francis chuckled, spinning me in beat with music. "Per-haps I am not used to dancing with masters like yourself." He winked, ignoring my never-ending glare.

The music slowed, every other instrument quieted, leav-ing the violin and piano to lead the piece. I wished I could enjoy the harmony, yet Francis had ruined even that; he spun us right to the center of the ballroom, stopping every oth-er pair in place. Dozens of eyes stung my skin, yet I refused them any acknowledgment.

"How are you enjoying my ball, Your Highness?" Fran-cis' voice cut through the violin.

"It's all right," I shrugged, painfully aware of all the strangers' ears around us. "There is clearly room for improve-ment," I added louder.

A grin spread across Francis' face. "I don't doubt that. I am open to suggestions, Your Highness."

"This music bores me." I almost heard a gasp from behind me. What in the Kingdom was I doing?

"And yet you agreed to a dance," Francis raised one brow.

"I believe you left me no choice." I cared not to hide the anger in my tone.

"I don't see a chain around your neck." Francis' face was just a few inches away from mine. "It's all right to enjoy my presence, Princess." He lowered his voice to a whisper, "Your secret is safe with me."

My skin flushed, though I didn't pay it any attention when I said my next words. "You and your foolish ball disgust me," I spat out. "Your arrogance blinds you, otherwise you could see how much I despise everything that involves you." My words silenced the musicians. Several people chuckled at my outburst; my eyes closed in embarrassment.

Francis' body pressed into mine, yet we did not move. The sweet burning feeling down in my stomach spread through my veins, spinning my head drunk.

A few moments of deathly silence passed before the musicians finally resumed their playing, making the strangers around us return to their dancing, forgetting about us altogether.

"Oh, I can see that, Princess, don't doubt." A small smile spread across Francis' face. "Thank you for allowing me the pleasure of your company." Francis slowly kissed both of my hands as he turned to leave without sparing me another glance.

"No more balls," I shouted after him, raising my chin. I turned back toward my table, though I couldn't help the feeling of foreign joy spreading through my chest despite my protests.

"Dear Gods, that was amazing," Florence planted her hand on my shoulder.

"Pardon me?" I slightly moved away from her reach.

"You totally humiliated him in front of everyone—" Florence grinned at me. "Oh—you must give me a lesson."

I sent Francis a quick glance, noting he was still watching me, a glass in his hand.

"On—humiliating Francis?" My brows furrowed.

"No silly!" she laughed. "Dancing! You were fabulous, you must tutor me."

"Oh. Of course," I replied to Florence, not exactly confident in what I'd just agreed to, but the bright smile spread across her face let me know my answer had satisfied her.

"Splendid!" Florence put a glass in my hand, urging me to drink. "You should have some."

"I think I've had enough for tonight." The idea of having any more alcohol in my veins made me nauseous. I should keep my head clear.

"It is not wine, Cordelia." Florence whispered, "You must have some before humans arrive."

My eyes flew toward her. Had I heard her correctly? The hair on my neck rose.

"Why would the humans come here?" I asked her, already guessing the answer.

Florence sighed as if trying to explain to a child why fire was hot, yet she stayed quiet. Shaking my head, I took a step backwards, my mind went into stupor.

"Take it," Florence shoved the drink into my hand, the smile on her face was long gone, and I could not remember if I'd ever seen her glum before.

My mind was occupied with dozens of awful images. My mouth went numb; nausea came in with great force, covering my skin in an icy sweat.

The doors to the ballroom flew wide open, letting a dozen people through.

My throat itched; I instinctively covered it with my hand. Their smell reached my nostrils, my lungs ached. The delightful aroma overwhelmed me, somehow I immediately knew the smell was of the human flesh.

It had not yet crossed my mind where the blood Florence brought me had come from. I'd been so worried for my own sanity, I'd cared not for the formalities of my new state.

No.

My head shook: in disapproval or disbelief—I was not sure. I would rather set myself on fire than participate in this nonsense.

Though Florence did not seem to care, trying to put the glass to my lips. "Drink it," she hissed at me. "Before you do something you will regret." She said, her stern tone left no room for an argument. Nothing of sunshine-Florence was left on her face. "Drink, Cordelia."

My trembling hands took the drink from her, obeying her requests. I emptied it, immediately noting that the drink she'd given me did not taste quite as good as the aroma coming from the group standing by the entrance of the ballroom.

"Good," Florence nodded, sighing in relief. She took the empty glass from my hand, hugging me tightly; although I could not return the hug this time. Paralyzed, all I was capable of doing was watching the scene that played out in front of me.

A dozen humans were at the mercy of the devil's creatures, their throats were on display before sharp teeth pierced their smooth skin.

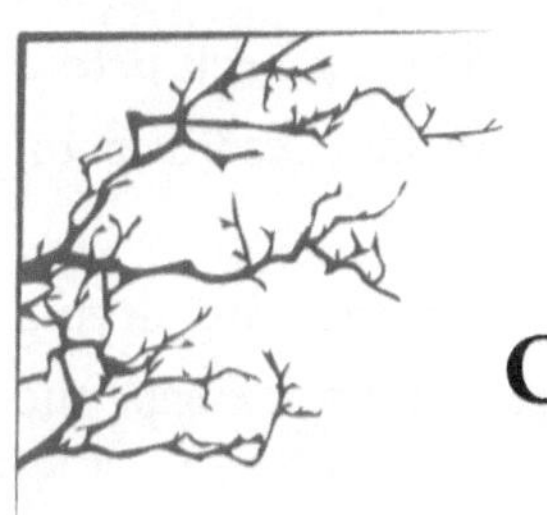

Chapter 9
A Gift

The shock left my eyes unable to close, unable to look away, revealing everything I had only seen in my nightmares as a child.

I didn't see pain in these people's eyes, just indifference and... enjoyment.

Perhaps, they'd gone mad in the moments of anticipation, unable to process what was happening to them. Perhaps, some of them had been prepared for such an outcome, and were patiently waiting for their endless dream.

Would they be dried empty of any thoughts? Would their hearts stop pumping, realizing there was nothing left to pump? Would some of them become the very thing they were victims of?

"Cordelia?"

Thunder broke into the room, making the windows shudder in protest.

The buzz in my head grew louder, as I watched a human leaning against a vampire's chest. Simon's chest. The woman threw her head back, allowing him closer.

I wanted to scream, run for her, take her away; though my body didn't move—paralyzed.

Simon moved his victim's hair, kissing her neck before piercing the skin with force. The woman squeaked in pain, her eyes rolling back.

Simon drank the woman's blood with pleasure, drying her empty. My head spun, but my eyes could not escape the horrific scene.

"Cordelia?" Cold hands gently held my face. "Please, look at me." Florence's worried eyes found mine.

"I will take her, go enjoy yourself, Florence." A voice came from behind me, making the back of my neck prickle.

Florence nodded, letting free of my face as I closed my eyes, not wanting to witness that spectacle again.

Strong hands held me by my shoulders, moving me towards the exit. My vision blurred, forcing nausea upon me: weakness entered every inch of my being.

"Princess?" The voice exclaimed. "I know you wouldn't want me to carry you out, so please walk."

The bitter words made my heart race with anger. His annoyed tone made me push him away, but I did as he said—I walked.

The sound of rain calmed my nerves; I focused on the noise, forcing the dark images out of my mind.

"Almost there," Francis said, making me realize he was not taking me to my room.

"Where are we going?" I asked him. I was in no position to protect myself, and the longer we walked, the less people I saw.

"Outside," Francis pulled on the large metal handle. "I figured you would like some fresh air, you haven't been outside in months."

The back door of the castle opened with a horrible squeak. A wave of air brushed over my skin, hitting my face with relief.

The rain drizzled into my hair, relaxing my wandering mind. I closed my eyes, putting my face directly into a stream of rain.

Francis' hand left my shoulder, reminding me of his presence.

I faced the man, meeting his gaze. "How can you allow this?" I accused him. My hands turned into fists, even the rain couldn't calm my fire.

"We need to feed." Francis shrugged, immediately understanding the subject of my question.

I took a deep breath, refusing to acknowledge the calmness of his answer. "Who are these people?"

"Someone who needs gold, someone who broke the law on human grounds, although, most of them are just lunatics."

My brows furrowed.

"They think of us as their high beings, gods sent by the Moon, if you will." He rolled his eyes at the absurdity of such words. "They bring themselves as sacrifices." He chuckled, as a new wave of nausea threatened to end me.

I staggered backwards, leaning against the wall of the castle. "You are no Gods, just monsters," I bit out through clenched teeth.

"We *are* higher beings, Princess, despite what you wish to believe." Francis took a step closer. "Besides, when did you hear about *good* gods? They're all just as gruesome as we are. Might as well call ourselves ones."

I shook my head in disbelief. "Your arrogance has no limits."

"So you've said." Francis took out a pipe from his jacket, covering it with his hand from the rain. "Do you mind?" He pointed at the pipe he'd already lit.

"Why just not give them gold? You have plenty." I gestured back towards the castle. "This is cruel."

"Again, we need to feed, Princess. It is what it is." The air filled with the smell of tobacco as Francis inhaled it. "It is very hypocritical, hearing it from a royal. How is this any different than people coming to court with *gifts*, offering their last goods? What about those knights who put their lives for your family's well-being?" Francis' eyebrows shot up.

"This is different!" I screamed in disbelief. How could he have compared the two? "We are not ending the lives of those who supply the castle." I added. "As for the knights, they protect the whole Kingdom, not just Royals. Moreover, they are paid to do so."

Francis laughed so hard, it made my blood boil. The urge to hit him just increased with new power. "When's the last time you've seen a knight beyond the royal grounds. Those humans you saw," he said through his laughter. "No knights protect them. Their villages are too poor for your crown to care about." He added seriously, "And we do not kill them either, not all of them at least." He shrugged. "Only those who broke the law and were sentenced to death. Anyone here on their own accord may leave this castle whenever they please.

"They know the risk of entering our castle, but no one is dragging them down here against their will. We offer safety to their children, we give them gold, and they give us just enough blood for us to survive without giving up their lives." Francis paused, filling his lungs with tobacco. "It is a simple transaction. We have a treaty. No innocent soul gets hurt if they act upon their part of the deal."

"They will turn into vampires!" I screamed at him again, disgusted by his calmness.

"Do they not teach you about our kind in your realm anymore?" Francis shook his head, taking a deep breath before continuing. "They will not turn from a bite unless that is what their souls wish to happen; they certainly will not turn from simply giving us blood."

My lungs refused to work as though someone hit my chest, forcing the air out. What in the Kingdom was he saying? *If they wish for it to happen.*

There was only one book I'd found in the library that had any kind of information besides the brief history we were given in our lessons. Of course, everyone at the castle knew the basics, but no one bothered to study the topic deeper. Nothing about the choice had been mentioned in the book.

"What—" My brows furrowed. "What are you saying?"

Francis grinned, as he let the tobacco escape his mouth. "Unless you are a reborn vampire, in order to turn, a bite has to be presented as a gift. Nothing should be taken in return: no blood."

I held onto the wall of the castle, steadying myself as the rain hardened, making my gown soaking wet. The lightning interrupted our conversation, dividing the starlit sky into two.

"Then," Francis continued quietly as I held my breath, dreading his next words. "The one who got bitten will only turn if they aren't willing to fight for their human nature. Someone who is unhappy with their being, per se." I shook my head at his words, not believing in them. "Otherwise the bite will heal on its own, as any animal bite would." Francis said, watching my reaction carefully. "Odd they don't teach you that at the royal palace, don't you think? Sounds pretty important to me. Every human at this village knows it." He took another inhale from his pipe.

It couldn't be true. He had to be lying to me. My whole body shook in unison with the thunder. My mind traveled, unable to comprehend the words Francis threw at me.

Surely I had not wished to become my greatest enemy.

I stared at the ceiling of my new room, deep in my thoughts.

A whole week had passed since my conversation with Francis, yet his words were still loud and clear in my mind, taking the ability to rest from me. *The one who got bitten will turn only if they aren't willing to fight for their human nature.* Had he told me the lie to redeem his choice of creating me—blaming me perhaps?

The bite has to be presented as a gift, nothing should be taken in return. A gift. What kind of gift was that, where your life is taken from you? Had my human life truly been so disastrous that my consciousness chose a different form?

A week in the room with all the questions floating above me like a heavy cloud, yet I still hadn't found any answers. The walls narrowed down on me with every passing second. My thoughts slowly drove me mad. Everytime I lost the battle of staying awake, my mind was invaded by dozens of humans bleeding dry before me.

I understood the extremes and necessities of such a treaty, although my heart refused to accept it. How could I participate in such gruesomeness?

No innocent soul gets hurt, if they act upon their part of the deal. What kind of hardship had one faced to be willing to put their lives at the mercy of whomever had gold and safety? How could the crown allow this?

I'd always known my mother only gave time to those she deemed worthy, but as a ruler, how could she allow innocent people—her people—to take such risks to feed their own children.

Could I really take the lives of those who were forced to come here because of a broken law?

Darkness slowly creeped into my vision, making my eyelids heavy. No matter my best attempts at staying awake, my consciousness abandoned me.

"What are you doing?" My whisper echoed through the hall of the Royal palace. "Someone will see."

"No one is here," he rolled his eyes. "Stop being so prude, Cordelia."

My chest squeezed tight. My trembling hands caught his, forcing them away.

Run. *As though a statue, my body did not move. My legs were frozen in place.*

Scream. *A scream escaped my lips. The sound did not reach my ears. As though under water, my voice was silent.*

The music from the ballroom grew louder.

And louder. And louder, and louder, and louder.

My eyes frantically searched for an exit when bright red covered my vision.

"Stop fighting me," he roared into my ear.

Dozens of lifeless bodies laid all over the floor. Their empty eyes did not leave mine when Timothy's hands wrapped around the fabric of my birthday gown.

The knife shimmered under the candle light. A woman's empty eyes stared at me from the reflection of the blade. Her crimson lips stretched out in a slow smile.

Timothy brought the knife closer to my flesh. "Don't you trust me?"

"Stop!" My voice finally broke through the heavy fog, forcing me awake. "Stop!" My eyes flew open, searching the room for any kind of invasion.

No one was here. He was not here. He would never hurt me again.

Nausea creeped into my being, turning my insides upside down. I barely made it to the bathing chambers before my stomach emptied itself out. I desperately needed a wash.

My skin cried in pain from all the scrubbing, though I still felt the shadows of his fingers on my flesh. My mind still felt his shadows hiding in the corners.

I needed to get out of this room.

Chapter 10
Prejudice

The castle was quiet at this late hour, only my steps and the unstopping rain interrupted the silence, as if to keep me company on this adventure.

For the first time since I'd gotten here, I was completely by myself walking through the dark corridors.

The darkness of this place made my mind wander to the scary stories I'd read as a child, sending a cool chill of awareness through my body; though I did not feel threatened, the opposite—I felt surprisingly calm. As if the darkness belonged to me, welcomed me to the depths of its secrets.

My candle lit up the walls of the castle, introducing me to the arts of this foreign place. Paintings of eerie, sinful images occupied every inch of the staircase walls, and I couldn't help studying the art longer than I should have. The wicked and erotic nature of the work publicized so freely made my face heat.

I walked through every open door, every hall that allowed me in. Art was everywhere; I had to force myself to continue my exploration without stopping every moment to study the interesting sculptures and paintings.

The red wooden door creaked in protest when I pushed it open. Taking a step forward I entered—what looked to be—a music room. Musical instruments occupied every corner of the space: from clarinets scattered across the walls to a grand piano standing proudly in the center. Vases with long dead jasmine took up every corner, delighting the space with its aroma.

The room was messy, books and music sheets were displayed on every surface. Empty bottles of wine gave away the owner of this room, although I couldn't be absolutely certain.

Studying the sheet on the music stand, I hummed the notes scribbled with passion. The melody was sad, set in a minor scale, making my heart melt with sorrow. I memorized the melody, wishing to bring it into life on my violin one day. Perhaps they had a violin in here, though I was not eager to touch anyone else's instruments—whoever the owner was.

I continued my observation, flipping through the book on the table nearby. The handwriting was barely legible, full of rage and tragedy. I read through the pages until my eyes spotted a signature at the bottom of the page. *To Issac,* it read. I quickly closed the book, realizing it was an unsent letter.

Ashamed of my actions, my legs carried me out the room, not wishing to continue my adventures snooping around a space that felt so intimate.

I'd wandered around for what seemed to be hours, and still there were so many floors I hadn't discovered yet.

As I walked through the long corridors, a huge wooden door entered my view.

A big hall overflowed with dozens of weapons and training equipment I once saw the knights at home use. This must've been a training hall, but who trained here? How many people lived here exactly?

Sets of axes, bows, daggers, and swords proudly decorated the hall. My hand extended toward a sword that looked just like mine before my mind had an opportunity to stop it.

This sword was longer than I was used to, and a lot heavier. I wielded it around, just like my father had taught me to, remembering his hands on my shoulder fixing my stance. *Hold it like it's an extension of your hand, little pearl,* he used to say to me.

Lost in the memory, I wielded the sword slicing my invisible opponent's neck. A smile of joy spread across my face from my little triumph, until the sound of slow clapping interrupted the peacefulness of the room, forcing my head towards the sound.

Two pairs of eyes watched me from a distance.

Roxanne stood next to the man who kept clapping, eyeing me with unmistakable annoyance. They both wore some kind of training attire: long trousers and tunics. Roxanne's fiery hair was braided into a crown, revealing her long neck.

"You shouldn't be here," the man said at last, his eyes shot lightning at me.

His black hair and brown eyes reminded me of the day I'd tried to escape this place. He was the one standing by the door of my room when I'd ran off, he was the one talking to Francis just moments earlier.

"Well?" The man brought me back from my observation and for the first time I felt true terror being in the presence of a vampire. He looked as if he was holding himself back from lunging towards me and draining me empty of any thought.

"I was just leaving," I made sure my voice sounded steady as I put away the sword back in its place. The man just snickered in reply.

"Leave her be, Caleb." Roxanne grabbed a bow and arrow from its stand.

My eyes never left Caleb's, searching for any sign he wouldn't charge me the moment Roxanne was distracted. Perhaps I put the sword away too early.

Caleb eyed me expectedly, assessing my own appearance this time. "Duel with me," he spat out.

"What?" I didn't bother hiding my confusion. The man had at least a foot on me, and a moment ago he looked at me as though his gaze alone could make me disappear.

Caleb started towards me and despite my better judgment I took a step back. He grabbed the sword I just put away, flashing an ugly scar that marked his hand. "Prove you can be more than a waste of space in this castle," he snickered, shoving the weapon towards me.

"Caleb," Roxanne called out in warning from the other side of the room while effortlessly sending the arrow flying straight into the center of the hay target.

I stared back at him still in disbelief, though his cruel words dared me to take the challenge.

What in the Kingdom was I thinking? There was no way I could possibly win—I hadn't trained in years, and even if I had I stood no chance against the warrior he certainly was. "I am out of practice," I finally said.

"Does it look like I care?" He shoved the sword into my chest. "I won't draw blood, I swear on the Moon. Not this time, at least," he whispered. "Prove you are more than a useless royal."

My vision blurred in rage when I grabbed the sword from him. My recklessness would be my end.

Caleb's cruel smile did not leave his face as he unsheathed his dagger. *A dagger!*

I took my stance, squeezing the hilt of the weapon. If I wanted any chance at surviving this I had to attack first. The weapon advantage was on my side, since Caleb thought I was too weak for him to arm himself accordingly.

I swung my sword to the right, holding it with both hands, preparing to strike my first blow. Caleb did not stop smiling down at me.

The sword was meant to be used with one hand, although I was not used to such weight. I cared not how inexperienced I might have seemed.

Absolutely no part of me believed Caleb's promise to not draw blood. Nevertheless, I'd made no such vows. I went straight for open skin.

Caleb staggered backwards—surprised at my skill or boldness, I was not sure—but quickly collected himself.

A lazy grin appeared on Caleb's face as he put himself back into his stance.

A rich smell of sour and sweet invaded my senses; my eyes traced the source of the smell: a thin red line was located right above Caleb's tunic.

A shiver went through me at the sight of a fresh wound, I could only hope it would not distract me. The uncomfortable prickling in my throat increased, but the anger in me refused to give into the feeling.

Caleb followed my gaze, tracing his fingers across the injury. The triumph of a small victory spread through my chest, although I could not allow myself to celebrate until this nonsense was over. Caleb's cocky smile had finally disappeared, leaving anger to take its place.

If he had not considered killing me before, I knew now the promise was long gone. I'd provoked him further by cutting his skin, though there was no part of me that regretted the move.

Caleb attempted to assess me once again, but I charged, preventing him from doing so. This time Caleb blocked every blow I threw at him with ease.

The sound of banging metal rang in my ears. Caleb got closer with each move, trapping me against the wall. Panic overwhelmed my senses, and I chided myself for letting him get his way.

My back hit the wall, yet Caleb had no intention of stepping away. Although his blade had not touched my flesh, it was inches away from doing so.

Each blow became harder to set back; my arms screamed in protest. Stray strands of hair flew into my face. Cold sweat broke through my skin, causing my palms to lose their grip. *He is going to end me, right here, right now.*

Everything slowed when the loud sound of metal hitting the marble stopped my movements in place.

My sword had fallen to the floor and with it my heart had as well.

Caleb's dagger met my uncovered neck; my mind wandered, waiting to meet the Gods.

I drew a small breath, and wondered if it was my last.

Chapter 11
Twelfth Moon

"Enough, Caleb." Roxanne rushed toward us. "Leave her alone." Her voice stayed calm, yet the coldness in her tone left no room for debate.

Caleb's blade did not leave my neck, though it did not touch it either. Our gazes locked. The fire in his eyes met my own.

"I know you," I mumbled in a whisper, studying this man's sickly familiar features.

"I highly doubt it," he hissed through gritted teeth. "I don't consort with royalty," Caleb spat out the last word.

"Put your weapon down. Now!" Roxanne barked at the man, forcing herself between us.

Caleb reluctantly lowered his weapon without taking his eyes off me.

"Would you give us a moment?" Roxanne glanced in my direction; nothing in her tone was nice nor polite.

I managed a slow nod, using the opportunity to flee.

Despite the numbness in my legs, I walked as fast as I possibly could. The shock was still fresh in my mind, paralyzing every other thought.

Closing the door behind me, I leaned on it, allowing myself a moment to calm.

I could have died was it not for Roxanne. What had I been thinking? The moment he'd entered the room, looking at me like that, I should have made my exit immediately.

Shaking my head in disbelief, I drew a shaky breath in.

"What do you think you are doing, Caleb?" Roxanne's voice traveled through the closed door. "You are lucky no one else was here to see this," she hissed at him. "I do not care how much you hate her, she can help us. Stop acting so foolish. Do you understand me, Caleb? Don't let this happen again."

Help us? Even if I'd been capable of helping them with whatever they needed, I was not sure I wanted to—not after this introduction.

The sound of steps behind the closed door grew louder, shortening the distance between us, forcing my legs to carry me back to my room.

The inside of the castle got darker—the sun must've set by now. The corridors did not seem welcoming anymore, the art on the walls glared at me menacingly.

Hoping I would find my room before meeting anyone else, I rushed up the stairs when a gleam of candle light appeared at the end of the corridor.

Did Roxanne and Caleb follow after me? What will they do to me? I held my breath, freezing in the shadows.

"Cordelia?" Florence's voice exclaimed, peaking past the candle.

I emerged from the darkness, relieved by my company.

Florence bestowed me with her sunshine smile. "I was looking for you, actually." She took a step forward. "Would you like to go to the Faris Village with me tonight? I wanted to visit the orphanage, and maybe give you a proper tour." The tone of her voice was full of hope. "Or I could show you around our castle, introduce you to everyone—whatever you would like."

Heavy footsteps echoing in the distance reminded me exactly who resided in this castle.

"The tour of the village sounds wonderful." I started down the stairs once again. "I would love to go right now."

My enthusiasm took Florence off guard; her eyes widened in confusion, yet she still followed me down—out of the castle: away from Caleb, Roxanne, and Francis.

"You can take this one, her name is Annabelle." Florence gestured toward a horse in the stables, setting up the saddle. "Do you like her?"

"Annabelle," I repeated, nodding in reply, petting the black horse standing in front of me.

The horse was lovely and reminded me of my own back home. I hadn't ridden in a long time and missed the speed and freedom that came with it.

"She's yours!" Florence exclaimed.

I wanted to argue, yet could not find it in me to say the words. It would've been wonderful to own a horse again: having the freedom of going anywhere I wished. Perhaps even more freedom than I'd had at home.

Florence mounted her white mare, waiting for me to follow. "We should definitely stop by some shops," she changed the topic, starting towards the small path in the woods. "Get you new clothes," she glanced at my dress.

I smiled at her suggestion; I definitely needed something else to wear. As much as I loved the red-golden dress I'd worn since the ball, it was far too luxurious for everyday wear. Moreover, Francis bought it for me, and I would've liked some independence, especially when it came to him.

"I have no gold, Florence," I suddenly realized.

"No need," she glanced back at me: the path was so narrow, two horses could not fit to walk side by side. "We do not exchange currencies here—we exchange services." Florence said proudly.

Services?

Florence grinned at my puzzled expression, as though she was about to tell me the biggest secret there was. "We host balls and different kinds of social events that allow the whole village to feed. In return, we get to use the services others have to offer: human food, drinks, clothes, horses." Florence shrugged, turning back on her path. "No gold is involved, as long as the ones you exchange with are vampires. Humans, on the other hand, wish to have gold. For some reason they see more value in a few coins."

Exchange services. Interesting. I had never heard of such an arrangement, yet it did sound appealing. More humane, somehow.

For a little while we fell into silence. The moon lit up our pathway, glowing just as brightly as the night I'd gone to the cemetery. The trees were now completely naked, prepared to wear their white attires.

My brows furrowed.

If my calculations were correct, winter should've been upon us with full force. There was no trace of snow yet.

I'd been bitten right after the autumn harvest, at the beginning of the ninth moon. The season had been changing with drastic speed even then, making everyone believe the winter would be long and cold this year. If Francis hadn't lied about me being here for months it should've been at least the eleventh moon right now: which always meant a lot of snow.

"What month is it?" I called after Florence.

"We have not yet entered the twelfth full moon," she replied quietly. "The weather is funny this year." She shrugged, the smile still on her face.

"Funny, indeed."

Though, something told me Florence knew a lot more about this anomaly than she showed me.

We continued the rest of our trip in silence until the forest surrounding us thinned.

Florence halted her mare, slowing Annabelle to a stop. She stared into the distance, her eyes lit up in excitement.

Gorgeous castles and estates settled down the hill, decorating the space with its astonishing architecture, inviting wandering souls into its mystery.

Chapter 12
Wandering Souls

Firelight illuminated every corner of the street. The stone roads overflowed with ravishing architecture and castle-like estates. Various shops occupied every corner, overwhelming me with their diversity.

Some sold clothes, some jewelry; some even sold poison potions. My eyes wandered, trying to catch a glimpse of every single part of this peculiar place.

"This way!" Florence tugged on my sleeve, leading me toward a shop she insisted we visit.

Hours later—and four new dresses—I still hadn't seen every street of this magical village.

The square was filled with laughter, loud conversations, and music. I watched the musicians skilfully play their instruments; their music traveled through the crowd, enticing people to dance.

"I promised the children at the orphanage I would pay them a visit tonight. They will be so excited to meet you," Florence interrupted my observation. "It is not far from here."

"Orphanage?" My eyebrows flew up.

"Yes, the children who haven't found their permanent houses yet live there." Florence held my hand as she pulled me down the street in the opposite direction of the musicians. "They are the sweetest! Let's go!"

Were the children at this orphanage bitten? I wanted to ask her, yet something told me I did not wish to know the answer.

The orphanage was a glorious castle located at the end of the main street, each window was rainbow colored stained glass. Children's laughter was heard even from outside the castle.

I did not know what I expected to witness, yet my imagination could've never done a justice to what was presented in front of me.

The place was truly enchanting; the ceiling was painted blue, displaying many stars with the Moon right in the center.

"Florence! Florence is here!" Dozens of children sang in unison, running toward Florence, embracing her in tight hugs.

"I brought you a friend!" Florence exclaimed, chuckling. "Her name is Cordelia," She nudged me towards the group.

"Cordelia," the children slowly repeated my name in awe, as though tasting the sound of it. They all stared at me, expectancy in their eyes.

"May I braid your hair, Miss?" A girl in a dark green dress asked, gazing at me with huge—inhumanly glowing—green eyes. She looked to be around seven years of age, although given the knowledge I possessed, she very well could've been much older than me.

I found myself nodding at her question, unable to deny her any requests. A big smile spread across her face as she took my hand, walking me deep inside the rainbow castle.

I undid my already braided hair. *She is just a child.* I told myself. *Timothy is not here.* I repeated it in my head as a mantra.

The green dress girl, who'd introduced herself as Charlotte, braided my hair with so much care, happily telling me all about her night. "We were not allowed outside tonight," Charlotte sighed. "Miss Morella said it rained a lot the day before, and the streets were still too muddy to play."

Charlotte picked a dried bouquet, carefully adding the wildflowers into my hair. When I'd asked how old she was, Charlotte just shrugged. "It was my hundred and thirty-first birthday last full moon, although Miss Morella says I will always be eight." She rolled her eyes.

Dear Gods. A hundred and thirty-one years of age, and still lived here, at the orphanage. An elder spirit trapped in a child's mind forever. *I will always be eight,* she'd said. Always a child no matter the time passing. Who could've possibly done this to a pure, innocent soul? Who'd been evil enough to doom a child to such a fate of eternity.

I glanced at Florence in the center of the hall, who now spun the jumping rope for the children. I wanted to ask her all about these precious, beautiful souls. What had happened to them? How had they found themselves here, in this magical, yet, all the same, dangerous village?

Deep in thought I didn't notice Charlotte standing in front of me at first. She studied me with her beautiful bright eyes, staring at me in awe. "You look like a princess," she said at last.

Charlotte's words broke something inside of my chest—perhaps it'd been my heart, though I could not be certain—as I smiled back at her.

"That she is," the voice behind me broke through all the children's laughter. I spun towards the sound, spotting Francis leaning against the wall. He wore the same vest he'd worn at the Royal ball all those months ago. His hair fell in a perfect mess, barely touching his shoulders when he grinned at me.

"Oh, Francis, back so soon? Where's Roxanne? I thought she went with you." Florence turned to face him, without slowing the jumping rope. "How did the meeting with the Barrens go?"

My heart stopped at the mention of Timothy's family name.

I smiled back at Charlotte, pretending I had no interest in their conversation, though I could feel Francis' withering gaze on my back.

"The meeting—" Francis trailed off. "Went as usual." He finished after a brief pause, as though choosing his words carefully. "Roxanne went home right after, she wanted me to let you know not to wait for her."

"It couldn't possibly be this bad," Florence's voice was barely a whisper.

Francis shrugged. "I will see you both at home," he said, turning towards the exit.

What meeting? What in the Kingdom is going on? I wanted to ask, but before I got a chance Charlotte took my hands into hers once again. "Could we please dance now?" She jumped up and down in excitement.

"Yes! Yes, please!" The children all around me yelped in unison, clapping their hands, as they dragged me to the center of the hall.

The clatter of hooves onto the gravel was the only sound occupying the forest. According to Florence we had at least an hour to get back before the sun rose.

On the way home, all I thought about was the mysterious meeting, though I could not ask Florence about it just yet. She was the only one I could possibly trust here, yet I was not confident she wouldn't keep anything from me. No. I had to take a different approach if I wanted to know the truth.

Instead, I asked her something less alarming. "How did those children end up at the orphanage?" I called after her. "Were they bitten at such a young age?"

"No, they were not bitten, Cordelia. We are not actually allowed to bite children; we have a treaty." Florence looked back at me. "They are like me—reborn." She smiled.

"Reborn?" I asked, remembering Francis mentioned something about reborn vampires.

"Yes. It is a bit complicated to explain, and being totally honest, I still do not fully understand it, but in order to become a reborn, the human body that hosted the soul had to have been killed by unnatural means." Florence took a long breath before continuing. "The souls who felt like their satisfactions were not met in their—often very short—lives, will return to our kingdom in a different form—in the form of a Vampire—to finish their duties."

I stared at her, my brows knitted together.

Florence sighed, returning her attention back to the pathway. "We died at the hands of others, Cordelia. Unnatural deaths." She cleared her throat. "Our human souls were not ready to leave this world, so we have been reborn in the form of a vampire."

Killed. All of those children had been murdered by gruesome human beings. Every single one of them.

My stomach turned upside down at the idea of it, nausea settled deep in my chest. "I am sorry that happened to you."

Florence sent me a half smile, "It's all right."

Silence fell in between us. I wished to ask her what had happened, but kept my mouth shut. I had no right to request such vulnerability from the person I'd been nothing but rude to these past months.

"It's all right to wonder, Cordelia." She read into my expression. "It's in the past," she shrugged. "My human family were travelers: never stayed in one place for long."

I held my breath in, catching her every word.

"On one of those trips, some hunters tried to rob our carriage. My dearest father got into a fight with them, protecting me and my siblings."

My fingers tightened around the reins.

"They killed him first," she said calmly. "Then the hunters cut my mother's throat, along with my young siblings, leaving me for last.

"I was nineteen then, the hunters thought I would be a great use for them, but seeing what they had done to my family I couldn't take it anymore. I took out the knife my father gifted me, and ended my suffering myself."

An icy chill ran down my skin.

"The next thing I remembered was waking in the cemetery, seeing the unnamed cold stones, lying next to the grave I must have dug out from. I didn't understand what had happened, I was all by myself." Florence sighed. "For a while I was convinced my siblings shared the same destiny; I wandered around the world for the longest time hoping to find them.

"Perhaps their souls chose to rest in the end."

I stared at Florence in horror, unable to say a word.

"My life got better after I met Roxanne, Caleb, and Francis. They offered me a place to stay, food, and companionship. I found the love of my life in this new being." The sunshine smile was back on her face. "I know you had a rough beginning here, Cordelia, but time will heal your wounds. I really hope you can find happiness here."

The distraught I had felt when Francis first brought me here seemed childish after hearing Florence's story, although she never seemed to judge me for it. I could not imagine what she had to go through before finally finding her peace.

The first sunray glanced from the horizon when we arrived at the castle. For the first time I saw it from the outside in its full glory.

The castle looked to be abandoned—only a few windows shimmered with firelight, giving this place some sense of life within.

Leaving our horses in the stable, I followed Florence through the front gate, passing the ballroom I'd danced in last week. Had it really only been a week? Somehow it felt like eternity.

Florence entered a room I had yet to discover, holding the door open for me. I hesitated entering, fighting the urge to find my own room, not interested in meeting Caleb again; though Florence didn't let me get away that easily as she pulled on my sleeve to enter.

I walked into the pitch black room, unable to see anything beyond my outstretched hand. Unwelcome fear grew deep in my stomach, forcing my eyes to adjust to new conditions. A few seconds passed before the pitch black room took on a new light. It was still dark, though I could see everything nearly perfectly.

I blinked rapidly, not believing in such abnormality.

The sound of matches being struck interrupted the silence, forcing my head to instinctively turn in its direction.

The room gained color, the fireplace in the center of the stone wall bestowed us with its beauty. Florence's eyes glowed, reflecting the firelight, as she stared at the dark green settee in front of the fireplace.

A huge wooden table settled to my right, twelve chairs encircling it. Right in the center of the table sat long dead roses, as if darkness itself rushed through the room, sucking the life out of them.

I walked towards Florence whose smile dropped as if it never even belonged on her face. Walking around six settees facing the fireplace in a half circle, I followed Florence's gaze, and saw the reason for the worry in her eyes.

Fiery hair fell in beautiful waves all around the cushions of the settee. Roxanne laid on her side, staring into the fire with blank eyes.

"I will bring us all some blood, make yourself comfortable," Florence told me, gesturing toward the settee next to the one Roxanne occupied.

I nodded, even though the last thing I wanted was to be left alone in the room with Roxanne.

Florence turned on one heel, walking out the door after I took my designated seat near her beloved.

Roxanne's empty eyes did not leave the fire's flames as she moved to sit upright. Without sparing me a glance—as though I was not even there—she let out an exhausted sigh. Perhaps I was lucky she paid me no attention. I did not wish to be in the middle of whatever forced Roxanne into such distress.

Was this about the mysterious meeting she and Francis had attended earlier? Why would they need to meet with the Barrens of all people? I had to know what the subject of these discussions was without anyone withholding the information from me.

Perhaps Roxanne would've been a perfect candidate to tell me all I needed to know; we only properly met this morning, she wouldn't have been aware of how little I knew of the situation with the Barrens.

I had the perfect chance at succeeding if I played my role well.

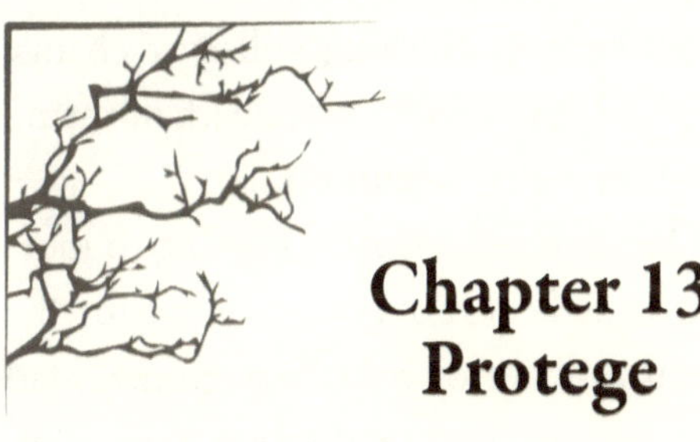

Chapter 13
Protege

Gathering myself, I prepared for the likely unpleasant conversation. *Just say the words, Cordelia.* I chided myself, annoyed at my own uncertainty.

"I see the meeting didn't go as planned?" I asked her, ensuring I kept my voice steady. I could not show her I cared about her answer. I definitely could not show her I had no idea what was going on.

"Huh," she snorted, noticing me for the first time. "*Didn't go as planned* is an understatement," Roxanne's soft accent swept through the room as she rolled her eyes.

Her answer did not give me much to work with. I had to do better than this. *Think, Cordelia, think.*

They'd met the Barrens, just like they'd met someone in my garden. What had they talked about then? My memory failed me at my attempt to recall the events that took place months ago.

A meeting with a noble can only mean one thing. The sudden realization hit me right before I gave up on my weak attempts at this manipulation.

They'd tried to come to some kind of agreement, bargained perhaps. If the meeting hadn't gone well, the Barrens must have refused whatever was offered.

"Barrens are foolish people. Nothing will ever change their minds. Their own selfishness will be the death of them," I said, praying I reached the right conclusion.

"Foolish, indeed," Roxanne said slowly, turning to meet my gaze. Her brows frowned, as though seeing me for the first time. Her gaze sent a shiver of cold through me. Had I already given myself away? "They will never believe us, thanks to your mother." Roxanne glared at me.

"My mother?" I failed to hold my tongue from asking. What did Mother have to do with the meeting? Had she been there as well?

"What?" Roxanne laughed at me. "Did you think the information about the Wurdulacs' attacks was public? Not everyone is a royal daughter with access to such knowledge."

Wurdulacs' attack? My breathing quickened at the reminder of the vampires that took my brother and father from me. Were they attacking humans again? What about our treaty? How many people had already suffered from their invasion?

Mother knew.

She knew and did nothing to prevent it.

Suddenly everything finally fell into place. All the rejections from joining the council meetings despite being allowed before. All the secrecy in her study. The Vanishing List.

"You had no idea, did you?" Roxanne narrowed her eyes on me.

"Of course I did," I replied defensively, trying to hold my mask of indifference.

"The look on your face suggests otherwise." Roxanne snickered. "Our dearest Queen truly outdid herself if she didn't even tell her protege."

"I am not her protege," I bit out in protest, yet Roxanne just shrugged at my outburst. "So, why do you need the Barrens' support?" I asked openly—no point in lying anymore. Not that I'm good at it anyway.

"For their army, of course," Roxanne scoffed. "We need their weapons."

"Why do you care anyway? Aren't they just attacking humans?" I cared not to come out as ignorant, my curiosity won over my pride.

"'Tis a common misconception among humans, although I thought a royal would know better." Roxanne rolled her eyes. I ignored the insult, patiently waiting for an answer. Roxanne let out an exhausted sigh before continuing. "No, they are not just attacking humans. They want full power of the land, that includes whoever does not agree with such terms. They want humans to be nothing more than a meal, sure, but they want some of us to serve them, become their slaves.

"And humans are too foolish to recognize the threat. When they finally realize we were correct all along, it will be too late."

"So you just need proof then?" I asked.

"Easier said than done—" Roxanne scoffed. "But yes, we need some kind of proof that they stand behind all the disorders."

My mind wandered to all of the possibilities. If what Roxanne had told me was the truth, my siblings were in great danger. The Royal family and their army had been the only barrier that had stopped the Wurdulacs from achieving their goals seven years ago. Surely they had learned from their failure, and would eliminate their biggest enemy first. My family would be the first to fall.

The sound of footsteps behind the door grew louder, interrupting my worrisome mind. Francis casually made his way into the room, taking the seat closest to the fire.

He wore the same black and gold vest he'd been in at the orphanage earlier. His eyes reflected the firelight, making them the most beautiful amber I had ever seen. The room fell into awkward silence as he took a small sip, getting comfortable on the chair.

Roxanne turned towards me, putting her back at Francis as though he was invisible. The move only made him roll his eyes in reply.

My brows shot up, unsure of what to make of the strange interaction. Had they gotten into an argument at the meeting like they had at my garden? Why was it always these two that met nobles anyway? They didn't appear to be the most compatible duo. How had they even met?

Suddenly, I needed to know. "How did you turn into a vampire?" I asked Roxanne. The question left my mouth before I thought better of it.

Roxanne shot me a look which made me regret the question immediately, but when her gaze fell onto Francis' clenched jaw, a small smile spread across her face. "My own foolishness got me here, you see," she replied, grinning. "Francis, Isaac, and I thought we could outwit a vampire without any consequences. We failed." Roxanne smirked ominously.

"Rox," Francis' sharp tone interrupted her, yet she just grinned, turning to face him.

"It is my story too, Francis," Roxanne smiled down at him, nothing about that smile felt genuine. "I get to tell *my* story to whomever I wish," she added angrily this time.

Isaac? It took me a moment to remember where I'd heard that name before. All those letters in the music room were addressed to him.

The awkward silence returned into the room as Francis and Roxanne stared at each other without saying a word. Only the sound of the door creaking broke through the veil.

"I am back with our dessert!" Florence exclaimed happily, making her way towards us, three glasses of crimson liquid in her hands. Simon followed her into the room, taking a seat beside Francis. The fresh memory of his teeth piercing through that woman's neck sent a shiver through me.

Florence offered me a drink before settling down on Roxanne's settee, bestowing her with a smile brighter than the full Moon herself; to my surprise Roxanne returned the smile, quietly thanking Florence.

I glanced at the glass in my hands before deliberately setting it down on the floor. The beast inside of me fought for its way out, yet I refused it any satisfaction. Not in front of everyone. Not when everyone drank it for their own pleasure and not merely as a means of survival.

"Did I interrupt the conversation?" Florence took Roxanne's hand into hers, kissing it gently. She looked between me and Roxanne, expecting an answer.

"We were talking about the Wurdulacs." Roxanne shrugged, causing Francis to almost choke on his drink as his eyes shot fire at her.

"What?" Roxanne smiled innocently. "I wasn't aware it was a secret. Besides, she is in danger too," she added, taking a sip of her drink. "Perhaps instead of wasting your time on dancing, you could actually inform our—" Her gaze traveled up and down my body. "*Guest* on the current situation."

Guest.

"Stop it, you two!" Florence shot Roxanne a look that made Roxanne lean back on the chair in defeat. "I am tired of both of you constantly fighting." Florence's eyes moved from Roxanne to Francis.

Francis touched the bridge of his nose, taking a deep breath, as though putting all of his energy into staying calm. If I hadn't known better I would think Roxanne took great pleasure in making Francis mad.

"Bring me to one of those meetings." I blurted out before thinking my plans through. Although, if my siblings' lives were in danger—and they absolutely were given the circumstance—it was not a hard choice for me to make. I might've failed my father and Brian by becoming the creature they gave their lives against, but I would not fail their grave by hiding from hardship. I could not fail them by allowing my siblings to suffer.

All of the eyes in the room fell on me with surprise and confusion, as if I'd told them the most ridiculous tale there was.

"I know all the nobles in this Kingdom well. I know how to approach them. They will listen to me." I looked Francis straight in the eyes, raising my chin high. "Isn't that what you meant by *she can help us* when you talked to Caleb in the training room?" I turned to Roxanne.

"Eavesdropping?" She narrowed her eyes on me.

"You talk louder than you think." I shrugged.

"And why—" Roxanne started, but was quickly interrupted by Francis.

"The answer is *no*, Your Highness," he told me sweetly, casually taking a sip of his drink.

Frustration filled my veins, turning my hands into fists. I stared at Francis, imagining him ignited by the fire he sat so close to. His eyes bored into my own.

Who did he think he was to refuse my offering? I would not sit here doing nothing when it came to my siblings' well-being. I would do as I wished, I was not a child who needed permission, especially not from him.

"What are you doing here, Simon?" Roxanne changed the subject. Her voice carried across the silent room, forcing Francis and I to quit our staring match. "Some might think you live here at this point," she teased Simon.

"What can I say? You have delicious refreshments." Simon grinned, showing off his crimson painted teeth.

The conversation carried on, yet I could barely hear anything being said.

We need some kind of proof. Roxanne's words were fresh in my mind. Something that could prove Wurdulacs were back after seven years of peace, and perhaps I knew just where to find it.

My plan—if you could even call it that, more of an idea, really—was madness indeed, but I was determined to follow through with this scheme.

If Francis wanted me to stay away, I would put myself right in the center of this disaster in spite of him.

A small smile spread across my face. I would get the proof they needed.

Chapter 14
Thieves and Wine

The dark green sheets of my bedding were cool on my skin. The fear of sleeping through my only chance to leave unnoticed barely allowed me any rest. For my plan to work I had to leave the moment the sun hid behind the horizon, before anyone got a chance to wake.

This was madness.

Moving the black curtains that blocked any light from coming into my room, I peeked out of the window. The twilight sky was covered in dark gray clouds, protecting me from the sun rays that were rapidly disappearing from my view. It was time.

I grabbed the old map from my nightstand, studying it for the hundredth time. Spending the last couple of days secretly searching their library for that map was the easiest part of this plan: from this point forward nothing would be this simple. Yet I was determined to succeed.

The map was not very detailed, but at least it showed the direction of the palace. South.

To my big disappointment, the trip would take longer than I wished. A full night's ride. A full night in foreign woods all by myself. Had Francis really carried me all the way here the night I'd been bitten?

Putting my new cloak on, I hid my hair under the hood. Anxiety rushed through my veins, my heart beat faster.

For Sandra, for Eleanor and Frederik, I could do this.

Making my way down to the stables, I checked every corner of the castle for unwanted eyes. The castle was still asleep, longing for the lively conversations of its residents. Bright moonlight intruded the empty rooms, indicating the start of a new day. I had to hurry.

One of the many useful skills my Royal life had taught me was to walk silent. Though, hiding from trained Royal knights for some privacy had been somehow easier than leaving a castle full of vampires undetected. Nevertheless, I managed to make my way down to the stables without anyone spotting me.

The weather was colder than before, as though the winter itself warned me to stay away from the insanity I was about to walk into. *Should I go back before it is too late?* The unwelcome thought crossed my mind. *For Sandra, for Frederik, for Eleanor.* I repeated the words, forcing my legs farther into the stables.

My trembling hands blindly fought with the straps of the saddle; too afraid of being caught, I had not taken a candle from my room: a decision I deeply regretted now.

"Going for another run, Your Highness?" The voice froze my body in place.

Damnation. I was so close!

Forcing my hands to obey, I slowly managed to get the straps in the right place, aware of the gaze on the back of my head. I swallowed the lump in my throat, slowly turning toward my intruder. "For a ride," I shrugged innocently, taking my seat in the saddle.

I could only hope the saddle would not fall down during my journey, but that would be a problem for later. Right now I just needed to get rid of Francis: who now grinned at me as though he'd found a naughty child stealing sweets from the kitchen.

"Is that so?" Francis smiled, crooking his head to the side. "Did no one teach you proper manners, Princess? Lying is rude." He frowned at me. "Let's try this again, shall we? Where are you going?"

My mind wandered, trying to come up with some kind of believable excuse. Why hadn't I thought of this earlier? My planning skills surely needed some practice.

"Save me the trouble, and just tell the truth, Princess."

Groaning at my own foolishness, I gave up. "I am going to get the proof you need."

My honest answer made Francis' brows frown in confusion.

I rolled my eyes at him. "I will get the documentation my mother keeps in her study about all of the attacks. Roxanne said you need proof for the nobles. I know where to get it." Getting comfortable on the saddle, I tried to adjust my dress.

For a moment Francis just stared at me, pure disbelief written on his face. "Are you out of your mind?" he whispered at last. "That is not your responsibility."

"I thought you wanted me out of my room," I countered. "I know where the Queen keeps them, I can do it."

Francis laughed so hard that, for a moment, I wished to run him over with my horse. "What?" He finally said. "You think you can just knock on the front door, and kindly ask them to let you in for old times' sake?" His teasing tone challenged me to act upon my wish.

Did he think me a fool? Ridiculous.

"No," I groaned. "I know every hidden passage in the palace. If you would move out of the way, by the time I get there everyone will be going to rest. No one would even know I took a step inside."

Francis massaged the bridge of his nose. "Moon, please help me," he murmured, as if actually praying. "And where are you going to hide when the sun is out?" He did not give up. To be frank I had not thought about this part yet, but surely I would've found shelter. Francis narrowed his eyes on me when I didn't reply. "Why do you care anyway? It is not like you care about the well being of our kind. And human villages were never in the interest of a *royal*." He spat out the last word.

Did he truly think that simply because I'd been born Royal, I cared not for humans? *Of course I do!* I wanted to scream at him, yet perhaps he wasn't completely wrong. The only reason I'd decided on this dangerous adventure was the thought of my siblings suffering. Perhaps I was the egocentric Royal he painted me to be. Nevertheless I wanted to help, even if it were selfish motives enticing me to act. "I will not stand aside while my siblings are in danger," I admitted.

Sighing, he put a saddle on the brown horse beside Annabelle. "All right then," he said after a long pause.

"What are you doing?" I narrowed my eyes.

"You think I am cruel enough to let you go straight into a death mission without my protection?"

"I do not need protection!" I absolutely did.

"'Tis not for you, Princess. The documents you are about to carry cost a fortune, someone must be there in case of trouble. We don't want your little adventure to be in vain, now do we?"

My lips turned into a thin line. "Fine," I agreed reluctantly, preparing for the longest night ahead of me.

A few hours into our very awkwardly quiet trip Francis took out a glass flask filled with some clear liquid: as though he'd been prepared for the trip. Or perhaps he always had a bottle with him no matter where he was: something told me it's the latter.

"Would you like some?" he asked me, catching my gaze.

I shook my head in reply. Whatever he drank, I certainly would not share with him.

Turning away from him, I tried to focus on the pathway that was now barely visible as the night fully settled down.

"So tell me, what exactly is our plan?" Francis asked me, intruding on my quiet night I became accustomed to.

The truth was I had no real plan, but I was not about to let Francis know that—he would turn me back around and lock me in his castle forever.

"Where is the entrance to the passage?" he persisted, not accepting silence as a suitable response. "Does it lead directly to where your mother keeps the documents?"

My eyebrows flew up in question. Did he really expect me to give him the most secret information about the Royal palace? What did he intend to do with all the information he was about to learn? I had to be careful if I wanted to keep my family safe.

"I suppose I could just be your guard dog then." Francis rolled his eyes at me, growing tired of my distance.

I was not opposed to the idea. Perhaps it would be good for Francis' arrogance to follow someone around for once.

"So tell me..." He crooked his eyes at me. "What is it like to live in our humble community after consorting with *royalty*?" Francis did not allow me the luxury of a peaceful night.

What was the purpose of this disruption? I let him come with me for protection, not to make my night miserable.

I took a deep breath. Francis knew all too well that the castle he resided in was far more luxurious than one any Royal family could afford. As if I cared how expensive the art I owned was. Arrogant, rude man.

"I am starting to think I might be the problem here," he continued despite my clear lack of interest. "You don't seem to struggle chatting with anyone but me. Why is that, Princess?" Francis looked at me before taking a sip of his drink. "You even managed to befriend Roxanne of all people, surely that took a lot of effort," he smirked.

Befriend was an exaggeration, but he was right: he was the problem here. How did he expect me to talk to him, when we both knew he was the one responsible for the destruction of my life?

"You cannot ignore me forever," Francis didn't give up. "We have a long night ahead of us."

This man truly loved the sound of his own voice, didn't he? Fine, he wanted me to talk. I would talk.

"Who is Issac?" I asked, expecting the question would finally grant me the quiet night I'd been hoping for.

He took another sip of his drink, starting straight ahead. A triumphant smile spread across my face, though it was short-lived for Francis' low voice reached my ears once again. "Issac is my younger brother—" he trailed off. "Well, he was my brother. Issac died at the end of the Crimson War, fighting alongside human soldiers."

My brows shot up, I wondered if I heard him right. His brother had fought in the war against his own kind? I stared at him waiting for more, yet he didn't spare another word. Had Francis fought in that war?

"Is that why you are doing all of this?" I asked him instead.

"I have an eternity to spare," Francis shrugged. "It gets boring eventually."

Obviously. He risked his life because he was bored. "How did you end up here?" I dared asking him.

"Roxanne already told you," the annoyance in his voice was unmistakable. "We were arrogant—"

"*Were*?" I laughed at Francis, making him roll his eyes.

"—desperate humans." He continued. "Eventually, we had to pay the price for our risks." He finished his drink, bestowing me with the most annoyed face I had ever seen him wear.

"I thought you wanted to chat," I shrugged, offended by his reaction.

Francis let out a sigh of exhaustion—as though I was the one to start the conversation in the first place—before reluctantly continuing. "Roxanne, Issac and I were thieves. One day I convinced them to steal from a vampire; the plan obviously did not unfold as expected. The end."

"How do you know Roxanne?"

Francis's eyes narrowed on me. "Do you always ask this many questions?"

"As I already said, I was enjoying the silence, you were the one to start this."

A grin made its way onto Francis' face. "How about this: I will tell you the whole story if you tell me about those hidden passages we are to enter?"

"Is bargaining your only skill?"

"Bargaining is a weapon of royalty, perhaps I would fit right in," he smirked, making my eyes roll this time. "Come now, Princess, I know you are curious, and I'm going to see the passages eventually. This way you get something in return."

"Doesn't sound like a very valuable bargain for you to make, don't you think?"

"Oh, but it is indeed. How can I protect the documents in a passage I know nothing about? Unlike you, I am not reckless enough to enter my enemy's grounds without any preparation."

Annabelle snorted as though participating in our odd banter. Perhaps he was right, it was irresponsible of me to leave him this helpless against the underground labyrinth of the palace. "Very well then. I accept."

A small smile made its way across Francis' face. "Issac and I met Roxanne at the orphanage; our parents died when we were still young," he started. "She was devastated when she first arrived: refused to talk to anyone.

"My brother, being his true self, eventually found a way to befriend Roxanne. He shared his desserts with her, protected her from older children in school: they were inseparable. I believe he even stole a kiss or two, although neither of them ever admitted to it." Francis laughed at the memory, though his laughter fell short just a moment later.

The clattering of hooves was the only sound heard in this eerie forest and I started to wonder if Francis had changed his mind and did not wish to continue the story. "The passage leads straight to my rooms," I sighed. "No one has used it for years. It is not far from the Queen's study." I answered his question from earlier, attempting to buy his words with my own.

My candor made Francis grin. "When Isaac and Roxanne turned sixteen, everything changed," Francis' voice got darker. "The orphanage deemed us old enough to live on our own, kicking us out on the street with our shy belongings. We had no place to go, no real skill, and no coin." His hands turned into fists around the reins. Yet, it was his only sign of distress: for his features stayed the same, as though he was merely telling me about the weather.

"We started stealing from those who did not know poverty," he smirked. "We would travel to the most expensive parts of human villages, take what we could and flee, never staying in one place for long.

"We were truly good at it too, skilled thieves," Francis laughed at himself. "We did it for years, never got caught, until I ruined it all." Francis trailed off, looking at me expectedly: clearly not willing to proceed until I held up my end of the bargain.

My lips turned into a thin line, annoyed by the foolish game he was playing. Yet the curiosity in me won the battle with my stubbornness. "The passage is located in the Royal cemetery. It is the only entrance—other than the one connected to the Queen's rooms—that is accessible from outside of the Royal grounds." I closed my eyes, not believing I actually revealed secrets that could endanger my family.

Francis nodded once before continuing. "I convinced Issac and Roxanne to steal from Faris. The Vampire Village. I was over confident in my own skills: I didn't think anything could go wrong. I led them straight to their deaths."

Francis took a deep breath before turning to look at me. "You can imagine the rest of the story." He finished his drink. "The vampire we stole from decided to teach us a lesson. He bit us, leaving us alone on the street. I tried to save my family, tried to get them away from Faris, but it wasn't long before the pain deprived me of any strength."

A shiver went through me at the memory of the pain I had to endure after the bite. My throat ached.

"Caleb found us." Francis turned away from me, staring back into nothingness. "He brought us to the castle, convinced his father to let us stay. He saved us, taught us, and protected us until we were capable of doing so ourselves."

I wanted to feel sorry for him, wanted to comfort him, yet the only emotion I had left in my possession was anger.

Anger for the injustice they had to endure and anger for the injustice Francis shoved upon me. "If you are so regretful of the fate your family had to suffer, why would you do this to me? Why did you bite me, knowing the burden one has to carry?"

"I wasn't the one to create you, Your Highness," he rolled his eyes. "I am not nearly responsible enough to commit to such a liability," Francis winked. "Although it seems your creator isn't very responsible either, leaving you all by yourself in the forest."

My heart nearly stopped at his declaration, yet my mind refused to accept his words. Shaking my head, I looked him straight in the eyes. "If it wasn't you, then who did this?" I asked, trying to catch him in a lie.

"I wish I knew the answer, Princess," he replied simply.

No! This could not be true. He'd been the one to find me in the woods. If he was not responsible for my fate, then why had he been in the woods by the palace at all?

"I did not bite you, Your Highness," Francis said, as though reading my thoughts. "I was nearby, trying to get home after the meeting. I heard your wails," Francis rolled his eyes. "When I found you, I searched the perimeter of the cemetery, but whoever gifted you the bite had already left."

"Why didn't you tell me this earlier?" I asked him, still not convinced of his words.

"Would you have believed me then?" he asked me. "Do you even believe me now?"

I stared at the ground beneath me, opting to focus on Annabelle's moderate steps rather than my own thoughts. The sound of night interrupted our silence, distracting me from my own miserable mind. I needed time. I needed time to think about all of this, decide for myself what to believe.

"It is your turn, Your Highness," Francis smiled at me. "Tell me about your infamous royal life. Did you have unlimited amounts of chocolate?"

I laughed before I could stop myself. "I suppose we did," I nodded, when the memory of Sandra entered my mind. "Though my sister and I always tried to steal the caramel fudge from the kitchen." The words left my mouth before I could stop them.

I wished I could have some fudge with Sandra right then, maybe it would've made this new life more bearable.

"I see you are a thief too," Francis replied. "I knew we had more in common than you let on." He smirked at me.

I rolled my eyes, smiling back at him when Francis turned his horse to the left—away from the path—gesturing for me to do the same. "This way."

My brows furrowed when I took the map out from my cloak. "According to the map, the palace is in that direction." I pointed south.

Francis laughed, staring at the very stolen map in my hands. "Where in the Kingdom did you get this?"

"Your library," I shrugged.

"A thief," he winked, riding away from the direction I just pointed at.

"Where are you going?" I stopped Annabelle altogether, refusing to go any further.

"Come now, you didn't think it would be a good idea to go to the palace now. You need rest, Princess."

"I am well, thank you," I argued.

"Our horses need rest to make the trip back." Francis turned to glare at me. "We don't know what hurry we'll need to leave in. Besides, when was the last time you've fed?" he asked me.

My face flushed at the mention of blood and I thanked the darkness for hiding my embarrassment. My throat ached from the reminder of the crimson liquid and my hands instinctively flew to cover it.

"That's what I thought," Francis chuckled. "You want to endanger humans now? I thought this whole adventure was supposed to do the exact opposite."

There was definitely logic in his words, although I was not convinced of his true motives. "That doesn't answer my question. Where are you going?" I demanded.

"Have some faith in me, Your Highness." He started his horse once again without waiting for me to follow. "We are going to my cabin."

Leaving me alone in these foreign woods, he did not give me much of a choice but to follow after him, into the unknown.

In the middle of the meadow, hidden by dense spruce, settled down a small—two story—wooden cabin. A short, broken fence encircled the house. Its every window was painted black.

"My human family used to live here," Francis said quietly, opening the metal lock. "Make yourself comfortable." Francis gestured for me to enter.

A small kitchenette was set right by the entrance door to the right. A long extinguished fireplace took up the majority of the space. Only one person could fit in this corridor.

"You can take this room," Francis pointed out the black door by the ladder that led to the second floor. "Let me see if we have any blood stored here." He lit up the candles set along the walls of the corridor.

The floor creaked underneath my steps as I set a foot inside the room. Taking off my cloak, I closed the door behind me when the sound of every cabinet door opening reached my ears.

My eyes adjusted to the unnatural darkness almost immediately, leaving my brows to frown in confusion. Although I could not see any color, my vision allowed me to assess the space I would reside in.

The room was tiny, a small bed was set across from the black painted window. The room was crowded, overflowing with books and children's paintings. Spider webs covered every corner of the furniture.

"Here, I found some for you." Turning to the sound of his voice, I spotted Francis at the threshold of the room. Francis froze in his place, looking me straight in the eyes. I spotted the bottle with crimson liquid in his hand, yet my eyes traveled straight to his neck.

I swallowed the lump in my throat, as my heart rushed inside of my chest. My nostrils flared, my lungs ached.

An unknown desire within me fought for its way out.

Chapter 15
Snowdrop

My eyes were captivated on the neck of the man in front of me.

The sound of his heartbeat quickened. I had to leave before I did something I would regret. Yet, I could not move, could not escape the temptation.

"Do it," Francis' raspy accent swept through the room, as he took a step forward. "We both know you want to," he whispered.

My nostrils flared, taking in the aroma. The smell of jasmine and dew in his veins welcomed me in. Failing to calm my treasonous mind, I closed my eyes shut.

"It's all right," Francis' breath tickled my ear. "This is how it should be, Princess." His hand brushed over mine, sending fire through my skin.

My head shook in disagreement or simply in an attempt to strip my restless mind of any thought—I was unsure.

The sound of the clasp on his tunic being undone reached my ears. Despite the winter, my whole body felt like the sun itself. My stomach ached and twisted with new desire.

Good Gods.

My treasonous body was at this man's mercy despite my mind's protests.

Who was this stranger living inside of me? Where was the delicate self control I'd been taught since birth? Where was my dignity and self preservation?

Like a starved man, the beast within me longed for its next meal.

My eyes flew open. Francis' tunic slid down his shoulder, revealing his smooth bronze skin: revealing his neck. His pulse sang serenades as I lost this unfair battle. In a mere second I stood before him, unable to refuse my body's demands any longer.

I devoured his blood as my teeth pierced his thin, soft skin.

Pleasure overwhelmed me, refusing me any clarity. His blood was as fresh as a dewdrop on a summer morning, as fresh as the rain, and as cold as the snow. It melted on my tongue in delightful satisfaction, corrupting me into the unknown. Sweet as honey, raw as briar, it consumed me, depriving me of my own mind: how could one go a whole life without this pleasure?

Slowly I relinquished any remaining control left within me. What a luxury it was to let go of everything and just be. A luxury I'd just been granted and was taking every bit of, not letting a drop go to waste.

Suddenly so aware of our bodies in the embrace, I felt Francis' heartbeat slowing. The sound of his pulse excited the beast within me, and I begged this joy to never end. Like the rain after a hurricane, we found our peace.

I was at peace.

A peace I already longed for, addicted to it, willing to exchange my own life for it. *More.*

My mind calmed, allowing clear thoughts to reenter my nature, allowing me the privy of his low moan.

Oh, Moon! Did I hurt him? The realization hit me in my chest, the danger of the situation I'd welcomed made my body freeze.

I slowly opened my eyes, ashamed of my desires, ashamed of what I'd allowed to happen. I slowly pushed myself from his neck, fighting through the craving, fighting with my own hands to let go.

The crimson wound I'd left on his neck challenged me to repeat our ritual: bright red, deep, delightful wound.

"Are you all right?" He cleared out his throat. *Me?* I should've been asking *him* this question. "You didn't hurt me." He read into my expression.

Francis let his hands fall from my waist slowly, as though afraid I would collapse without his support. Our gazes collided. Mesmerized by the intensity of his hypnotic amber eyes, my heart stopped.

You are a fool, Cordelia. A fool indeed. Yet I could not force my body away.

"Cordelia?" He crooked his head.

His low voice vibrated through my chest, warming my heart, poisoning my mind. My name on his lips sounded heavenly and peculiar all the same. Like the first snowdrop flower blooming in the cold winter, decorating nature with its beauty despite the cool cruelty of the surroundings. I wanted him to say my name again. And again.

Francis' gaze dropped to my lips before his hand gently grabbed my chin. I held my breath in anticipation and excitement. *What would his lips taste like,* I wondered, as he cleaned the blood off my lips with his thumb.

His gentle touch sent a chill through my body, my lips parted at the impact without my permission when a shaky breath escaped them.

The room suddenly felt small. Or infinite.

"Cordelia?" Francis said again, making me drunk on the word alone. Yet his worried expression forced me to sober up.

Only then I realized I hadn't said a word since he walked into the room.

Say something. I screamed at myself, but the words didn't come.

"I was shocked too the first time I bit someone." He let go of my lips; I already missed his cold rough fingers.

The bite. I'd just bitten someone for the first time, yet my mind was somewhere else entirely. What was wrong with me?

Fool, fool, fool!

You are a fool, Cordelia! Moon help me, stop this nonsense.

"You will be all right," Francis offered a small smile. "I promise, Your Highness."

Your Highness.

"It is time." The voice pulled me out of my dreamless sleep. Francis shook me by my shoulder, forcing my eyes to open. "Your Highness, we have to leave now if you want to get home by dawn."

The moment he'd left the room this morning I'd fallen asleep almost immediately, not wanting to spend another moment alone with my own thoughts. Thankfully, the trip to the cabin had exhausted me enough for my mind to have mercy on me and allow me the rest I desperately needed.

Sitting up on the bed I'd claimed as mine for the day, I wondered where Francis had slept. Was there another room upstairs?

"I will go prepare our horses for the trip. I will be waiting outside. Hurry up!" Francis ordered me on his way out of the room, without waiting for my reply: as if I was a puppy that would follow him around.

Francis being back to his rude, arrogant self was nothing new to me, yet somehow it made me upset. How could he act as though nothing had happened? *Had* something happened? I thought we... *We what?* I shook my head, laughing at the ridiculous line of thoughts.

He'd told me about his past, let me drink the blood from his throat—that had to mean something, right? Did it mean anything to him, or did he do this with everyone?

Well, what did you expect, Cordelia? That you are going to talk about what happened, share your feelings perhaps? I rolled my eyes at my own foolishness. I needed to quit thinking about him right this moment! Tonight was not the night to allow any distractions into our already very dangerous journey.

Putting on my cloak, I checked if the map was still in my pocket. I studied it for a moment, memorizing the quickest route back home in case something did indeed go wrong.

Home. Calling Francis' castle my home felt odd, even in my own thoughts. Was it my home, or was Francis waiting for me to learn how to tend for myself in my new being to finally throw me out? *Guest* was what Roxanne had called me.

Stop it, Cordelia! Why was I suddenly so sentimental on such an important night? Getting the documents needed to be the only thing on my mind: I would figure out the rest later!

If I survived.

Rebraiding my hair into a tight bun, I secured it with a hair pin, hiding it underneath the hood. By dawn I would either be dead or happily celebrating my success. I could do it. I *would* do it! For Sandra, for Frederick, for Eleanor... for every human my mother chose to neglect.

"Princess, we have to go!" Francis's voice brought me back to reality. "Hurry up!" He loudly knocked on the door.

The banging did not stop until I opened the door with more force than it required. I officially loathed this man. What was his problem? I walked right past him, ignoring his outburst altogether.

Getting up on my horse, I sent Francis an annoyed, impatient look that he returned with even more force. Splendid!

If this interaction was any indication of how our night was going to go—it would be really bad.

Chapter 16
Royal Dungeons

"This way," I whispered to Francis, turning off the trail to the cemetery.

We'd left our horses hidden behind a line of dense spruce, making the rest of the trip by foot.

Thankfully, the trip had not been long, leaving us no opportunity to fight. The cabin—I had no idea existed—settled down just beyond the palace grounds.

The air of the cemetery was impregnated with unwelcome memories. I wiped the sweat off my hands on my cloak, forcing my lungs to expand. Fidgeting with my sleeves, I focused on the passage ahead, determined to ignore my surroundings.

"Are we almost there?" Francis asked, scanning the cemetery for any unwelcome company.

"Yes," I whispered as something caught my gaze.

Dozens of bright red flowers settled on the grave nearest to my brother's. My brows furrowed as I took a step toward it. But before I got close to the stone Francis caught my hand, squeezing it tight. "Don't look at it." He gently pulled me back on our pathway.

Why? I wanted to ask him before the realization knocked the air out of my lungs.

My grave. My empty grave was now resting next to my brother and father. My stomach turned upside down, threatening to empty its contents.

Not tonight. My breathing quickened in unison with my heart beat. Not tonight.

"Look at me," Francis held my face, forcing my gaze to meet his. "We must go, Princess. Every moment counts." His cold hands were settled on my cheeks. "Take a deep breath and keep moving." His stern commanding voice emptied my mind of any thought.

I nodded, swallowing the lump in my throat. Francis was right—in a few moments there would be no turning back. I had to stay focused.

"Good." Francis let go of my face. "We can do this, Your Highness." He winked, giving me a reassuring smile.

We can do this.

Carefully moving the branches that covered the passage from unwelcome eyes, I slightly opened the door ajar.

We can do this.

The door creaked in protest. The passage was pitch black, though I had taken it so often as a child I could make the trip blind folded.

The passage only connected a few chambers: Sandra's, Brian's, and mine. If Francis and I were lucky, we would not meet anyone on our way to my rooms.

I brought a finger to my mouth, gesturing for Francis to be as quiet as possible—if anyone heard us here, we were trapped.

Step by step, we silently made our way through the darkness. The passage of my childhood now felt foreign, as though I had no business setting a foot inside of it. I supposed I did not. Familiar walls stared back at me, scolding me for intruding into their quiet night.

One, two, three, four. I counted the turns of the passage, afraid of ending up elsewhere. *Five.* The entrance to my bedchamber should've been on the left.

My shaky hands felt the wall, desperately searching for the handle. The smell of mold made my eyes water. *Where is it?* The longer we stayed in the passage, the more danger we put ourselves into. There were plenty of places to hide inside of the palace, but if someone saw us here—

Panic filled my mind, making me shake even more.

A cold hand covered mine, moving it to the left where the metal handle scratched my fingers. "Calm down, Princess," Francis' breath tickled my ear. "Trust your instincts. Our kind can see in the dark if your human nature would stop fighting it."

With Francis' hand still atop mine, I pushed the door open, taking a careful step into my old wardrobe.

"Your Highness, you should get back to your chambers." Mories' voice came from the room and my heart stopped in place. *She knows I am here!* My gaze found Francis' when Mories' voice broke through the wardrobe door. "Your Highness, the Queen requested for you to leave."

"No," a broken voice whispered in reply.

Icy sweat swept across my skin, making my palms sticky. What could Mories possibly have been doing in my room at this hour? Who was she talking to? She'd said *Your Highness.*

I slowly moved toward the light coming from the small gap in the door, hoping to assess the situation.

"Dear, we both will get in trouble if you don't leave." Mories added softly, taking a few steps toward my old bed.

My gaze collided with Francis'. *What do we do now?* We should have left, gone through Brian's chambers perhaps, but I could not force myself to move.

The sounds of footsteps made Mories take another step closer to the bed, as if protecting whoever was underneath the blankets. "Your Majesty," she bowed.

Damnation!

Francis covered his face with a palm in pure annoyance. We were doomed. Only one door separated us from my room. One wooden door could be the reason for our execution.

"Leave us." The Queen addressed Mories, though I could not see her from this angle.

Mories nodded once, sending a quick glance toward the bed before taking her leave.

"Get up, Sandra, right this moment." Mother's voice shook my body, as if I was the one who angered her.

Sandra.

"Get up right now, and leave this room for good." The Queen walked up to the bed, angrily pulling away all the blankets that hid Sandra from the world. "You have no reason to be here. Stop this foolish behavior."

"I am hurting no one by staying here, Mother." Sandra's voice sounded so different than I remembered: as if the storm had passed through her, depriving her of any color within. My full-of-life Sandra now sounded drained of any emotion.

"Hold your tongue, child," the Queen bit out. "I am tired of your childish behavior. You are a disgrace to this dynasty just like Cordelia now." Her features were collected, despite her harsh words.

Sandra stared straight into the Queen's eyes, no fear shown on her face. *Sandra, please just do what she tells you to. I told her in my mind, praying that the Moon would kindly send her my message. I could not see Sandra get hurt. Not my Sandra.*

"Get off the bed right this moment, before I call the knights to drag you out," the Queen interrupted their staring match.

"Why are you doing this to me?" Sandra shouted in reply. Something I had never heard her do. "Why do you hate me?"

I was going to be sick. I could not continue watching this, yet my eyes refused to leave the scene that played out in front of me.

"Get! Out!" The Queen pointed at the door.

"No," Sandra whispered.

My heart was about to jump out of my chest. My body shook as though the cold ocean enveloped me in its embrace.

"Pardon me?" Mother's voice sent a chill through me.

"I said *no*," Sandra repeated slowly, emphasizing each word.

"You can either go to your rooms right now, or spend the night in the dungeon."

Francis moved toward me, gesturing for us to leave. I shook my head in refusal. Francis' lips turned into a thin line, yet he did not force me out.

Sandra's loud laugh brought me back to the scene in my old room. "Dear Gods," she whispered with a wild smile on her face. "Is that what you told Cordelia when she didn't want to marry him? Is that what you will do when I refuse his hand?"

For the first time in my entire life I witnessed my mother taken off guard, but she quickly masked it. I was not the only one to notice her change of emotions: the smile on Sandra's face grew wider. "Yes, I know what he's done to her," she nodded at the Queen. "He told me so himself, and was sickly proud of it." Sandra's face turned, as though she smelled spoiled milk.

What in the Kingdom had Sandra been doing with Timothy for them to have this conversation? *Gods, no.*

"You will marry him for this dynasty," Mother said firmly. "If you want your place at the throne after my death, you will do as I say," she finished, confirming my biggest fear.

No, no, no.

"I don't want to be a queen!" my sister screamed from the top of her lungs. "Just let me leave! Let me go! I don't want to marry him! He hurts me! He hurts me, Mother! Is that why Cordelia ran away? Was it because of him? Because of you?"

Quiet tears fell from my eyes. If only I could return and take Sandra's place to the throne. If only I could keep her safe once again.

The Queen leaned towards my sister as she slapped her hard across the face.

Despite my mind's hardest efforts to stay logical, my heart won this battle. My hand flew toward the door that separated me from my sister, prepared to open it. I cared not for the consequences I would have faced. I cared not if this was my greeting to death herself. My sweaty hand held the handle firmly—

Francis grasped my hand with so much strength it hurt. I turned to look at him through my blurred vision. He shook his head in horror, gently rubbing my palm. More tears fell from my face, wetting my dress. Francis moved closer, holding me firmly in one place.

"You have no right to talk to your Queen this way," Mother raised her voice. "I will not discuss my decisions with you. You do as I say without any questions or complaints." The Queen shook her head in disgust. "You are even worse than she was."

"If you force me to marry Timothy I will jump off the tower!" Sandra's words broke my heart into small pieces. "I will do it!" she shrieked. "I will do it!"

The Queen walked towards the door, uncovering my view of Sandra's—full of hurt—face. This was not my Sandra. Not anymore. This was the face of a woman who did not know peace, who did not know joy.

A knock on the door rang through the room. "Take her down to the dungeon, she shall spend the night there," the Queen gave the order calmly. "Guard this room. Do not let anyone in again: especially her."

Several pairs of steps barged into the room, walking straight toward my sister when she started bellowing in hysteria.

I tried to free myself of Francis' embrace, tried to get to the handle, yet his strong hands did not let me. His hand covered my mouth, as my tears fell down in helplessness.

Sandra's screeches filled the room—a sound I'd never heard her make. A sound that would haunt me for eternity. Her voice became hoarse as the guards dragged her from the room.

"Let me go!" she cried, kicking and pushing the guards. "Let me go!" She turned to look at our mother. "She is dead because of you! She is dead because of all of you!"

Chapter 17
Intruders

S ilence.

For the longest few minutes of my life, we just sat in silence. Francis did not let go of me, although his grip had loosened. He was the only reason my whole body had not shattered into small pieces, yet he could not save my heart.

"I am sorry," he whispered into my ear.

My soul wanted to run and hide, though my mind felt empty. My body did not feel like my own, my eyes studied the wooden door through the glass that covered my vision.

This was a dream. A nightmare.

Perhaps I had died and was in purgatory, answering for my sins before the Moon. Perhaps my Sandra was safe, and this was no more than a twisted jest of my consciousness, punishing me for all the wrongs I'd committed throughout my life.

Even if it was a lie, the thought brought me comfort.

"Tell me where the Queen's study is," Francis whispered. "I will get the documents and come back for you."

I shook my head, "No. I am fine."

I could not allow any distractions: not when we were so close to our target, not when we were playing hide and seek with death herself.

For Sandra.

The wardrobe door opened with an uncomfortable screech, bringing me back to my surroundings as I barged into the room that once was my own. Francis quietly followed after.

My eyes scanned the room that used to be my only shield from the outside world. The only thing that had been safe and certain in my life was now full of grief. It smelled like home and suffering. No matter the fact that all of my things were in places where I'd left them last; no matter the comforting darkness of my old surroundings, the room was not mine—not anymore.

Despite the tears that threatened to break loose, my trembling body made it to the door Sandra had been dragged out of.

Leaning on the wooden barrier that separated me from the main hallway, I tried to catch the sound of any proof Mother's order was actually being followed.

The sound of guards pacing behind the door made it clear the order was indeed being fulfilled; the guards were in their designated spots, waiting for anyone foolish enough to intrude on their Queen's new rule.

This was our only way out of this room. The only way that was now guarded. Damnation.

I turned to find Francis patiently waiting at my side. His brows flew up in question, which I replied to with a slight shake of my head: we could not get through it unnoticed. Francis' lips turned into a thin line.

A small voice in my mind screamed at me to leave the palace, admit failure and find safety once again, yet I ignored it, determined to succeed no matter what—

The sound of several steps from the hallway broke through the room; our gazes met in pure terror. Francis gestured for me to go, yet I was frozen in place, scanning my old room for anything useful.

One wrong move would mean our immediate execution, or worse. How could I have come here this unprepared? How could I have let my own impulsiveness lead us into jeopardy? My foolishness would get us killed.

As quietly as possible, my legs carried me in the opposite direction of the passage. Kneeling on the floor before my old bed, I prayed to the Moon and all the Gods that my sword was still in its designated place: safely hidden from unwelcome eyes, underneath the bed frame. I reached for the scabbard, dragging it toward me from the corner.

Quickly strapping it around my waist, I managed to get it into place as the sound of several steps got terrifyingly close.

I flew towards Francis, who guarded the entrance of the passage, waiting for me to go through it. He had unleashed his own dagger, glaring at the main door.

We rushed through the wardrobe, closing the door tightly behind us, separating ourselves from the intruders of my old room. Just like that I said goodbye to my childhood.

Just like that I said goodbye to my old life.

"Are there any other entrances?" Francis whispered as we made our way through the darkness.

"Yes, but it's dangerous," I replied just as quietly. "We don't have a choice." I said more to myself than to him.

Although I knew Sandra was not in her room, my sister's room was not abandoned. Her servants might still be there, yet somehow this option was more appealing than wandering the infinite hallways of the palace—Brian's chambers were much farther from the Queen's studies than Sandra's.

"We have to go through Sandra's bedchambers," I made the decision.

Francis nodded, although I could tell he was not fond of the idea.

The door of the passage to Sandra's room opened silently, as if it had never been used before. The room was painfully empty.

Despite my relief, part of me refused to believe Sandra was truly spending the night in the dungeon. I closed my eyes, taking slow steps toward the main entrance. The idea of being so close to my sister broke me in half.

Leaning on the door, I took a deep breath, listening carefully for any sign of movement in the hallway.

Francis squeezed his dagger as I slowly opened the door ajar. The hallways were quiet, dark, and... empty, thank the Moon. I pointed at Mother's study, meeting Francis' gaze. About a hundred yards separated us from the documents.

No guards were seen on our path. We only had one chance, and no room for any more mistakes.

Please let the study be empty, please, I kept repeating in my head. That was the only risk we could not be prepared for. *Please be empty,* I begged.

Francis and I shared a determined nod. There was no fear shown on his face, and I could only hope my features did not give my true feelings away. *Breathe.* I ordered myself, setting my feet toward the darkness.

Everything slowed. Like in a nightmare, I ran, yet could not feel my body move. Every step felt as though it separated me from my target.

The ringing in my ears was as loud as the bells of the church. My mind felt as though it was in the depths of the ocean—quiet and loud all the same.

We rushed through the door of the study, closing it tight behind us. Anxiety broke through the wall I'd built in my mind, depriving me of any other emotion.

The only source of light in the study was the bright moon peeking out of curtains. Terror refused me the sweet relief of some luck. We were still in a very dangerous position here. No passageways led out of this room, if someone entered we were as good as dead. We had to make it quick.

I moved toward Mother's table, leaving Francis to guard the door. I grabbed the matches from the Queen's bookshelf when anxiety hit me with an even stronger force. The shaking in my hands made me lose at the weak attempt to light the candle. *Come on!* I screamed at the match. *I do not have time for this!*

When the fire finally illuminated the room, I released the air from my lungs.

Rushing through the endless amounts of paper, I tried to find something—anything—useful. Part of me wanted to take them all and go through the papers when we were in the safety of our home, although the logic in me did not allow such foolishness.

Of course whatever we took would be noticed eventually; but if I took it all, the search for it would start immediately.

Budget, allies agreements, lists of prisoners…

Nothing about the missing people. *Damnation!* Had we come here for nothing? Had we risked our heads only to leave empty handed? I knew Mother kept the *Vanishing List*. I'd seen it when searching for Duke Barren's proposition for his son's marriage: right before Mother permanently banished me from her study.

"We have to hurry, Princess," Francis whispered.

Anxiety tightened my heart into a painful knot as my hands flipped through the never-ending stack of papers.

Wedding budget, the list of guests…

I wanted to scream!

Weaponry, army, Wurdulacs…

Wurdulacs.

"Princess," Francis shot me a worried gaze.

The attacks on our kingdom grew in the last few months, Your Majesty. I am sorry to inform you of the details of recent invasions on our borders. The bodies of the victims were not found, we are forced to believe the assaulters are associated with the Wurdulac society. Your youngests are in grave danger, Your Majesty.

I flipped to the next page, finding dozens of letters of the same character.

"Princess!" Francis hissed at me.

The papers crinkled as I folded them into my pocket—

The banging on the marble floor echoed into the room. My gaze slid to Francis' when I blew out the candle, freezing in place. The ringing thud of heels grew louder from the hallway.

Francis mouthed a curse, squeezing his dagger until his knuckles whitened. He took a slow step toward me, his free hand caught my wrist, pulling me close.

Several more heavy slaps of boots raced toward the study.

My hand instinctively flew to the handle of my sword as I held a deep breath, afraid to make a sound. Someone must have seen us come in here. We were doomed.

The steps stopped right in front of the door to the study, the eternity of silence entered the room.

"Your Majesty, we think there are intruders in the castle," the voice from the hallway announced when Francis pressed my body against the wall by the door, placing himself beside me. "We heard someone go through the passage in Your oldest daughter's room."

I closed my eyes tight, separating myself from the reality of my surroundings.

"You *think*?" Mother's voice cut through the air, as though it'd grown blades of its own. "Why are you here?" she bit out. "I want the intruders alive before me."

The icy sweat from my forehead fell down on my eyelashes. They did not know we were in the study, but they would soon enough. We were trapped here. We were trapped!

"Now!" the Queen yelled at the knights, turning the handle of the door to the study.

Several pairs of boots rushed down the hallway when the door creaked open, shielding us in the corner.

My hand found Francis' as the Queen entered the study, making her way across the room. Francis' overly calm eyes met mine when his thumb stroked across my palm. My lungs froze.

The firelight illuminated the room seconds later; my heart fell to my heels. The sound of rustling paper reached my ears. I closed my eyes shut—

Silence.

As though the world froze in place, deathly silence fell upon the study.

My eyes flew open in an instant, meeting Francis' imperturbable gaze.

One glance at our shadows behind the door was enough for my mother to realize. One glance for her to know the intruders were right in the heart of her palace.

The shaking in my hands increased, my body was mere seconds from collapsing—

Mother put out the candle—enveloping the room in a pitch black embrace—when her loud, deliberate steps slowly disappeared.

She'd left. We were alive. My body shook, filling my paralyzed lungs with air. She didn't see us.

"We have to go," Francis whispered, dragging me out of the study when a shimmer from my mother's table stopped me in place.

"Wait," I rushed toward the object.

"Princess, we have to go!" Francis hissed at me as I let the golden Royal stamp slide into my pocket. His grip around my wrist hardened, pulling me after him.

We flew out the room, back to Sandra's bedchambers. Running straight for the passage, we spared no time making sure the pathway was clear.

My stomach creaked with pain when the passage illuminated in candlelight behind us. The sound of dozens of steps following after us covered my skin in a freezing sweat.

Francis held my hand tight, urging me to run faster. "Don't look back," he said, pushing me ahead of him.

The exit of the passage entered my view just before my legs were ready to give up. A few more steps, just a few more steps!

My hand flew to the handle when Francis shoved me out of the way. I staggered backward from the impact, hitting the stoned cold wall of the passage. He yanked the door wide open, fleeing out.

Francis abandoned me after all.

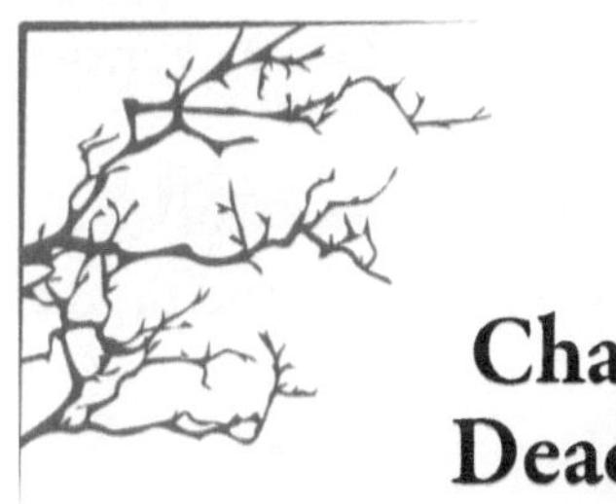

Chapter 18
Deadly Path

He abandoned me here. He used me as a distraction for the knights, while he found himself shelter.

The steps behind me grew terrifyingly close, shortening the distance between us.

I fought through the terror inside of my stomach, jerking the door open. The sound of banging metal occupied the cemetery.

Francis deftly dodged all of the blades that flew his way, cutting the throats of two knights that blocked our path in a single move. The smell of crimson reached my nostrils, my head spun in anticipation.

"Let's go!" He caught my arm, his face covered in blood. "Before we have to kill anyone else."

The night was oddly quiet, but it did not last long.

My lungs were on fire, yet I refused myself the luxury of stopping.

Heavy steps pounded against the ground; my head flew in their direction.

Five—no, six—guards followed after us. They all wore their Royal attires: armed from head to toe.

"They are following us!" I yelled, facing Francis.

A whistle broke through the air when dozens of arrows flew past us, barely missing our flesh.

"Don't look back!" Francis screamed at me. "Go!"

Our followers were blinded by the darkness and the distance. Only pure luck would allow our enemies to achieve their goal.

Adrenaline filled my veins, forcing my legs to move faster. The world had gone silent: only the sounds of my heavy breathing and my heartbeat broke through.

"Do not go to the cabin!" Francis yelled as he pushed me onto Annabelle before mounting his own horse.

"Why?" I screamed back, yet my voice got lost in the loud sea of galloping.

The arrows did not stop, flying past us, making my heart jump out of my rib cage with each blow.

"Fuck!" Francis howled.

I turned to look for the reason for his distress when my eyes fell onto his right leg. The arrow shone bright under the moonlight; drops of crimson fell down onto the road.

"Do not look back!" he caught my worried gaze.

"Your leg!" I bellowed.

More arrows flew towards us. The calm trees of the forest were laughing at the absurdity of our situation. It seemed even the winter had decided to injure us with its glory, letting the first snowflakes fall down on our faces.

Everything slowed. A loud neigh echoed through the forest. Francis' *riderless* stallion passed me with mad speed, sending a powerful wave of air in our direction. My hands squeezed the reins tightly, keeping control over Annabelle when she tried to follow up with the terrified horse.

The arrow in Francis' stallion shone bright from its ribs when it hid behind the tree line.

"Francis!" I shrieked, searching for him.

A faint groan came in reply about a hundred yards behind me.

Every cell in my body stilled, my mind became vacant when I turned Annabelle back towards Francis: back towards the guards.

Arrows flew in a powerful rain. The wind rushed Annabelle faster.

"Francis," my hand stretched out to the figure on the ground when he grumbled, forcing his body up.

"You sure you wouldn't rather save the horse," he smirked, struggling to his feet.

Francis reached for my outstretched hand and I held onto him as though my own life depended on it. "We have no time for your jokes right now," I screamed out in frustration as I helped him mount my horse; though a part of me was relieved—perhaps his wound wasn't as bad as it looked.

"If you don't mind me—ah—" Francis' words turned into a muffled scream as his hand flew to his injured leg. "I—I am fine." His, covered in blood, hands wrapped around my waist. "Let's go."

The voices of the Royal knights reached my ears when my hold on the reins hardened, turning Annabelle into the depths of the foreign forest—off the pathway. I could only hope my memory of the map would not fail me.

"Silver," Francis mumbled, leaning on me when the heavy steps of the knights finally quieted. "Do not go to the cabin," he whispered into my ear, dropping his head on my shoulder.

"You have to stay awake." I held his hands tightly around my waist. "Stay awake!" I ordered. "Francis—"

I did not have any time to react. On the ground, Francis' limp body laid upon me, pinching me to the cold soil.

"Francis," I bellowed, yet the reply never came.

Putting all my strength into holding the reins, I fought Annabelle who tried to escape this vacant place: tried to leave us behind.

"Francis!"

Chapter 19
Silver Blood

"Francis?" Groaning, I got to my feet.

Tightening Annabelle's reins to a nearby tree, I refused to move my gaze away from Francis' limp body, as if he would disappear the moment I looked away. "Francis!"

I rushed toward him. Dropping to my knees, I frantically shook his shoulders in a weak attempt to bring his consciousness back.

The wind whispered to me, sending dozens of sharp, cold needles straight into my face.

The wind whispered for me to leave Francis behind, find safety for myself while I still could. I wanted to scream in reply.

A few minutes—that was all we had before the knights would find our crimson path on the fresh white snow. The wind whispered to me, and I begged it to cover our tracks with its powerful force.

For a few moments I just kneeled before Francis, my mind rushed through every possible solution. There was absolutely no way I would be able to sit him atop the horse myself—I needed him awake.

Swallowing the lump in my throat, I gathered any strength that remained to stay calm.

The silver arrow shimmered under the Moon's presence. The crimson drops painted the freshly fallen snow in a color of death. The crimson prickled my throat, challenging me to give up control. I held my breath to stop the urge, yet the aroma drew me in with the most delightful flavor.

Focus!

My cold fingers made contact with Francis'—just as cold—skin. The cotton of Francis' trousers had dried out on the wound, hiding the injury within. *Gods, have mercy.*

The arrow had not gone through his leg fully, therefore the arrow head was still inside, keeping the blood from escaping. I did not dare take out the arrow from the wound myself: it would only damage the tissue further. That was the only thing I knew for a fact when it came to treating any kind of wound—do not touch anything, and go to a healer.

The nearby healer was a whole night away.

I looked around, desperate to find something—anything!—useful. Yet, nothing but the snow and naked trees surrounded me. *All right, then.*

My trembling hands reached for Francis' coat. "Please," I whispered to no one in particular, uncovering the bottle of alcohol from his inside pocket. The flask was surprisingly half full, thank the Gods.

Setting the flask aside, I ripped the inside hem of my dress.

I'd seen the healers do bandages before, surely it could not be that difficult.

Every muscle in me tightened as I poured the alcohol onto the wound, waiting for his screams to come—yet they did not. Perhaps it was for the best—the quieter we were the better.

Wrapping the cloth tightly around his leg, I placed snow in between the material before tying the ends in a strong knot—this had to do for now.

Now I just need to wake him. Putting the remains of the alcohol underneath Francis' nose, I waited. I waited, and waited, and waited! Francis' eyes stayed shut. The panic overwhelmed me; my whole body shivered, sending me a fresh dose of nausea.

He could not die from a wound like this one. Then, why wasn't he waking up? I shook his shoulders again as my vision began to blur. *Please!*

Silver. Francis' words fought their way through the chaos of my thoughts. Silver. What in the Kingdom did that mean? How would you even treat a silver wound anyway? How would you treat a *vampire* wound?

Dear Gods.

The realization hit me, the nausea worsened. There was only one way out of this—only one solution.

My hands shook, unsheathing the sword from its scabbard. My heart galloped.

I had no choice.

The wind quieted down, as if intrigued by what I was going to do next.

I made a long cut across my arm. If this would not work, I might've just signed my deal with the Moon herself. If this would not work, we would both bleed out dry, doomed to lay here in the darkness of the forest until its residents found and devoured our long dead flesh.

As the blood from my arm dripped down his lips, I begged him to wake up. He could not have saved my life and then *died* because of my foolish plan to break into the Royal palace! He could not! I refused!

Please, Francis, please open your eyes.

For what seemed to be an eternity, I held my arm above Francis' lips, committed to make this work. My arm shook when cold air brushed the open wound I drew with my sword. *Please!*

Crimson lips slightly moved before a force of sharp, excruciating pain deprived me of any thoughts. A suppressed cry escaped my lips when Francis' sharp, long fangs pierced my flesh, sending goosebumps down my skin.

My arm became limp in the strong hold of his hands. The agony spread through my body, setting my bones on fire. Trapped, I could not escape the torture, could not endure it either. The fire spread with such speed, it made me want to beg for a quicker death.

The pain reached my heart right before stopping all together, allowing the sweet, strange warmth to envelope me from the inside out.

My breathing quickened, my pulse spiraled.

Dozens of roses grew in the depths of my stomach, their thorns prickled and scratched my insides in an odd satisfaction.

I wanted more.

I cared not if I survived this long, dark night; I cared not if Francis would never stop, drying me empty, killing me so slowly.

Joy overwhelmed me, refusing my mind any say in the situation. My chest tightened as a quiet whimper left my mouth without permission.

The sound made Francis freeze in place; his sharp teeth deserted my flesh as the brightness in his eyes slowly creeped in.

"I am—" Francis stared at the bite he just left me in pure horror. "Sorry." He coughed, wiping my blood off his lips. His strong hands held my arm so gently; the roses in my stomach bloomed with more power.

His face was so close to mine, his breath brushed my lips. I watched his perfect eyes, unable to look away.

Francis took out a cloth from his coat, wrapping it around my wound—just like I had for him a few minutes ago. His strong, soft hands gently touched my cheek, and I had to stop myself from leaning into the temptation. "Princess?"

His husky voice sucked the air out of my lungs, his amber eyes hypnotized me, welcoming me into the depths of his soul. The smell of my blood on his lips made my head spin.

"Cordelia?"

I could see every curve of his perfect, soft, crimson lips.

My dear Gods! I shook my head. *What is wrong with me?*

"We need to get out of here," I quickly exclaimed, rushing to my feet—away from him. "I am certain the knights will trace us here soon." Untightening Annabelle's reins, I avoided Francis' gaze at all cost. "Can you mount the horse?"

"I can try," Francis groaned, attempting to get to his feet.

After a few failed attempts we'd finally managed to mount the horse. I had Francis sit in front of me this time: in case he lost consciousness again.

If we were lucky, we would get home without any more obstacles, yet I did not dare to spoil myself with such dreams. Luck was definitely not on our side tonight.

The trip back was much quicker than our way there. We did not stop for rest, we did not slow for even a moment. I could feel the frustration in Annabelle's every step, yet I also could not allow her the break she desperately needed.

"A little bit more," I patted her on the back as we continued our long journey.

Francis was in and out of the oblivion despite my best attempts at keeping him awake. If we fell again, we might've never gotten back up.

Just a little longer and Francis would get the treatment he needed, just a little longer and this disaster would come to an end.

Seconds, minutes, hours later I could finally see the silhouette of the castle. The early sun rays slowly crept in, forcing me to cover every inch of my skin; Francis did the same.

"Please stay awake, we are almost there," I told him.

"I am trying my best, Your Highness."

The horizon was now bright pink, fighting with the darkness behind the forest, forcing it to give place to the beginning of a new day. We had to make it before the sun fully uncovered itself.

Francis' castle was gorgeous in the early morning light. Glorious stained glass art now shimmered with dozens of rainbows, brightening the misery of our night.

I urged Annabelle faster, not believing we'd actually made our way here. We'd done it.

The excitement and relief filled my blood—

Francis' low growl dropped the reality of our situation back on me, his body shook from all the pain he'd endured throughout our journey.

"We are almost there," I kept telling him—or myself, I was not sure. My voice sounded hoarse after tonight's events. "Almost there," I whispered, turning Annabelle to the closest entrance of the castle.

"I got this," Francis stated, as he dismounted.

Despite his childish refusal, I stretched out my hand to him for support.

"What have you done?" A voice traveled from behind me. I turned toward the sound, and my already bad mood darkened.

"What have you done?" Caleb screamed at me, pushing me aside with such force I stumbled over my feet. "What have you done to him!"

Chapter 20
Dull Daggers

Every instinct in me screamed at me to run, yet I could not—would not— leave Francis until I knew he was indeed safe.

"I am fine," Francis' voice dropped a few octaves as he fought his way between Caleb and I. "She did not do anything." His fist firmly planted at Caleb's chest as he staggered from side to side. "Leave her alone," Francis growled right before he collapsed.

Caleb's strong hands caught Francis' weak body, my own hands stretched out in a feeble attempt to help.

"What in the Kingdom—" Roxanne's scream flew through the courtyard as she ran down the stairs. "Dear Gods, Francis!"

"I just need rest," Francis groaned, his eyes fluttering before shutting closed.

"Help me get him inside," Caleb addressed Roxanne without sparing me a glance.

Slowly, they made their way up the stairs, leaving me to watch them disappear into the darkness of the castle.

The sun extended its powerful hands toward me, touching my cheek, burning my skin with an uncomfortable ache. Holding the reins tightly as if my life depended on it, I wished to stand and stare at it forever: unwilling to say another goodbye.

"Let's get you inside, the sun is almost out." The voice made me jump. So deep in my thoughts, I hadn't even noticed my company. "I am so glad you are alive, we were so worried when we realized you were gone." Florence hugged my shoulders tightly.

She pried the reins from my hands, walking Annabelle back to the stables.

I wanted to protest, tell her I could take care of myself and my horse. I wanted to thank her for the kindness of her heart, yet all I could do was stare into the darkness Francis had disappeared into.

"You need rest, Cordelia." Florence carefully touched my back as if I was made of the most delicate glass.

"Will he be okay?" I finally found my voice.

"He will be," Florence nodded, gently ushering me toward the castle. "It is not the first time he got shot with silver. Caleb can treat his wound."

The idea of Caleb doing anything to Francis made me feel uneasy.

"Caleb can be a lot of things, but he loves his family." Florence read the emotions on my face. "We have nothing to worry about." She sent me a weak smile. "Let's get you settled. Shall we?"

"Thank you."

A loud knock on the door pulled me from my dreamless sleep. My eyes slowly opened, despite their best wishes to stay shut forever.

Two silhouettes stood at the threshold of my room. The candles shone brightly in their hands, reminding me of the warm loving sun.

It took a few moments for my eyes to adjust to the darkness of my room, yet I could not trust the clarity of my vision. Perhaps I was still asleep.

Roxanne took a few deliberate steps into the room, handing me a glass of fresh blood. "You must be starving."

Her dark blue dress shimmered under the candlelight in a dozen rainbows. Her bright red hair was braided into a crown. She looked as though she appeared from the most magical fairy tale.

I took the glass, still not believing the sanity of my mind.

Florence placed her candle upon the dresser, taking a seat on my bed.

"How are you feeling?" Florence's dark brown eyes watched me with curiosity. Dried wild flowers decorated her beautiful curls, her olive dress reminded me of a summer forest. "You've slept for nearly two nights."

"Is he well?" I whispered.

"Francis is well," her soft hands covered mine. "He just needs to rest now."

For the first time since I began my journey, I took a full breath. My eyes closed as the relief washed over me, my aching heart finally calmed.

"Where did you two go?" Roxanne broke a moment of silence. "What happened?"

They had no knowledge of anything that had occurred at the Royal palace. For them we'd just disappeared in the middle of the night, and I'd returned Francis on the brink of death.

No wonder Caleb acted the way he had. Perhaps I understood. If something like that happened to Sandra I would've been furious too.

"We got the documents," my voice cracked, as I rushed out of bed.

"What?" Roxanne's frowned.

My eyes scanned the room, searching for the cloak I'd worn that night. I hadn't even checked if the documents were still where I'd left them when the fatigue had claimed me. After the knights had attacked, all I thought about was finding safety.

My fingers brushed over the papers that were now crumpled. I smoothed out the corners of the documents before handing them over to Roxanne and Florence. "Here."

They took the papers from my hands, holding it carefully as though it'd grown fangs.

I watched their facial expressions change, as they carefully read the contents: from pure confusion to realization, from realization to disbelief.

"Good Gods!" Roxanne laughed. "How did you—" she trailed off, her eyes full of shock.

"This is it—" Florence chimed in, her smile as bright as the sun itself.

"We must set up the meeting immediately," Roxanne's gaze met mine. "Thank you."

"I wouldn't have been able to do it without Francis."

"At least he is good for something," she rolled her eyes. "Nevertheless, I am in your debt. I have been begging him to break into the royal palace for months." Roxanne held the papers close to her heart. "Whatever did you do to convince him? Thank you."

Convince him? My brows frowned.

"I should send the letter to the Barrens now." Roxanne gave Florence a kiss before charging toward the door.

Despite my best attempts at sharing their excitement, my mind wandered to dark places, ignoring my pleas. The reminder of the Barrens' name hurt. My sister's screams were still fresh in my mind. My heart wailed, as if a dull dagger crashed through my chest.

"Do you have caramel fudge?" I suddenly asked Florence who studied my face carefully.

"No," her eyes found mine. "But I know where to find it." She smiled mischievously.

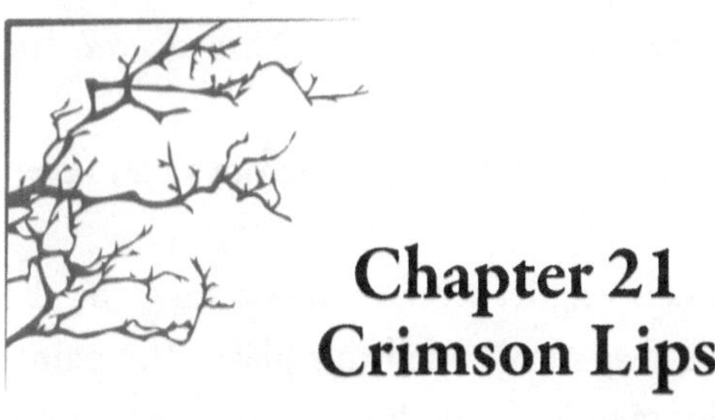

Chapter 21
Crimson Lips

My eyes reflected the light from the candles, glowing in the darkness. I could not find it in me to hate the abnormality, instead, I studied my irises in the mirror with curiosity. The shimmering reminded me of a starlit sky: infinite, full of secrets and mysteries.

The warm bath had scared away the exhaustion I was greeted with when I woke. Clean clothing and freshly braided hair made my lungs breathe with ease.

I will be waiting in the common area, Florence had told me before leaving me to the privacy of my room. She still hadn't told me where we would be going: just looked at my ripped to shreds dress, kindly telling me to change.

I studied myself in the mirror. My eyes glowed inhumanly bright, my clean hair shone like fine silk. The amber dress covered the ugly scar on my chest.

For the first time in a while, I did not look frightened.

The common area was all the way down the stairs by the exit to the castle. I held the candle near my heart, taking slow steps down.

The memory of walking in these halls when we'd arrived that night was still raw in my mind. The hushed screams and whispers did not leave me. *Let's take the arrow out first,* the voice had said. *Then burn the poison out of the wound,* the other had agreed.

The suppressed screams had stopped before I had fallen asleep.

The castle was eerily quiet now, as if listening for the whispers and secrets that surrounded this place. The paintings on the walls gloomed in the darkness, glaring pointedly at me.

"Cordelia," the paintings whispered. "Cordelia."

The murmurs did not stop, my heart beat faster. I spun around, searching for the origin of the echo. Dozens of candles quietly watched me from afar.

I followed the candles to the very end of the hall. I had yet to explore this part of the Castle, thinking it must've been the private rooms of the residents within.

The candles led me through the ajar door. "Cordelia."

Candles covered every surface of the room, illuminating every hidden corner. A variety of books, paintings, and sculptures chaotically laid upon different tables and shelves, spilling onto the floor. As if a hurricane went through this room, every piece of furniture was occupied by wild disorganization.

I walked past the bookshelf that separated the room into two. Despite the peculiarity of the scene, my pulse had quieted, my breathing steadied.

I turned around the bookshelf.

Relief and fear washed over me at the exact same time, mixed into one bewildering emotion. My legs carried me toward the sound of Francis' quiet breathing as if my body had a mind of its own.

Francis laid upon a massive wooden bed. Sheets the color of night and shadows were wrinkled underneath him. His chest rose and fell in a steady rhythm.

I took a step closer.

"Cordelia," he mumbled.

I hurried to apologize for the intrusion of his space when I realized he was fast asleep.

I should've left. I should've left this room, yet I did not. Instead I took another step, then another, and another, until only inches separated us.

My gaze could not escape the capture of this prison, unable to move away from his immaculate features: his messy—covered in blood—hair, his full brows, his soft pink lips.

I swallowed the lump in my throat, moving closer and closer as if my eyes could not handle the distance, could not capture the perfection of his skin in its greatness. I moved closer until my face was right above his.

I breathed in jasmine, smoke, wine, and blood. My blood. My blood was still on his lips.

I should leave.

His lips were so soft.

I have no business being here.

His skin was flawless.

A princess knows prudence.

My lips covered his.

Chapter 22
Crimson Fudge

"We must celebrate!" Simon threw his hands in the air.

Simon's tavern definitely hadn't been on my list of possible places serving caramel fudge, yet Florence insisted it was the only place around here that had a great variety of *human desserts*—as she called it.

The tavern was fairly small; the place overflowed with guests. Every table was occupied, others stood by the bar, some even outside. Laughter and lively conversations filled the establishment, leaving no room for sadness nor tears.

"We must indeed!" Florence agreed. She and Roxanne sat across from me, their hands in a tight embrace.

Florence had been eager to share the news the moment the three of us set foot inside the tavern with their best friend. Simon was thrilled there had been progress with the war efforts; he barely kept his hands from hugging the living spirit out of me. "I will get us some celebratory drinks," he winked at our table. "Would you like anything specific?" Simon carefully turned to me.

Aware he had been asking whether or not I would drink blood on such an occasion, embarrassment creeped into my flesh. If only Simon had known what I'd done at the cabin.

"Would you happen to have caramel fudge?" I avoided his true question entirely.

"Why, don't insult me now." He shoved his palm onto his heart, forcing a small smile across my face. "I will fetch you the finest caramel fudge ever made." He winked as he turned toward the kitchen door that carried a big *no entrance* sign.

"Did you have a chance to check on Francis before leaving?" Florence quietly asked Roxanne.

My chest tightened at the mention of his name, my neck grew warm. My fingers involuntarily flew toward my lips: the trace of Francis was still fresh on my skin.

As if keeping the most precious secret there was, I pretended I cared not to hear the reply.

"I did, he should wake within a few nights," Roxanne nodded. "Thank generous Gods and the Moon it was silver, not Royal steel."

"Thank generous Gods and the Moon," Florence repeated Roxanne's words, glancing at me carefully. "Are you feeling any better?" she asked. "Has your arm healed?"

Cold sweat covered my skin within seconds, ice wrapped around my heart unabling it from any movement. Shame spread through my veins, settling down deep in my stomach.

She'd seen the bite Francis had left me. Of course she had.

Have they seen the bite I left Francis as well?

I wished I could disappear into nothingness, fall into the depths of the ground underneath this building.

Instead, I put a smile on my face and pretended her question did not affect me in any way.

"I am well, thank you." I managed to keep my voice steady. "How are the children at the orphanage?" I cared not how obvious my intentions seemed when I changed the subject.

"Oh, they are great!" Florence exclaimed. "Charlotte has been asking about you. You must visit them soon."

"The best caramel fudge has arrived!" Simon interrupted our awkward interaction as he placed a huge plate of dessert before me. "And so are our drinks." He dropped at the seat near me, clapping his hands once. "Let our celebration begin!"

Four glasses of crimson liquid glared at me.

"To Cordelia and Francis, and their foolish—but very valuable—mission!" Roxanne met my gaze, raising her glass.

Everyone cheered. I followed their lead, but could not bring myself to drink the contents of my own. I knew it was bad manners, yet could not seem to force my hands to put the glass near my lips. The red liquid brought my mind back to the cabin, back to the red I saw on his lips before I left. Before I had kissed him.

For Moon's sake, stop it, Cordelia.

"I added moonshine into your drink," Simon whispered into my ear, pointing at my untouched glass.

A surprised laugh escaped my lips as I shook my head.

"I always keep my promises," Simon shrugged with a serious look on his face.

"That is a very good trait to have." I played along, keeping my own features as though we were discussing a very important topic until a genuine smile spread across my face. "Thank you."

"Of course," he smiled back at me. "How are you adjusting to our way of living?" he added quietly after a small pause.

I glanced at Roxanne and Florence before answering. They held each other's hands as though invisible rope tied them together. The pair seemed to have forgotten everyone else's presence.

"It's overwhelming," I admitted. "But I am all right."

"I am glad to hear that." He put his hand atop mine and for a moment he just looked at me, understanding written on his face. "Well, try your fudge, don't languish!" he broke the spell.

"All right, all right." I grabbed a spoon, smiling at his impatience.

The soft fudge melted on my tongue. I waited for the taste to reach my mind, I waited for the sweetness to overwhelm my senses. Yet nothing happened.

Frowning, I looked up at Simon.

"I figured you wouldn't want any blood on it, so—" he answered my silent question. "Human food tastes little to us without blood on it."

"Oh," was all I said.

"Here," Simon sighed. "Let me fix it for you." He reached for his drink, pouring half of it on the fudge. "Try it now. It should taste just as good as before." He grinned, "or probably even better, since I was the one to cook it."

Despite my disappointment, I managed to put a smile on my face.

Taking a spoonful of fudge, I studied it carefully as though it could bite me. Crimson liquid dripped down my spoon, coloring the plate red. My stomach turned in disgust, yet the aroma reached my nostrils. The aching in my throat increased, urging me to feed the monster within. I put the spoon into my mouth.

"Heavens." A moan escaped my lips without permission as I took another spoonful of my dessert. "This is the best fudge I have had in my entire existence," I said out loud before I could stop myself. Everyone at the table burst into laughter.

"I am glad you like it!" Simon chuckled. "Or should I say *love it*?"

"I love it," I said with my mouth full, making everyone laugh even harder.

"I see you all are enjoying yourselves without me," a low voice froze me in place.

Francis stood at the head of our table, amusement shining in his eyes.

Chapter 23
Unique Use of
Swords

"What in the Kingdom are you doing here?" The worry in Florence's voice was unmistakable.

Francis made his way around the table, taking the empty seat by my side. His eyes never left mine.

Does he remember?

My mind was on fire. A navy blue blazer stopped just above the bite I'd left him. I returned my eyes back to my dessert, unable to hold his gaze any longer.

Anxiety creeped in, settling down in my chest. *What was I thinking?* I wanted to scream at myself. *Fool. I must keep my distance.*

"Francis?" Florence persisted.

"Yes?" He finally acknowledged her.

"Are you—" she frowned. "What are you doing here? You need rest."

"I've rested plenty." Francis took my glass without my permission. "Besides—" he choked on my drink before he could finish. I pretended not to notice his curious gaze on me, though I could not stop a slight smile of amusement from spreading across my face. "I woke to the empty house and assumed you all would be here." Francis took a more careful sip from my glass this time.

"Where is Caleb?" Roxanne's brows furrowed.

"How would I know?" Francis shrugged, finally putting my drink down. "So—" He looked over our table. "Anything interesting happened while I was busy?"

"Everything tends to be rather peaceful when you're not around," Simon crooked his head.

The conversation carried on, yet I could not pay attention to any words being spoken. As if an invisible barrier separated me from the world, I looked at my companions through thick glass. Too aware of who sat beside me, my mind was unable to break free from the prison of my thoughts.

"Never took you for a moonshine lover, Princess," a whisper broke through the wall around me.

"I shall get back to the castle. It has been a long night." I smiled at the table, putting the silverware back on the table with more force than I intended.

"I will join you." Francis got up from his chair, stretching out his hand to help me up.

"No need, I remember the way back." I ignored his hand. "Thank you for the fudge," I smiled at Simon, getting up. "And the drink."

"Of—" Simon's brows furrowed in confusion. It took him a second to collect himself before trying again. "Of course!"

The whole table stared, their eyes jumping from Francis' outstretched hand to my face.

Enjoying the spectacle he had created, Francis theatrically dropped his hands when he said, "Why, I might need help getting back." The smirk did not leave his face. "It's a pity you do not have your fancy sword with you. I really enjoyed that part."

Was he mocking me for saving his life? How dared he!

I put a sweet smile on my face. "I am sure you meant to say *thank you, Cordelia, for not leaving me in the middle of the forest to die*, and also," I crooked my head to the side, looking him straight in the eyes. "Who said I needed a sword?"

A wide grin slowly spread across his face as he bestowed me with an approving nod.

I wished to set him on fire.

"Good night, everyone." I looked at the confused faces of my company.

Francis' childish behavior would definitely make me act upon my wish one night. Not tonight though, tonight I turned around and stormed out of the tavern.

"What in the Kingdom was that about?" Roxanne's hushed voice reached me right before I escaped the building. *If only I knew.* I wished to reply to her question, walking towards Annabelle.

"Wait up, Princess."

A groan escaped me. I did not need to turn around to know that Francis was walking directly behind me.

"What do you need?" I said, looking straight ahead.

"Would you please slow down?" He chuckled. "It is quite hard to walk when your leg has been shot through. I was serious. Let me escort you back home." He caught up to me, limping. "It is not safe for either of us to be alone in the woods: not after what happened."

"Even if I say no, you will still follow after me, won't you?" My brows flew up.

"Aye, I will."

I shrugged, mounting my horse. "Then why even ask?"

"I am merely being nice, that is all."

I rolled my eyes at his comment. "Clearly, we have different definitions of nice."

The night had settled down in the ice that painted the forest light blue. The snowy ground crunched under the weight of hooves, waking up the creatures that called these woods home.

We'd almost made it all the way to the castle, when Francis broke our silence.

"How did you enjoy your night?" his voice echoed from behind me.

The narrow pathway was my only salvation on our trip back: I could not face Francis' eyes were he to walk beside me.

"It was great before you showed up," I muttered.

"Is that so?" A bright laugh reached my ears. "Am I truly that horrible to be around?"

"Could we get back in silence?" I sighed. "I am begging you."

"You see," Francis did not pay any attention to my pleas. "I thought we had a great time together. I even think there is a part of you that really enjoyed my company."

I did not need to see his face to know he was smirking.

"Don't get ahead of yourself." I let out a small laugh. "I only let you come for protection." The words burned in my throat.

"And yet, you couldn't resist the urge to feed me," he said so easily, as though we were talking about the weather. Perhaps for him it was indeed so easy. "Saved my life even—"

"I pitied you," I quickly interrupted. "It would be an embarrassment to die like that—even for you. I knew that death couldn't live up to your name."

He laughed even harder now. "Pity, huh?"

"Precisely." My heart galloped.

"Why, thank you," Francis teased. "Was it at least nice?"

"Was *what* nice?" I asked, my brows furrowed.

"Me drinking your blood, of course," he replied as though it was obvious. "Was it nice? I hope you enjoyed it." His playful tone made my head turn his direction despite my wishes. "I've been told I am great at it," he winked.

Blood rushed to my face, coloring my cheeks bright pink. "You are surrounded by liars," I scoffed, turning away from him.

My eyes stared straight ahead; the bright blue moon smiled down at me. I asked the moon to clear my head of this nonsense, yet it seemed it enjoyed my reaction as much as Francis did.

"I beg to differ," he whispered as though telling me a secret. "How come your face is bright red?"

"You think too highly of yourself," I shook my head.

"I've been told that too, but, as you said, I am surrounded by liars." The most genuine laugh I had ever heard from him reached me. "Thank you, Princess," Francis added more seriously this time. "I will be forever grateful for your unique use of the sword."

I glanced at him and spotted a soft smile on his face. The moon lit up his features. My eyes bored into the lips I'd kissed this morning.

"Seriously, though, wear a sword on you from now on." He caught my gaze. "For protection—" He cleared his throat. "I mean, wear your sword on you for protection."

"I don't exactly know how to wield it." The truth slipped my lips before I could catch it.

"Of course," he laughed once again.

I glared at him, the seriousness in my features cut his laughter short.

"You weren't joking," Francis' brows flew high.

"My father used to teach me when I was a child." I turned away from him. "I stopped practicing after his death."

The silence in between us stretched out for what seemed to be an eternity. Only the moderate slow steps of our horses were heard in this night forest until Francis' voice broke free.

"Well," he cleared out his throat. "I suggest you resume your training. Especially if you wish to walk out of the castle alone." Francis paused, before adding quietly. "People go missing, Your Highness. It is not safe." His voice cracked as he spoke. "Each night becomes more dangerous than the night before. I suggest you not leave the castle by yourself at all."

"I see I am a prisoner now."

"Of course not, but perhaps walk in the company of someone you trust."

"I do not trust a single soul here," I shrugged, turning Annabelle off the pathway, toward the stables of his castle.

Something about Francis' presence prevented me from being truthful. Of course there was a small part of me that trusted him, Florence, and even Roxanne—a small, almost nonexistent, part of me...

Yet I could not bring myself to say it out loud, could not let him know my vulnerabilities, my weaknesses. For it was certainly a weakness. My Royal upbringing had taught me that lesson a long while ago: everyone kept secrets and would use you for their own gain.

"Not even me?" Francis dismounted his horse.

"Especially not you," I smiled, following his lead.

"Allow me to help, Your Highness." Francis rushed toward me, his hand outstretched in a graceful gesture.

I rolled my eyes at him, yet still took the offer. Francis bestowed me with a smile, his eyes full of amusement.

So aware of his closeness, a shaky breath escaped me. His touch forced dozens of thorns to scratch the insides of my stomach, and despite my vow to keep my distance, my treasonous body enjoyed the long forgotten sensation.

My eyes met his, trying to find the hidden truth in them. *What are you doing to me?* I wanted to ask him.

His hand stretched out toward my face. *How would his fingers feel on my cheek?* My treasonous mind wondered. *How would they feel on my lips?* He gently moved a stray strand of hair behind my ear, sending panic piercing through my body.

Everything in my body stilled in fear.

Don't you trust me, Cordelia? Timothy's laugh was loud and clear in my mind. My long hair was in his firm grasp, forcing my face up.

"Princess?" Francis' voice traveled through the fog in my mind, his whisper brushed my lips. Francis' brows furrowed, pure worry written on his face.

Stop moving! He roared at me, freezing every bone in my body.

"Princess?" Francis' voice pulled me out of the memory as I jumped out of his reach, storming out of the stables. "Are you well?" He rushed after me.

"Yes!" I put all of my energy into forcing my birthday ball out of my mind. "Just need some rest," I offered over my shoulder.

Timothy is not here. I calmed my breathing, walking towards the castle. *He cannot hurt me anymore.* I ignored Francis' worried stare on my back.

"I am all right," I said more to myself than to him.

The sound of our steps occupied the heavy silence in between us. My eyes were locked on the castle before me, though I could not tend to my surroundings for a heavy fog invaded my vision: I was blinded by my own thoughts.

"What in the Kingdom—" Francis' voice echoed behind me.

Chapter 24
Royal Steel

Francis' eyes traveled past me, an odd smile spread across his face. "What is a cat doing in your lap?" he yelled, laughing.

"I found him in the kitchen, trying to steal our dinner. Poor thing was freezing to death." Caleb sat atop the stairs by the front entrance of the castle. A gray hairball settled down in his lap, slowly eating a huge chunk of raw meat. A pair of gold eyes met mine.

"Silver?" I took a few careful steps forward.

The cat let out a loud *mew* before rushing toward me: his dinner completely forgotten.

"Silver!" I dropped to my knees, catching the creature tight in my arms. "Hello, my friend!" I pet under his chin. "How did you find me?"

"You named your cat Silver?" Francis' brows furrowed down at me.

"You have a cat?" Caleb chimed in.

"I missed you too," A genuine laugh escaped my lips when Silver licked my hands.

Francis' voice dropped a few octaves, "A word?" he gestured Caleb inside.

"Of course," Caleb pursed his lips.

"Thank you," I called after Caleb as he reached the entrance.

He nodded before disappearing into the castle.

For being an outdoor cat, Silver quickly adjusted to his new home. Just one hour later—after inspecting every corner of my room—he deemed it safe to take a nap. Laying next to me on the bed, Silver purred in his sleep, bringing a small smile to my face every time I glanced at my companion.

But even he couldn't ease my mind tonight.

With a book borrowed from Francis' library in my hands, my eyes could barely focus on the text. The book was not boring by any means: it was my thoughts that refused me any distraction.

My mind was occupied by Francis' lips so close to mine, and memories of Timothy following right after. Will I ever kiss another—conscious—person in my life? Could I ever trust another soul?

Groaning, I began rereading the same page I'd read at least a dozen times when a shimmer from the corner of my room caught my gaze.

My sword laid upon a small table, its handle sparkled under the candlelight. I set the book aside as my legs carried me toward the weapon, my hands stretched out grabbing the blade.

UNKINDNESS OF CRIMSON RAVENS

The sun was far from making its appearance: I had hours to practice. Francis was right, I did indeed need to know how to protect myself.

A princess should not trouble herself with swords and war play. Mother's voice screamed in my mind.

Everyone should know how to protect themselves and their loved ones. Especially in the time of war. Father's voice countered.

Securing the scabbard onto my waist, I closed the door of my room behind me.

The wooden door of the training room creaked when I pushed it open. The unsettling darkness of the place covered my skin in ice. I rushed toward the candles, lightning them one by one.

The room overflowed with weapons, armors, and bags of hay resembling human targets.

Walking toward the nearest hay doll, I took my stance.

Shoulders down, eyes on the opponent, left leg to the side for balance. Father's words instructed me. *The sword is an extension of your arm; it is now a part of you, little pearl.*

I inhaled through my nose, forcing my lungs to expand. I imagined air reaching every part of my body, healing every crack of my soul, filling my heart. *Breathe out.* Every worry, every unwanted thought escaped my mind as I emptied my lungs. My head spun with sweet satisfaction, every muscle in me relaxed.

Like an unstoppable force, my hand was as strong as steel when I extended my blade before me. I lifted my dominant leg, transferring my weight forward as I lunged. As though I weighed no more than feathers, I flew toward my target with ease and power.

The sound of pierced material brought satisfaction to my ears. Excitement overwhelmed me when I freed my blade from my pretend opponent's heart. Blood rushed through my body, reaching every cell of my being, setting my insides aflame.

"Your position is too unsteady. You need to fix it before you get killed."

My shoulders straightened, my hands slowly dropped to my side as I turned to face my intruder. I raised my chin high.

"Your blade is also dull," Caleb pointed at my sword. "I can see it from here."

He wore a white tunic, and long black trousers. His face was impossible to read as he smiled at me, although the smile did not reach his eyes.

Despite Florence's kind words of this man, and the fact that he'd found Silver, I narrowed my eyes anticipating his next move. "I am not in the mood to be mocked or yelled at right now." My grip tightened around the hilt of my sword as I stormed toward the exit. My teeth clenched.

"Wait," Caleb's hand stretched out, blocking my way.

My body was caught up in a burning flame, the fire in me grew faster than the falling star.

"I'm sorry for yelling at you that night," he said carefully.

My eyes found his troubled features.

"I wasn't aware of what had happened, and assumed—" Caleb trailed off, shaking his head. "It does not matter. I apologize for my behavior."

My eyebrows flew up at his confession.

"As for the time we first met," he continued, "I am sorry for acting that way." Caleb closed his eyes. "I can be rather protective of my found family, although that is not an excuse."

There were only a few feet in between us, yet I still questioned my vision's sanity.

My head moved in a slow silent nod. *Am I asleep?*

"Thank you for saving my brother," Caleb said softly. "I am in your debt."

"I didn't do it for you." The bitter words left my mouth before I could catch them.

Caleb's lips turned into a thin line when he nodded. "Would you like me to teach you some sword wielding? As a payment for your troubles."

My mouth opened and closed a few times, as I vacantly stared at the man before me. *He must be jesting.*

"I am all right," my voice finally found its way out. "I appreciate the offer..." I mumbled, staggering to the side in an attempt to walk away once again.

His hand gently caught my shoulder. "Your stance is great, but you lose it the moment the actual fighting starts." His eyes bored into mine. "Let me show you the proper way."

"I do not plan on fighting anyone." I freed my shoulder from his grip.

"No one plans such things," the man continued, ignoring my harsh tone. "The skill can come in handy with what we are dealing with," he persisted. "I heard you are to attend the next meeting. Anything can happen on human grounds."

My eyebrows furrowed together: no one had told me I was to attend the meeting. Sweat broke through my skin at the idea of seeing Timothy's parents again. *What if he will be there?* My muscles tensed, my heart skipped a beat.

"I will play nice, I swear." Caleb forced a kind smile. "You must know how to protect yourself. Humans can be dangerous for our kind. What they lack in strength they compensate with their expansive numbers and weaponry."

He was right, yet I could not find it in me to accept the offer no matter how childish my reasoning was. Pride was not a trait I would like to possess, however it was all that consumed me when facing this man.

Perhaps he was trying to make things right between us. Though, I was not to trust easily, not after how miserable he'd made me feel in my time here.

"Is that," Caleb interrupted my inner battle. "Royal steel?" His eyes froze on my blade.

"Yes." My grip tightened around the hilt.

"They do not make these anymore," Caleb declared.

"They do not," my voice was as cold as the winter lake. "This sword is quite old."

My father and brother had been the last people to make this kind of steel. The skill had died with them on the battlefield.

I was to learn when I turned twenty years of age, but my mother had refused to share the sacred papers with me.

A woman should not trouble herself with such things. I will pass the knowledge to my grandson and your future husband, she'd told me.

I'd cried a lot that night.

"May I take a look?" Caleb's eyes shone with curiosity.

I hesitated for a moment. I was not nearly naive enough to give away my only weapon when facing a person who'd forced me to duel just weeks ago. Roxanne was not here tonight to stop his nonsense.

Seeing my inner conflict, Caleb offered me his own weapons. "I was always fascinated by the only blade that can kill us at a mere touch with our blood."

Something in his eyes made me believe the sincerity of his words. My mind screamed at me for my foolishness as my hand stretched out to exchange weapons.

He studied the sword carefully as if it was made of fragile glass. "Exquisite," he whispered.

"What do you mean it can kill us by touching our blood?" I asked, glancing at my perfectly healed wrist.

Caleb followed my gaze as I quickly pulled down my sleeve. "I assume Francis sucked the poison out of your blood before it reached your heart, though I suggest making yourself bleed elsehow next time." He returned his gaze back to the sword.

My cheeks burned aflame. Does everyone at the Castle know about the bite now?

"Where silver only slows our healing," the man continued, "Royal steel will kill you the moment it reaches your heart: no herb will reverse the process." Caleb spun the sword once, making the blade shimmer under the candle light. "My father used to be a smith for the Royal family, but could never make a weapon like this despite his best attempts."

"Your father?" I crooked my head.

"Uh—" Caleb trailed off, his eyes met mine. "Yes. He was a Royal smith," he shrugged. "Before he was turned into a vampire."

"When was that?" I suddenly asked Caleb. "How old are you?"

"Old," Caleb chuckled, handing me my sword back. "I was bitten by my father on my seventeenth birthday."

"Your father bit you?" The terror in my voice rang dozens of bells.

"I wanted him to," Caleb smiled at my reaction, retrieving his blades. "When my father was first turned he had to leave me for my own safety." His voice was as calm as the morning breeze no matter the tragedy of his words. "I missed him greatly. So we made a deal: when I was to come of age, my father would bite me himself so we could spend the rest of our lives inseparable."

"Where is he now?" Surprised by how openly he answered every question I threw at him, I was glad to use this opportunity to its fullest. "What happened to your mother?"

"My mother died when I was young," Caleb shrugged. "As for my father, he does not enjoy crowds. He moved to Faris, and started working there as a local smith after Francis began to host the balls. He says he's too old to partake in such nonsense."

"How old is Francis?" The words left my mouth before I could stop myself.

A wide grin spread across Caleb's face before his bright laugh impregnated the training room. "Why don't you ask him yourself?" Caleb kept laughing.

Embarrassment washed over me, turning my lips into a thin line. My mouth was my biggest enemy.

"He is thirty-four." Caleb did not stop smirking. "So," his eyebrows flew up. "Would you like me to teach you sword wielding?"

Thirty-four. When was he bitten? I wondered, yet did not dare asking Caleb—who stared at me patiently—another question.

He did not seem like the Caleb I'd met. This Caleb was kind: reminded me a lot of Brian.

Perhaps Florence was right and Caleb just needed time to ensure his family was safe from me. Surely I could understand the concern. No one would want to be associated with the kidnapping of an heir, not even someone as powerful as a family of vampires.

I supposed I did not need to trust him to let him teach me some useful skills. He seemed to be a man who knew a lot about training. His broad, strong physique was proof of that.

As I was about to accept his offer, an excruciating scream flew through the walls. "Help!" A cry disturbed the peace of the castle. "Help me!" A shiver went through me when the familiarity of the voice stumbled through my mind. "Somebody help me!" Roxanne screamed.

Caleb was out of the door before I managed to force my body to obey. I charged through the room, fleeing toward the loud cries.

Everything stopped when I saw Florence's limp body in Roxanne's arms. Roxanne's hands were painted bright crimson, blood dripped down to the floor.

My hand covered my mouth. Florence's olive dress was now dark brown, blood did not stop flowing down her body. The wound on the stomach revealed her insides. My stomach turned.

My eyes found Roxanne's tearful face.

Francis rushed down the steps, pure horror written on his face.

"Help," Roxanne cried. "They attacked—" her lips trembled. "They attacked right after you left."

Caleb took Florence's unconscious, bloody body, carrying her up the stairs with ease and calm. Dozens of needles prickled my throat when he passed me.

Francis' heavy steps shortened the distance between him and Roxanne. His hands gently held Roxanne's shoulders, preventing her from collapsing.

"What did they attack with?" Francis' voice was as calm as the center of a hurricane.

"They—" Roxanne gasped for air. "They attacked when you left. They took the children." Roxanne kept repeating, staring into nothingness without blinking. "I cannot go through this again. I cannot." Her body started to shake. "Issac—"

"Rox," Francis said softly. "Look at me." He rubbed her cheeks with his thumbs. "What kind of blade did they use?"

"Silver," Roxanne whispered, nodding a few times before slowly turning her attention to Francis, her eyes as red as the flames of a candle. "They used silver."

"Then she will be all right." He held her face. "Tell me what happened?"

"The screams started right after you left." She glanced at me, swallowing hard. "We didn't know what was happening."

Francis carefully sat Roxanne on the floor, taking a seat next to her. His hands covered Roxanne in a tight embrace as though shielding her from the outside forces.

She met his eyes before continuing, "Florence insisted on checking the orphanage: ensure the children were safe." The quiet tears fell down her face. "We were too late," Roxanne whispered. "They took the children, Francis. Wurdulacs took the children and everyone who stood in their way."

Chapter 25
Brink of Death

Cold sweat broke through my skin. The frost enveloped my heart, squeezing it tight. "I don't understand," my voice shook. "What does that mean?"

Francis and Roxanne shared a concerned look.

"Why would they take the children?" I persisted, taking a step toward the pair.

A heavy silence filled the air when her—full of terror—eyes met mine.

The wind howled its loud serenades, shaking the castle with its force. Dozens of snowflakes hit the windows above us in a beautiful waltz.

Francis cleared his throat, taking Roxanne's crimson hand. "You need rest, let's get you to bed."

"No!" She shook her head rapidly. "I must stay." She tried to move away from Francis' embrace. "I have to be here. Florence needs me."

Francis lowered his voice to a whisper. "You will only be in Caleb's way and you know it." He helped Roxanne to get on her feet; her shaking legs barely kept her upright. "Come now, Rox. You are about to lose consciousness."

"No—I—No," she stuttered, losing her balance for a moment. "I can't—"

I caught her other hand for support. "I promise I will get you the moment Florence wakes."

Roxanne stared me straight in the eyes for what felt like an eternity before she finally gave in. "All right," she nodded slowly. "All right. Wake me if anything happens—anything at all."

"I swear." I squeezed her hand.

Francis' eyes met mine when he mouthed a silent *thank you* before walking Roxanne up the stairs.

I was left all by myself in the hall by the main entrance. The blood slowly dried on the floor, painting the marble in a color of death.

Florence's crimson body did not leave my mind, her frozen in place features made my lips tremble. Her bright smile had turned into a blue—as ice—sorrow. *She will be all right,* I told myself, not believing my own words. Everyone seemed confident in Caleb's ability to heal, but I'd seen the damage. No one could survive a wound like that: no human at least—

The front door flew open, inviting the storm inside. Snow rushed toward me, cutting my face. My hands shielded my skin from the impact when I saw a figure standing at the threshold of our home; my hand flew toward the weapon at my waist.

"I came as soon as I could," a familiar voice exclaimed. "How is she?" Simon forced the door closed behind him.

I took my hand off the sword, rushing toward our guest. "Caleb is healing her now."

"Good. That's good." He took his snowy coat off. "I was so worried when they left. I would've gone with them, but—" Simon paused, setting his coat on the handle. "They destroyed Faris. Many lost their lives."

I could not imagine the extent of horrors he had to witness firsthand.

"As long Florence is with Caleb, everything will be well." Simon put his hand on my shoulder; I wanted to laugh at the absurdity of his words.

How could he be so confident?

"Has Caleb treated wounds like this before?" I argued.

Panic threatened to stop my heart for eternity.

"He's treated worse," Simon's voice lowered.

"Worse?" I almost screamed in terror. "How much worse could it get? Florence was barely alive! Her stomach was cut open, her—"

As if the winter storm broke into the castle, my whole body shook like never before. The nausea crept into my flesh, sabotaging my well being.

"You need to sit down, Cordelia." Simon walked me down the hall to the common area. "Caleb is a great healer, believe me. He can treat anything as long as the heart is beating." He gestured for me to enter the room. "I will bring us something to drink."

I walked straight toward the fireplace.

Francis must have been here before the disaster crashed upon our castle. A few glasses of crimson liquid sat upon the table next to his settee. I took a careful sip of his long forgotten drink.

The warmth of human blood rushed down to my stomach, calming my aching heart. I took another sip, and another, until the glass was empty.

My body collapsed on the nearby settee: fatigue over-whelmed me. I didn't notice the figure standing in front of me until my hands were free of the glass.

Simon refilled my drink, his lips moving: he must be talking to me. I forced my mind to focus: in vain. *Wurdulacs took the children.* My mind repeated again and again until the words faded into one incoherent noise, ringing loudly in my ears. My head was going to explode.

"Cordelia?" The whisper finally forced my invisible wall to shatter.

I raised my head, meeting Simon's eyes. A bright red line decorated his cheek. "Are you hurt?" I pointed at his injury.

"Don't worry about it." He crouched in front of me. "Do you need anything?"

"Why would they take the children?" My gaze hardened.

Simon's troubled eyes moved to the fire as he took a seat beside me. "They are the best weapon for achieving their goal—" His voice froze the blood in my veins. "To wipe out the human population."

"What in the Kingdom are you saying?" My voice did not belong to me. "Can someone stop speaking in riddles and tell me what's going on?" I lashed out at him.

My head spun from all the anger and frustration that consumed me. Simon did not deserve the harshness of my tone, did not deserve the anger I put on him. "Sorry," I added quietly.

"That's all right." A sad smile found its way onto his face. "I understand. All of this must be a lot to take in for some-one in your position."

I wanted to argue that my position was no different from anyone else's, instead I simply nodded. "No one tells me anything," I told him. "I want to help, but I don't even know what is going on. My siblings are in danger."

Simon took a deep breath. "Vampire children are the easiest to control," he explained. "They are just as strong as we are, but they are easy to manipulate, easy to capture. And it doesn't take as long to starve them."

Simon sighed. "Wurdulacs will starve the children until they go so wild, they could drain anyone in an instant."

"Starve them," I repeated in disbelief.

"You must know by now: the hungrier you are, the harder it is to control the urge to drain out the first person you see." He sighed. "They will make the children so hungry, the moment they're unleashed on human grounds it will be over before it even begins."

My eyes burned. "Over," I whispered.

"They will wipe out the human village, so Faris would have no other choice but to go elsewhere—" Simon's gaze dropped.

"They are turning all humans against vampires." I guessed. "If they destroy the villages, no human will feel safe allowing Faris to feed."

Simon nodded. "Their goal is to destroy the treaty, weaken our alliance and our strength; so when they come we won't stand a chance."

"We must warn the humans about the attack." I refused to accept the calmness in his words.

"We will next week, during the meeting." Francis entered the room, heading straight toward me. He took an empty glass from my hands, pouring himself a drink.

"How is Roxanne?" I asked him.

"She will be alright," He shrugged, finishing the drink in one gulp before returning it to me. "Thankfully her wounds did not need Caleb's attention."

Hours passed as we sat in silence. I stared at the flames, imagining their powerful hands stretching out and brushing my skin. The fire was slowly dying out, yet no one seemed to care about the heat leaving the room.

Heavy steps grew louder against the marble, stopping just outside the room. Our heads flew towards the door, waiting for the owner to show their face.

The door creaked open, revealing a figure covered in blood. Caleb's white tunic was now bright red, the exhaustion reaching his eyes made him look a lot older.

"How is she?" Francis got up from his chair.

Caleb did not say anything as though his mind traveled into places we will never know about. Francis repeated his question, taking a step forward. Their gazes met before Caleb finally responded, "She will be alright."

I let out air from my lungs that I didn't know I was holding. *She will be alright.* I looked at Francis, his eyes were closed in silent relief.

"When will she wake?" Simon's voice carried through the room.

"In a week. Perhaps two." Caleb took a seat next to the fire. "It is hard to tell. She's lost a lot of blood."

"I should go tell Roxanne." I charged toward the door.

"I will tell her." Francis caught my hand, holding it firmly. "You go rest, Princess."

His thumb brushed over the back of my palm, burning my stomach aflame.

"I should go too." Simon looked at our hands' embrace and I immediately moved away. "Dawn is near." He sent me a curt smile.

"Good night," I said to no one in particular, rushing to the exit.

Simon's words did not leave me when sleep claimed me, nor did they leave me a whole week after when I was preparing to meet with the Barrens.

The shaking in my hands increased with every passing moment, making it more challenging to braid my hair.

I cannot do this! My thoughts screamed at me as I watched my reflection. The dark blue gown tightened around my ribs, around my neck. *I can't. I can't!* My irritated skin tingled when I pulled the fabric off of my neck. Perhaps I should change.

"Ready for another adventure, my Princess?" Francis knocked on my open door, making me jump in my chair.

"Cease calling me that," I spoke through clenched teeth, meeting his gaze through the mirror.

I wiped my sweaty hands on the gown before attempting to braid my hair for the tenth time.

"Why not?" Francis picked up Silver—who, I am sure, mewed at him to leave—with outstretched hands, studying the cat as though he'd never seen such an animal before.

I forced a lump down my throat, though it just grew bigger. "I am a princess no more." I tightened the braid around itself several times. "And certainly not yours."

Breathe in. Breathe out. I commanded myself. *I can't do this! What if he is there?* My lips trembled.

"Is she always this gloomy?" he asked the cat, tapping on its head.

Breathe in. Breathe out.

"Are you always this childish?" I rolled my eyes, securing the end of the braid with a pin. Thick air wouldn't let me breathe. My chest ached, yet I refrained from checking if my heart was still in its place.

I shook the invisible hands of my body, breathing way too fast.

"Are you alright?" Francis raised a brow, putting the cat down. When I didn't reply he added, "You have nothing to worry about, Princess. The Barrens are all bark and no bite," he smirked.

"I'm fine," I bit out, walking toward him. "What do you need from me, Francis?"

"Uh—" He crooked his head. "Nothing, I suppose."

"Then leave." I spat out, slamming the door in front of his nose.

My insides turned upside down—

My legs carried me to the bathing chambers just when my stomach emptied itself out.

I washed my face with warm water; my lungs finally expanded with relief.

I studied my expression in the mirror; barely visible dark circles under my eyes suggested the restless day I had. Nightmares had haunted me, begging me to not bring them into reality, yet I had no choice. I had to go.

William Barren would never believe the authenticity of the documents were I to choose to stay behind. I had to go if I wanted a chance at safety for the people I loved.

I put my cloak on, closing the door behind me.

Making my way down the hall, I stopped by the door Florence had told me was hers when I first arrived, with a goblet of blood in my hands.

The door creaked open, showing two figures lying atop the bed sheets. Red, matted hair lay upon the pillow as if in flames. Roxanne's sleepy eyes found mine.

"I just wanted to visit Florence before we left," I whispered, offering Roxanne the goblet.

She nodded slightly, propping herself up on the bed as she took the drink.

My eyes traveled past her, stopping on Florence's still features. Her dark, warm skin now looked lifeless. Her full bright lips were now pale.

I walked around the bed, taking Florence's lifeless hand into mine.

"She is strong, nothing could ever break her," Roxanne whispered.

"She is." I squeezed Florence's hand before heading for the door.

"Wait," Roxanne's hoarse voice called after me when I reached for the handle. "You have to make them believe," she rasped. "Promise you will do whatever it takes."

"You are not coming, then," I said more to myself than to her.

Roxanne shook her head, "I cannot leave her." Her eyes burned into mine. "Swear to me you will do everything possible."

Why would she think I was capable of something like that? "I swear," I said anyway.

"They will regret what they have done," she bit out. "I will make sure of that." She glanced at the figure by her side.

My hand grabbed the handle of the door when my eyes stopped on a beautiful painting staring at me from the wall. Two women were in a tight embrace, dancing through the empty ballroom. At the bottom of the painting it read, *To the love of my life, R.*

"You painted this?" I turned to Roxanne, who now gently brushed Florence's hair.

"She actually painted everything in the castle," Francis' voice brushed over my ear.

Dressed in fancy attire, he now stood by my side, at the threshold of Florence's room. "We have to go," he offered me a tight smile, leaving the room.

"It's beautiful," I sent Roxanne a small smile before following after him.

Our steps echoed through the corridor as we made our way down the stairs. The world increasingly spun the farther I strayed from safety. I drew a deep breath, reaching for the banister. Francis' worried gaze fell upon me, though he refrained from saying anything.

Our earlier encounter floated above us like a heavy cloud. I should apologize for my outburst, yet the words would not come.

"Give me a moment." Francis disappeared into—what looked to be—his study, without sparing me a glance when we reached the end of the stairs.

My heart burned, falling down to my stomach as I stared at Roxanne's painting resting on the wall. *Dear Moon, I cannot breathe.*

"Where are the documents?" Francis called out from the room.

I peeked into the study; Francis frantically searched through the stack of papers on the table. "I gave them to Roxanne," I told him carefully.

"They were here last night," he gestured in front of him. "I put the documents right here."

"What is going on?" Roxanne's voice echoed from behind as she pushed past me.

Francis' gaze met hers when he said, "The documents are gone."

Chapter 26
Guard Dog

Voices erupted in unison, turning into one incoherent sound.

"I left them in your study!" Roxanne shouted.

"They are not here!" Francis yelled back.

"Are you certain?" Roxanne rushed toward the table.

"Do you take me for a fool?" Francis shook his head.

Papers flew in every direction when Roxanne rummaged through the documents. "Fuck!" She finally gave up. "I put them right here. They were right here!"

Francis took a deep breath, collecting himself before speaking. "Who did you tell about the documents?" he said in a terrifyingly calm voice.

"I heard shouting." Caleb ran into the room, with an unsheathed dagger in his hand. "Is everything all right?" He scanned the room.

"We only told Simon," Roxanne shook her head.

"What is going on?" Caleb whispered to me, putting his dagger away.

"We can't find the documents," I replied quietly.

"Did you tell him at the tavern?" Francis took a deep breath as though using all of his energy to keep himself put.

Roxanne nodded, touching the bridge of her nose.

"Bloody hell." Francis sat down on the chair.

"Someone must have overheard you," Caleb chimed in.

"It doesn't matter," Francis finally acknowledged Caleb's presence. "What are we to do now? The meeting is in a few hours! How did we get the documents across the entire Kingdom just to lose them in a stack of papers?" Francis snickered. "We risked our lives stealing from the queen for nothing."

But the documents were not the only thing we stole from my mother. My legs carried me out of the study before I understood where I was headed. My legs screamed in protest as I flew up the staircase.

"Where in the Kingdom are you going?" Francis called after me. "Maybe this isn't the time for one of your runs, Your Highness."

Silver's gaze met mine when I charged across my room. He let out a loud mew, curiously following after me.

My heartbeat quickened as I swept through my drawer, desperate to find our only hope of salvation. My fingers brushed over the familiar shape, its golden engraving sparkled under the candle light.

"What is that?" Roxanne's voice traveled from behind me. She, Francis, and Caleb stood in the doorway of my room, eyeing me expectantly.

I spun the stamp in my hands, studying its curves. "The Royal stamp," I met her gaze. "We can forge the documents. They won't know the difference with a Royal stamp on it."

A wide grin spread across Roxanne's face; Francis stared at me in awe. It was Caleb who looked at me with suspicion. "If they catch us in a lie, it will ruin everything."

"They won't," I asserted. "Not with me present."

Earthy smells of spruce impregnated the air. The only way to reach the Barrens' estate from the vampire grounds was through the dark snowy woods, with no clear path to follow.

"Excited to reunite with your beloved friends?" Francis' voice cut through the cold air, making me flinch.

I bit my cheek when nausea turned my stomach upside down. My eyes scanned the surroundings, memorizing every branch's curve.

"What is going on with you?" Francis crooked his head.

"Nothing." The inside of my cheek started to bleed. The snow crushed under our horses' hooves.

"Come now, Princess," his voice softened. "I can tell something is bothering you. You've been gloomier than usual tonight."

"*You* are bothering me." My nails dug into my palm around Annabelle's reins.

"And what did I do?" Francis chuckled. When silence fell between us once again he sighed. "I don't understand you, Cordelia." He offered me a sad smile. "If you despise me so much, why did you kiss me?"

The words knocked the air out of my lungs, my face turned warm with embarrassment. He had been awake. Of course, he had been.

"It's all right," he shrugged. "I enjoyed the kiss, I just wish I was more conscious," he hummed.

"I am sorry." I closed my eyes.

"Don't be sorry, Princess, I'm sure I'll be more conscious next time."

"It's not—" I stared at the blood on my palms.

"Perhaps I misunderstood the kiss," Francis suggested, his eyes fell upon my hands. "I'm sorry if I—"

"We can't," I interrupted him, meeting his gaze. "We should not. It's wrong."

"Wrong?" Francis' brows furrowed. "Am I not of proper blood for you?"

"No!" I quickly exclaimed, shaking my head. "Moon, no!"

"Then," he sighed. "What is it, Cordelia?"

"I—" I filled my lungs, avoiding his gaze. "I can't," I whispered, a sad smile made it onto my face. "Perhaps with time, but—"

He nodded, seeming to understand the unspoken words. "May I ask—"

"No."

Francis offered a soft smile, handing me the flask. When my brows rose high he explained, "'Tis not wine, Princess. We are to enter human grounds, I figured you didn't have any before we left," he shrugged.

"Let me talk to the Barrens, all right?" I drank from the flask. "I know how to convince them."

"Care to share?" Francis crooked his head. When I didn't reply he chuckled. "Right, I'm just your guard dog." He reached for the flask.

"If I tell you my plan you will turn us around," I told him quietly, avoiding his gaze.

Francis choked on his drink. "I don't recall your last plan being very planned."

"My plan will work." I snatched the drink out of his hand.

"You are jesting, Princess," Francis shook his head. "If you don't tell me, I am turning *you* around."

"I've known these people since birth. I know what to do. Just—" I trailed off. "How can you expect me to start trusting you if you yourself don't trust me?"

His lips turned into a thin line. "Tell me what to do."

"Make sure no one touches me," I whispered.

The thought of Timothy being so close made me shiver.

"No one will touch you," Francis' voice grew colder, "I swear."

Chapter 27
Pretend Princess

Hiding our horses just beyond the treeline set a new wave of fear into my veins. Anxiety slowly made its way through my body with every step I took. No matter my best efforts at remaining collected, the storm inside of me grew, smashing peace on its way.

The Barrens' estate near Silverstone city peaked out of the horizon, reminding me of all the time I'd spent in its walls. Every part of me awoke, paying close attention to the details. I knew the estate like my own five fingers, yet still memorized every exit in case of danger.

To the right of the building, just by the long, high gates, three guards stood atop the tower. My hand went into my pocket, brushing the handle of the dagger Francis had given me. Three more guards were posted on the other side.

"Nice place," Francis muttered under his breath.

My gaze met the curious eyes of one of the guards as he gestured something to the others. My eyes did not leave him. I raised my chin, imagining I could burn them all with my gaze alone. *I can do it,* I told myself.

"I thought you'd been here before," I whispered to Francis.

"Nay, before tonight Barren only agreed to meet in the woods."

"What changed?" My gaze narrowed.

"Last time... did not go as planned," Francis snickered. "I'm assuming he would like some witnesses from now on." Francis' brows furrowed, his gaze locked on the guards. "Seems they were not notified of our visit."

"They were," I told him confidently. "They are just trying to make us believe we are invading their land. It's their tactic to force us into obedience." I couldn't help but roll my eyes.

Francis' curious gaze left a trace on my skin, yet I did not spare him a glance. I had to stay alert. "If something goes wrong, go downstairs: as far down as you can," I said in barely a whisper. "Their passages are not as complex as the ones in the Royal palace, they all lead into the underground exits."

"Understood."

The first gate slowly opened, revealing about a dozen guards standing in the middle of the courtyard before the estate. They looked at me puzzled, clearly noticing my new—inhuman—appearance. I waited, burning my gaze into their flesh. They all shared a quick glance at each other before slowly getting down to their knees. "Your Highness," they said quietly, uncertainty in their voices, as though unsure whether they were supposed to bow before me at all.

"Rise," my voice carried over the courtyard.

Like one, the guards got to their feet. Some blatantly stared at me in confusion, though the majority dropped their gazes as required.

"Your Highness, His Grace is waiting for the meeting in the court hall," one of the men said without meeting my gaze. "Allow me to escort you and your—" he looked up at Francis, his brows furrowed.

"Guard dog," Francis suggested, winking.

A small snicker escaped the guard's mouth, but he collected himself immediately when noticed my expression. "Forgive me, Your Highness," the man quickly bowed once again. "I meant to say your guest, Your Highness."

"No need to escort us." I walked past him, ignoring all the murmurs that grew louder the farther I got. Francis fell into step right behind me, keeping a few feet between us.

My shoulders straightened, my chin was raised. I put on my mask of indifference, focusing my gaze straight ahead, as though nothing and no one could possibly be of any interest to me. No one was worthy of a glance from a Royal.

The halls were filled with the smell of sickly sweet irises and cold. The strong aroma awakened the nausea in me. The irises reminded me of the stolen kisses these walls had witnessed. Kisses I wished to demand back.

The doors of the court hall were shut closed, two guards stood adjacent to the entrance.

"Let His Grace know, I am ready for him," I told the guards without sparing them a glance.

"Of—" The first guard trailed off, staring at me with no care in the Kingdom.

"Of course, Your Highness," the other guard finished the sentence, sending his partner a disapproving look.

After several knocks on the door, the man disappeared behind the giant doors. Hushed voices traveled through the barrier between us, though I could not make out the words. I stood there like a statue, waiting for my announcement.

Francis seemed to fall into the role I had given him with ease. His gaze—just like mine—was focused straight ahead, his features did not give away any emotion.

The door opened before us. My heavy, confident steps clattered on the marble as I made my way toward the table in the center of the room; the guards followed after us.

At the head of the table sat a man. His bright smile reached his eyes when he spotted me. His white—as snow—greasy hair fell down his shoulders, his wrinkled, oily skin made it difficult for me not to cringe.

He got up from his chair, sending me a curt nod; the smile did not leave his face.

I waited for him to bow—as etiquette required—yet he did not move a muscle. The fact that the guards fell into my perfect act should've been enough for me. Surely I wasn't expecting the Duke to show me any respect.

"Dearest Cordelia," William Barren exclaimed. His hands were outstretched as though he hoped for a hug. "What a pleasure it is to see you safe and sound. When the Queen announced our dearest princess had gone missing, mine and my son's hearts truly broke, I must say." He held his heart with theatrical hurt on his face. *Dear Moon, free me from this nonsense.* "The Queen told us you passed away, but when I learned the casket was empty..." A disgusting smile appeared on his face. "I knew you must have joined the dark side." He gestured toward the chair opposite him, "Please, take a seat. I believe we have much to discuss."

"Indeed we do," I finally said to him, ignoring his foolish monologue. Francis moved the chair out for me to sit, yet did not take a seat next to me. He stood a few feet behind, acting as though my personal guard. "I expect you are aware of the matter of our meeting?" I crooked my head so slightly.

"Of course, my dear." William said, taking his own seat. "But first allow me to offer you some wine." He flicked his fingers for the maid to come.

"We do not have time for such luxuries, Your Grace." My mouth went sour at the title I addressed him by.

"Surely one glass will not delay you from your—" he trailed off, studying me carefully. "What is it you are doing now, *Cordelia*?" His eyes narrowed. "Now that you have no duties to attend to." A smirk grew on his face, making me sick to my stomach. "Does the Queen know about your *new being*?"

"I am here on behalf of the Queen, *sir*." My patience was slowly running out with each word that left this man's mouth. "Our Queen personally sent me to attend to this matter."

"How disappointing," William tsked, pouring a glass of wine for himself. "And what about the orphan boy?" William addressed Francis and I prayed to all the Gods Francis knew not to anger the man. "So quiet, so collected." Duke crooked his head, smiling. "Unlike the usual Francis I'd met before," William laughed. "Surely, our dearest Cordelia's presence has nothing to do with that."

"Of course not." Francis' voice traveled past me. "You didn't seem to appreciate my true nature during our last meeting, perhaps I changed for your sake."

"Sir," I addressed the Duke, interrupting Francis before he could say anything else. "We have no time for this. Are you here to waste a Royal's time?"

A loud laughter broke through the room. "You are as much of a Royal as I am." William did not stop laughing. "If not less."

"Our Queen will be pleased to hear about how you've been disrespecting the first to the throne." My words cut through his laughter, stopping it all at once.

For a moment we just stared at each other, calculating our next moves. "Shall we get to the business now that we have settled our statuses?" I smiled.

"What do you want?" William Barren took a sip of his wine. "I already told your dog—" he nodded at Francis. "I am not interested in playing some imaginary war. Those missing people are your kind's fault and have nothing to do with me, those people are not even part of our court."

"They will be soon enough," I replied calmly. "Wurdulacs are building an army as we speak."

Barren just rolled his eyes at my words. "Wurdulacs left our territory for good seven years ago, dear. Surely, you are smarter than to fall for such a foolish tale."

My hands stretched out, handing the forged documents to the man before me. He skimmed through the paper as his smirk slowly disappeared. "What in the Kingdom is this?" He shoved the documents back into my hands. "Where did you get those from?"

"Our Queen demanded you see her personal documentation on the matter." I folded the papers back into my pocket.

"Where is the proof that they are indeed her papers?" Barren's narrowed eyes studied me. "The Queen is not the only one in the possession of a Royal stamp."

Damnation.

"Of course," I smiled sweetly at him, nodding. "I will inform the Queen you declined her request," I said, heading towards the exit; Francis followed after me. I refused to look at him, yet his confused expression did not leave unnoticed.

With each step I took toward the door, I began to doubt my judgment more and more. Perhaps I'd underestimated William's intelligence, perhaps no matter my act he could see right through my lies.

My fist rose to knock on the door when Barren's voice stopped me in place. "Wait!" William shouted after me, spreading a triumphant smile across my face. "Allow me to see those documents again," he spoke with indifference in his tone.

William walked toward us; Francis' muscles tensed when the Duke stopped just a step away.

He snatched the papers from my hand, ignoring Francis' reaction altogether. "What—" Duke's eyes found mine. "What does the Queen require of me?"

I stretched out my hand toward the papers, demanding them back. Only when William reluctantly handed me the documents did I reply to his question. "Your army must be ready for the war," I said. "Evacuate the residences of your region, give those in need shelter immediately. According to our sources, the first attack is planned to happen within a week."

"How can you give out such specific dates?" He narrowed his gaze.

"Wurdulacs attacked the vampire grounds, kidnapping children for their army," I told him the truth. "They are starving them to go after humans. According to our calculations the attack will happen within a week. The date is not certain, yet a very accurate estimation."

Dread was unmistaken in William's eyes, no matter him trying to hide his fear. "And if I refuse?" he challenged me, smirking.

"Then you shall fall first," I met his gaze, bestowing him with a smirk of my own. "I will make sure of that."

William's jaw clenched. "I will see what I can do," his muscles tensed. "Good travels, Cordelia."

I kept my composure as we followed the guards out of the estate. I should have felt relief—triumph even—yet my lungs squeezed tighter.

My heart shook in my chest as we made it across the courtyard. Dozens of eyes bored into my skin, though their owners did not wear the confusion I expected. Most of them watched me with anger, some even gripped their blades.

An odd rush of amusement swept through me. They were frightened; frightened of a princess that was not fit to rule, but to mindlessly follow her mother's orders. A weak, spoiled Royal who now posed a threat.

The guards dragged the gate open before us when I felt it. Dozens of eyes watched me carefully, yet only one pair bored so deeply it hurt.

"Your Highness," the gate men bowed, gesturing us out.

The hair on my nape rose.

His burning stare pained my back.

"What's the matter?" Francis asked quietly, realizing I was no longer following him out.

Everything calmed.

Painfully slowly, I turned my head in the direction of the window I used to search for the moment I took a step into the estate. Second floor, the last window on the left.

Our gazes locked.

With a blank expression, he just stared. The eyes that haunted my sleep now studied me carefully. I studied them back with the intention to forget them forever.

"Cordelia?" Francis' hand brushed over my shoulder.

His blond hair was brushed back, his blue eyes were now dull. The cruel smile was long gone from his face.

My gaze hardened. My heartbeat quickened, though not from anxiety.

I needed him to feel the pain he inflicted upon me, burn in it forever and be haunted by it every time he dared closing his eyes.

I wanted retribution.

I needed him to suffer.

He hurts me! My sister wailed. *He hurts me, Mother!*

Nothing could stop me from slicing his throat and drying him empty. Nothing could stop me from crushing every bone in his body.

My mouth watered in anticipation. The insides of my throat painfully ached.

"Princess, we have to leave." Francis got a hold of my wrist, tugging me out. "Now," he hissed.

Was it fear I saw in Timothy's eyes?

He moved the curtain, his silhouette slowly disappeared behind the window.

My lungs expanded.

The gate banged closed behind us as I freed myself from Francis' grip.

"Dear Gods and the Moon," Francis swore, falling into step behind me. "They were moments away from attacking," he groaned. "What's the matter with you?"

"I'm fine," I said, rushing towards our horses.

"You must have some before we go," Francis pressed the flask into my hand. "The last thing we need is you attacking anyone."

"I'm fine," I bit out, mounting Annabelle.

"You wanted to attack that man." Francis countered. "Who even was that?" he asked, mounting his horse.

"No one," I ordered Annabelle to take me home.

"Wait up, Princess!"

The nausea that had tortured me the whole day finally threatened to break loose. Even the cold winter couldn't calm my burning flesh. The air thickened.

"I'm fine," I mumbled, breathing in through my nose. "I'm fi—" A groan escaped me, forcing me to halt my horse.

Breathe! I ordered myself, dismounting. *Brea—*

My stomach emptied itself out.

Long-awaited relief washed over me as I sat on my knees, catching my breath. My hands pressed into the crunchy snow; the cold brought comfort to my skin.

"Cordelia?" Francis' cold hand felt my forehead. "You are paler than the snow."

"I'm fine." I closed my eyes, leaning into his hand. "I am fine," I said as my mind deprived me of any thought.

The smell of cool jasmine eased my mind as consciousness was slowly returning to me. Soft crunching of snow brought peace to my ears. Warm, rough fabric scratched my cheek.

"We are almost home, Princess," Francis' soft voice forced my mind out of oblivion.

My eyes fluttered open. My head spun, taking in the surroundings. I sat atop Francis' horse, his hands gently held me close to him.

I moved a few inches from the man, barely keeping on the horse. "What happened?" I tightened the cloak around myself, feeling exposed.

"When was the last time you slept?" Francis' hand wrapped around me tightly.

I couldn't recall a single night that wasn't riddled with constant screams and cold sweats, though I wasn't about to admit that to Francis. It was enough for him to see my disarray after a single meeting.

The moon hid behind the clouds. Bright snow fell onto my face; snowflakes melted, sliding down my cheek. This proximity felt wrong. "I am well enough to ride my own horse." I glanced at Annabelle falling into step behind us; her reins tight to Francis' saddle.

He sighed. "The castle is just a hundred yards away. I'm sure you can survive my presence for another minute." Francis' lips turned into a thin line. "Was that him?"

My eyes focused on a branch in front of me, desperately trying to avoid Francis' searching gaze. He sighed, taking my silence as an answer.

Francis knowing about Timothy was both a relief and distress. I needn't hide my past from him any longer, but he had no right to know something I tried to bury deep down.

For the first time, I didn't enjoy the silence that grew between us. I wished for him to talk, mock me even: anything.

My legs were ready to flee to my room the moment the castle entered my view. Francis turned his horse toward the stables; his hands gripped me tightly when he ordered for his mare to halt.

"Thank you," I mumbled as he helped me from the horse.

"Cordelia—" Francis called after me when I was halfway up the stairs of the main entrance.

I pushed the doors open, fighting with the wind that wouldn't let me in; the storm grew stronger. My fingers turned to ice when I rushed up the stairs toward my room.

The storm banged against the windows; the wind whistled, echoing through the halls.

"How did the meeting go?" Roxanne's voice reached me from Florence's room as I hurried down the corridor.

"Hey!" Roxanne called after me. "Wait up!" Her heavy steps followed.

I slammed the door behind me, sliding down the wood. Silent tears fell down my face as I curled into a ball right on the floor. Timothy glared at me when I closed my eyes; I wished to pry my eyes open forever.

The door creaked slightly, yet I cared not who stood at the threshold. "Go away," I croaked.

Silver rubbed his face against my neck, comforting me as tears damped my cheeks.

The roof shook as a new wave of the blizzard swept through the castle. The cold made its way to my uncovered skin. I forced my body up, hobbling to my bed. Woolen blankets could not bring warmth into my body nor my soul.

When the door swung open, I was ready to scream at whoever invaded my space, but when I turned to say the gruesome words, they got stuck in my throat.

Roxanne stood at the threshold of my room; a bottle of moonshine in her hands.

Chapter 28
Renascence

Roxanne made her way across the room, getting comfortable on my bed as though it was her own. "What happened?" She drank straight from the bottle before offering it to me.

"Nothing," I said dismissively. "I want to be alone."

"Do you, though?" She raised a brow, crooking her head. She shoved the bottle into my hands, ushering me to drink.

I glared at her, though I could not find it in me to order her out. "No." I snatched the bottle out of Roxanne's hand; the smell hit my nostrils. My eyes watered as I moved the bottle close to my lips. "I do not." I choked on the moonshine.

Roxanne snorted at my reaction. "Never thought I would be drinking with a royal herself." She chuckled when she met my glare. "I know we are not friends, but Florence—" Roxanne sighed. "She would want me to be here when she cannot."

I took another big sip, coughing, though not from the drink this time. "I am fine," I mumbled. "I can take care of myself."

"I hear you scream sometimes." Roxanne adjusted a pillow under her back. "We all do," her emotionless voice hit straight into my chest. "We don't have to talk; I prefer drinking anyway," she shrugged.

I swallowed the burning liquid, my eyes searched Roxanne's for any sign of mockery. "I don't need your pity," I spat out. I had no reason to be angry with Roxanne, yet I was all the same. "And I don't need a sitter."

Roxanne's gaze fell onto her lap when she whispered, "Maybe I don't want to be alone either."

My brows furrowed so slightly at her confession. I opened my mouth to reply, yet the words abandoned me.

I took a long sip of moonshine before handing the bottle to Roxanne.

The wind whistled through my room, bringing me out of the oblivion as my eyes fluttered open. The cold brushed over my uncovered skin; goosebumps traveled down my body. A long forgotten calmness swept through me.

Frowning, I wondered if perhaps I was still asleep when an unfamiliar serenity enveloped me whole.

I pulled the blankets higher when my gaze fell upon a small piece of paper lying atop the pillow next to me.

My brows furrowed as my hand stretched out to the rough parchment: a beautiful drawing of a woman with a gray cat in her hands. In the corner in a neat handwriting it read, *You snore. R.*

A grin spread across my face as my fingers brushed over the paper. After a whole bottle of moonshine split between the two of us, I couldn't recall the moment I had fallen asleep.

An impatient knock on the door made me drop the drawing. "Come in," my hoarse voice traveled through the room as I attempted to fix the dress I had fallen asleep in.

A few more loud thuds vibrated on the wood.

"Come in!" I said louder, clearing my throat; the knocks continued with new power.

A groan escaped me as I climbed out of the bed, making my way towards the door with the serenade of loud thuds. "Caleb?" I swung the door open.

The man frowned, scanning my appearance. "Get dressed," he said. "We are going to train."

My brows flew high. "Perhaps we could start tomorrow?" I suggested, attempting to close the door.

"Ask Roxanne for the proper attire." Caleb's boot stopped the door from closing. "The dress won't do," he simply said, walking away. "I will be waiting for you in the training hall," Caleb called over his shoulder.

Perhaps I was still asleep.

My gaze fell upon Florence peacefully sleeping on the bed by the window when Roxanne opened the door. "Caleb said you can give me something to wear," I told her. "He wants me to train with him."

Florence's chest rose and fell in a steady rhythm. Her soft features had brightened since the night I saw her last. A sigh of relief filled my lungs.

"You can take these," Roxanne offered me a pair of trousers and a tunic, looking me up and down. "They should fit."

I glanced at the wardrobe she took her clothes out of. "I thought this was Florence's room."

"We like to share our rooms," Roxanne shrugged. "Tell Caleb I won't train tonight." She offered as she disappeared into the bathing chambers.

I studied my new attire in the mirror. Roxanne's black trousers fit as though they were made specially for me. A small excited smile appeared on my face when I moved my legs, surprised how comfortable the trousers felt.

A woman cannot wear such outrageous clothing. A small laugh escaped my lips as though I was a naughty child that got away with mischief.

I attached a scabbard to my waist; my eyes couldn't get enough of the clothes I was gifted. Despite the fact I was yet to know how to wield it, I for sure looked as though I wouldn't need protection from anyone. Odd feelings of confidence filled me.

My confidence abandoned me when Caleb ordered me around the training hall for the next few nights.

"You have to stay calm." He swung his wooden stick against mine. "Your emotions are your greatest enemy." Not a trace of sweat on his skin.

Caleb looked as though this was no more than a warm up no matter the amount of hours we'd spent training; my skin was covered in sweat the moment my hands wrapped around the hilt of my wooden weapon. My heavy breathing echoed through the room as I dodged his blows.

"Have you fought on wooden sticks before?" Caleb asked.

"When I was five," I rolled my eyes, blocking his next attack.

"Whoever let you hold a real weapon so early made a real mistake." His stick almost touched my fingers.

"I know how to hold a weapon." I seethed through clenched teeth.

"Hold it?" Caleb's brows flew high. "Maybe. Fight with it?" He chuckled; his stick flew mere inches from my face. "I am surprised you haven't injured yourself with it before." His eyes narrowed. "Have you?"

"Once," I admitted quietly.

"Only once?" He laughed, almost knocking the weapon out of my hand. "Focus!"

"Stop distracting me with your chatter." My grip around the hilt tightened.

"If something as simple as *chatter* can distract you, you will lose the moment your opponent takes out their weapon." He laughed at my attempt to attack. "You have the skill of a ten year old. Who taught you this hideous technique?"

Blood rushed in my veins, my jaw clenched. I ignored his question as his stick landed on the back of my palm finally knocking the weapon out of my grasp.

I glanced at my reddened skin, picking up the stick. My hand wrapped around the hilt as I charged towards him. "Are you here to teach or insult me?" I seethed.

"Whatever gets the job done." Caleb snorted, shortening the distance between us: forcing me against the wall. "You seem to prefer the latter."

"What is that supposed to mean?" I spat out.

"We have been at it for hours and yet you only showed signs of strength when I angered you," Caleb retorted. "Though it also makes you distracted." His stick landed on my ribs. The air escaped my lungs. "Anger is good, but only when it's controlled."

"I loathe you," I said at last, swinging my weapon in his direction again with more power.

"Good," he nodded. "Now try to actually hit my stick and not the air."

A groan escaped me as I almost smashed the stick out of his hand.

"Better." Caleb lowered his weapon, charging toward the door. "We are done for tonight," he said as the door closed behind him.

Catching my breath, I slid down the wall. Cold stone floor calmed my heating flesh. I wiped the sweat off my forehead with the sleeve of my tunic when my gaze fell on the polished red bow.

My wobbly legs carried me towards the weapon; my fingers felt the smooth wood.

My hand wrapped around the grip. I'd never shot a bow before, but Brian had loved it. He often showed off his skill to me and Sandra.

I nocked an arrow, aiming it toward the hay target. The arrow swung to the side a few times before I managed to let it fly free.

The arrow bounced off the wall, barely missing the window, in a sharp ring.

A bright laugh echoed behind me. "Were you aiming for the window?" Francis walked towards my fallen weapon.

I narrowed my eyes, aiming another arrow at him.

Francis chuckled at my threat as he picked up the arrow from the floor. "Please don't hit the window when you shoot at me."

Fighting the smile that threatened to appear on my face, I rolled my eyes. The last time we talked was during our ride home after the meeting. An odd feeling of longing accompanied me the last couple of days.

A heavy sigh escaped my lips as I leaned against the wall.

"Tough practice?" Francis' brows rose as he put the missing arrow back into its quiver.

A peculiar timidity filled the air. "Not at all." I met his playful eyes when he leaned against the wall beside me. Jasmine spun my head drunk.

"Sure it was." A grin spread across his face. "Caleb was the one to tutor me as well. I know his style of teaching very well." His gaze bored into mine; suddenly the room narrowed down. "No need to lie, Princess."

I swallowed a lump in my throat that grew bigger with every passing moment. "He makes me want to strangle him." I smiled, sliding down the wall in an attempt to escape Francis' penetrating gaze: escape the bewildering emotions he brought out of me.

Francis laughed, taking a seat next to me on the floor. "I would offer you my help, but I'm afraid swords are not my expertise." His shoulder brushed over mine. My breathing hilted.

"What *is* your expertise?" I raised a brow at him, ignoring my foolish reaction.

"Daggers," Francis shrugged. "Though I am pretty good at everything, naturally."

"Of course you are." I rolled my eyes.

"You don't believe me?" Francis crooked his head, a slow grin made its way onto his face. "May I?" He pointed at the bow in my hand.

"Please." I handed him the weapon; his hand brushed against mine.

He sent me a quick smile as he got to his feet. Grabbing the arrow I'd nearly broken the window with, Francis graciously placed it across the bow. His hands held the weapon firmly, yet gently all the same, as he pulled on the bowstring. My eyes were unable to escape this prison.

The arrow landed straight in the middle of the target on the opposite side of this gigantic room. My brows shot up.

"Believe me now?" Francis tilted his head, placing the weapon where it belonged—far from my hands.

I shook my head. "Why don't you carry a bow with you, if you are this good?"

"Daggers are more practical." Francis took his abandoned place beside me. My body froze at the proximity. "And they are easier to hide: gives some sort of advantage. I can give you a lesson," he said, a trace of hope sang in his voice.

I swallowed a lump in my throat at the idea. "I've had enough lessons for one night," I shook my head; my eyes studied the stone floor, avoiding his gaze.

"Perhaps tomorrow?" Francis persisted.

"I think I will pass." I offered him a small smile. Though the words burned my tongue, for a strange feeling of disappointment at my reply washed over me.

"Come now, Princess," Francis leaned into me. "I thought we were friends. What's the matter?"

I should keep my distance, I wanted to say.

"I won't be as mean as Caleb, I promise," he didn't give up. "I will even give you a dagger of your own."

"Bargaining again?" I smiled.

Francis shrugged, "What do you say?"

"Perhaps tomorrow." The words flew out of my mouth as I lost the battle with my sanity.

A grin spread across Francis' face. "Can't wait."

Two voices carried from Florence's room as I made my way up the stairs, my legs froze in place. I pushed on the ajar door.

Dark curls, pink lips. "Florence?" My voice broke when the woman sitting on the bed had faced me.

My feet carried me towards Florence as I embraced her in the tightest hug I'd ever given anyone. "How are you feeling?" I searched her eyes for any sign of pain.

"Better." She bestowed me with the sunshine smile I'd thought I'd never see her wear again.

My hands squeezed her tighter until she squeaked. "Sorry!" I retreated; my eyes fell onto her wrapped wound.

Florence chuckled. "If only I knew all I had to do was almost die to get a hug out of you."

I wanted to roll my eyes, but the smile on my face refused to leave. "I was so worried," I whispered.

"I'm all right," she nodded, her hands found mine.

"Caleb said you must stay in bed for the rest of the night." Roxanne gestured for Florence to lay back down. "Let me bring you something to drink." She smiled, departing from the room.

"What happened while I was gone?" Florence rasped; her eyes met mine.

"Not much," I shrugged. "The Barrens agreed to help."

"So I heard," she smiled. "And how are you?"

My brows knitted together, realizing the truth. "I'm good."

Chapter 29
Poisonous Thorns

S now crushed under our steps as we made our way into the woods just behind the castle. The moon hid from our view, leaving us in the night forest alone. The cold riddled my lungs when the soft singing of an owl echoed from afar.

What a great mistake I'd made agreeing to this.

"Have you shot a dagger before?" Francis stopped before a huge oak, unsheathing four daggers. He skillfully spun one of them in his hand.

"No." I watched the snow fall onto my palms.

"It's fairly easy to learn." Francis handed me the blade. Beautiful patterns decorated the hilt. "Although, it does require a lot of practice." He carefully adjusted my fingers on the handle of the dagger; a shadow of a smile made it onto his face. "Put your right leg in front, keep your shoulders straight," Francis demonstrated. When I failed to recreate the stance his hands reached in my direction, stopping mere inches from me. "May I?"

I nodded; his hands softly fell onto my shoulders. The flowers bloomed deep in my stomach at his touch.

"The most important thing is to keep your mind clear." His hands gently adjusted my stance. "The blade should be facing you." He moved my hand in the correct position. "Now, throw it."

"That's it?" I frowned; my eyes met his piercing gaze.

Francis nodded slightly before adding, "Try not to miss the tree," he winked.

I scoffed, eyeing my enormous target.

The blade escaped my grip before I was ready to let go of it. Slicing the air, it spun; the hilt hit the oak with a loud thud before crashing onto the snow.

"Don't let it spin as much," Francis handed me another dagger. "Soften your hold, right here." His cold fingers gentled my wrist.

My skin burned under his touch. My mind drowned in lunacy. I wished to leave before it ended me, yet my legs refused to obey.

Enough! I ordered myself. My eyes closed, seeking salvation from this folly.

Francis' breath caressed my ear as his fingers wrapped around my wrist, adjusting my hold. "Take a deep breath," he whispered, letting go of my hand. "Now throw it."

I wished the ground could break into two, taking me straight to hell for my foolishness.

My eyes opened when Francis granted me some space I had silently begged for.

The dagger flew through the air, spinning towards the oak. The tip of the blade brushed the tree bark before collapsing onto the snow once again.

"Better." Francis slipped another dagger into my palm; his hand gently wrapped around mine. Francis raised our embraced hands, taking the throwing position. "It's all about the timing," his breathing tickled my ear.

I swallowed down the flowers that spiraled in my throat when I faced him. The thorns cut through my flesh, poisoning my mind. The cold had no power over the burning heat that enveloped me whole.

My back met his chest. My legs barely kept me upright as I tried to stop myself from leaning into his embrace.

What in the Kingdom was wrong with me?

Francis' hand guided our throw; my fingers barely remembered to let go of the dagger.

The dagger glided through the air, its tip smoothly cut through the tree. "See," Francis whispered into my ear.

My mind drunk on the poison urged my lips to part; his low voice willed my back to arch into him, depriving me of any lucidity.

Stop it, Cordelia! The thorns pierced my flesh. Francis ceased breathing when I put my face directly next to his. What a dangerous waltz I'd welcomed, though no drop of clarity could stop me. *Moon save me.* I choked on my own breathing as my body moved closer. My aflame hand fell onto his coat.

Frozen in place, we stood there. The snow danced around us, our lips brushed—

A whistle broke through the space, tearing my gaze off Francis. A loud thud tore me off his coat. A dagger landed straight into the tree in front of me.

My head flew in the direction the knife had come from.

"Did I interrupt?" Caleb smirked.

"Not at all," I smiled. "Thank you for the lesson," I offered to Francis before walking back toward the castle: away from whatever delusion I was about to engage in.

Words on the page finally blended into one when I gave up on an attempt to keep my mind busy. I shut the book, chiding myself for my weak ability to focus.

The sun was about to make its appearance when I closed the curtains.

I begged for sleep to take me away as darkness enveloped my room. Yet my mind spiraled, refusing me rest.

A groan escaped me when my insides tightened in an oddly comfortable ache, begging for salvation, longing for a touch.

I took a long breath in an attempt to stop this nonsense, yet my body refused. The feeling became unbearable.

Every time my lungs emptied the flowers begged for freedom, making their way down my stomach. Then lower, and lower.

Damnation!

I put the sheets aside, hoping for the cool air to calm my aching body. Yet even the small wind brushing against my skin sent my body aflame.

The soft blankets suddenly felt too soft, my skin longed for the sensation.

I cannot, I tried to convince myself, yet my eyes closed as the shadows of his lips atop mine invaded my peace. *I cannot allow such vulnerability,* I argued as the memory of his hands on my shoulders sucked the air out of my lungs.

The heat burned all fear out of my mind, daring me to act upon my wicked wish.

Before my treasonous mind could stop me, I put a cloak atop my nightgown, fleeing out of the room.

Before my treasonous mind could interrupt, my legs carried me to him.

Chapter 30
Orchestra of Two Souls

A sad piano accompanied the peacefulness of the castle. The same melody I'd found on the music sheets weeks ago vibrated through the walls.

My breathing quickened with anticipation as I made my way toward the melody.

My hands pushed on the doors to the music room.

Francis sat before the piano, his fingers skillfully striking the keys of the instrument. Every note filled the space with passion, with pain. The rolled up sleeves of his white tunic revealed his strong hands.

I had no business being here—intruding on what appeared to be a very intimate moment—yet the music captured my mind, imprisoning me in its warmth. My shaky legs took a step closer; my eyes closed, letting the melody sweep through me.

Every worry abandoned my mind as my hands stretched out toward the reddish-brown violin resting nearby. My fingers felt the instrument, studying its curves.

I held the neck of the violin as my legs carried me toward Francis. His gaze met mine as I skimmed through the sheet music on the rack of his piano.

Unknown fear overwhelmed me. Roses bloomed in my stomach, pressing against my lungs. The aroma of the man in front of me filled my veins with sweet satisfaction.

I raised the violin to my collar bone.

Francis' eyes bored into my skin when my bow touched the strings. I closed my eyes, unable to hold his gaze.

Embarrassment washed over me. The roses tightened against my lungs, depriving my mind of any thought. Every sense in me heightened. The room narrowed down as though it was only us two that existed in the entire Kingdom.

The music carried me away from the room, away from the castle. Each note bestowed me the bravery I'd never known before, every note urged me closer to him. The air filled with a passion and desire I was no longer able to ignore.

Our notes were wrapped in a tight embrace, our minds merged into one. I filled my lungs with his scent, drunk on it.

The notes of the piano became slower, quieter, longer until the very last key let the music flow between us. I dragged the bow against the strings in our last dance, letting the music fly free.

Francis' amber eyes met mine when he closed the fall board of his piano. He carefully took the violin from my hands, setting it down atop his instrument.

His hands embraced mine when he got up from the stool. Our faces were mere inches from each other as he stroked my palms. Thick air in between us made every breath a struggle.

My eyes traveled to his lips before finding them with my own.

His lips melted on my tongue. My head spun. The roses painfully tightened my insides, a quiet moan escaped my lips. My teeth pierced through Francis' thin skin; the blood interrupted our kiss, making it sweeter.

More. A silent plea intruded my mind. *More.*

"I have to tell you something," Francis broke our kiss, holding my face gently. His shaky voice covered my skin in goosebumps.

"Later," was all I was able to say, afraid that any passing moment would sober my mind up. "Tell me after."

I opened my eyes, meeting his amber irises. His eyes darkened under my gaze, his lips turned into a thin line, as though unsure of how to proceed with my demands.

My hands traveled toward his face as I broke his restraints with a kiss.

Our lips did not separate when Francis effortlessly picked me up into his embrace. Our lips did not separate when he carried me through the space, up the stairs, to my room.

Our lips did not separate when Francis closed the door shut.

Chapter 31
Crimson Touch

His soft lips tasted like cigars: bitter and sweet at the same time. Exquisite. The kiss woke every cell in my body, begging for more.

I put my trembling hands on his chest, unable to resist the urge to touch him.

We fought across the room, until my back was against the wall. Until his hands moved toward the back of my neck, toward my hair—

The fear knocked the air out of me; my own hand flew to his in an attempt to stop any further movement.

I gripped his wrist so tightly it hurt my own. I held it as if my life depended on it. My eyes met his when fear prevented my next breath. The room shook.

Francis moved his hands up. He nodded once at me in understanding without moving an inch. I focused on my breath, studying Francis' eyes. His beautiful eyes. His eyes, no one else's.

I swallowed the lump in my throat, fighting the battle with my mind. Slowly, I let go of his hand, trusting him not to touch my hair again. *It's just Francis, no one else,* I told myself, trying to calm my unresting heart.

Francis held out his own hands as if asking for a dance. Unsure what he intended to do, I took his offer.

Slowly, he kissed both of my hands gently before turning us around, until he was the one against the wall. He put my hands on his chest while placing his own against the wall.

My breathing hilted as I moved my face closer to his. He wanted me in control.

Our lips brushed together as we gazed into each other's eyes. His warm breath tickled my lips, patiently waiting for my next move.

I slowly closed the gap until my lips covered his. I kissed him with force I didn't know I had. I'd never kissed anyone on my own accord and I savored every moment of it. I let all restraint go as the fear departed my mind. Francis returned the kiss with so much passion and care that I could not help the sound of pure joy from escaping my throat.

I was no longer in control of my own body: my own thoughts. All I knew was that I wanted more. Collecting all the pieces of bravery I possessed, I undid the buttons of Francis' shirt. My fingers shook.

His skin was as smooth as a pearl, as cold as the morning of winter solstice. I ran my palms over his torso, memorizing every curve of his body. Every cut, every scar.

I broke the kiss, meeting Francis' eyes for a moment before turning my back to him. I could only hope Francis did not see how much my body trembled with anxiety as I undid the bow of my gown. I didn't want him to stop. I wanted this. I needed this.

Francis put his hands on the first button of my night-gown. "May I?" His voice sent a shiver down my spine for all the wrong reasons.

"Yes," my voice was barely a whisper, the anticipation burned me alive.

"Have you—" Francis whispered into my ear. "I mean, besides... him. Have you—"

"Yes," I interrupted him. "Before the engagement."

My gown slipped down my shoulders, covering my exposed chest in dozens of goosebumps. His breath tickled my ear, "Tell me what you want, my Princess."

A shaky breath escaped my lips. "I want your lips."

Roses bloomed deep down in my stomach, tightening my insides in their stems, scratching my skin in the most delightful way possible. The thorns pierced the bottom of my stomach, forcing a sweet sound of satisfaction from the depths of my throat.

A trace of his smile touched my skin when his lips brushed over my shoulder, gently making their way up my neck. Every kiss left my skin burning in fire, every breath left my soul demanding more. His hands held the sleeves of my dress, carefully avoiding my exposed skin.

My head flew backward, settling on Francis' shoulder. My lips were desperate to find his, my hands urgently stretched out to feel his skin.

I buried myself into this man's neck, counting every beat of his pulse. One, two, three. The dance made my head spin drunk.

Despite our small distance I wanted him closer. I wrapped his hands around my lower stomach, my back pressed against his chest. I needed him closer.

"What else, my Princess?" he said against my cheek.

His low voice woke up the part in me I'd never known existed. My mind quieted, leaving instinct to speak for me. I could not resist the urge to feel the forbidden desire any longer. I wanted it now, more than anything in my life.

I crooked my head, exposing my neck. "Please."

A low moan escaped his lip.

"Please," I begged.

My trembling hands slowly shifted the ends of my undone braid over my shoulder. Fear and excitement rushed through my veins as my heartbeat quickened.

"I will keep you safe," Francis said softly before his sharp teeth pierced my thin skin, forcing my lungs empty.

A quiet cry escaped me as the sweet pain rushed across my body: straight into my mind. My breathing hilted with every passing moment, my eyes rolled back.

The blood rushed toward my open wound, happily departing my body. Unable to keep quiet any longer, I let out a loud moan that echoed through the room.

More. I wanted to tell Francis, yet I forgot how to speak.

My throat itched and burned at the idea of my blood on Francis' lips. I brought his hand toward my lips.

My mouth opened, anxious to feed the foreign creature within the depths of my soul. My lips wrapped around his thumb; his hand gently grasped my chin. I sucked on it until my teeth broke through his skin, letting the blood flow onto my tongue.

I gasped when the first drop reached my throat, cooling the fire that grew within. My tongue danced across his open wound, absorbing his blood like a sponge.

His blood melted in my mouth like honey. Everything spun. I almost fainted.

Francis' loud moan interrupted my racing thoughts as he leaned against the wall.

My neck immediately longed for his mouth. "More," I cried out without relinquishing his thumb.

His tongue brushed across my sickly wound, licking every drop of blood from my skin. "Patience, Princess."

I all but lost my mind, for tears of joy flowed down my cheeks. "Please."

"You will faint if I don't stop," Francis whispered, his fingers wrapped around my own. "What's the matter?" His crimson thumb stroked my lips, turning me to face him.

My lips devoured his.

The taste of his blood mixed with mine destroyed any restraint left in me.

Without breaking our kiss, I forced us toward my bed. The back of my knees hit the frame as I dragged Francis' body atop my own.

Our gazes met. His amber irises bored into my skin, burning every cell of my body. "Tell me what you need, Princess." He leaned into me.

"You." I caught my breath. Every cell in my body screamed for his touch. "I need you." My hands reached for his trousers, undoing them.

"Are you certain?" he asked me carefully, yet did not stop my hands from sliding his trousers down.

"I am." I wrapped my legs around his waist.

A loud moan escaped me without my permission as he entered my body. My hands clung onto his shoulders like a drowning person would to a straw. His lips covered every inch of my neck, his tongue cleaned my fresh wound dry. My back arched from the sensation, exposing my chest for Francis' lips.

More. I wanted to cry.

The creature inside of me was not yet satisfied. My skin burned as his lips swept across my scar. My chest ached as his mouth covered the center of my breast. His teeth gently brushed my nipple with every thrust of his hips. *Good Gods.*

Each thrust attempted to tame the neverending thorns deep in my stomach, each thrust made flowers bloom with new power.

The creature demanded its orders be followed.

"Please," a hoarse moan echoed through the room. I had no idea what I begged for.

Francis' thumb journeyed its way to my mouth; my teeth wrapped around his finger, reinjuring his healing wound.

Francis' moans sung in unison with my own, engulfing the room in pleasure.

His free hand drove into my thigh in a painful delight; but he retreated it in an instant, depriving my exposed skin of his touch. I swallowed the blood in my mouth as my trembling hand guided his near my bud. I drew a breath.

"I will keep you safe," he whispered. "Just tell me to stop and I will."

I nodded, swallowing hard. My grasp did not loosen when I placed his fingers onto my flesh. Controlling their every move, I allowed Francis' fingers to touch me.

Each stroke healed a long broken part of me, every touch calmed my racing mind.

His hips slammed against mine, forcing the air out of me; his blood soaked my tongue, bringing me back to life.

I sucked onto his finger, refusing any drop of crimson go to waste as he buried himself deep inside of me, stretching my entrance in sweet satisfaction.

"You are divine, my Princess." Francis' breathing heaved.

"Francis—" My body exploded in a delightful euphoria. Relief washed over me when the room filled with the sound of pleasure.

"Cordelia," Francis' hoarse voice stumbled through the fog in my mind when his relief filled my insides.

Chapter 32
Emerald

The knock on the door pulled me out of the sweet dream—a dream that made me blush—yet I refused to let my eyes open.

The woolen blankets fondled my bare skin, the winter storm whistled through the ceiling, calming my mind. A slow smile tugged on my lips.

"Cordelia—" The door creaked open.

"Go away, Florence," Francis rasped. My eyes flew open.

"Oh—" she mumbled, shutting the door.

I faced Francis, confirming I was indeed awake. His dark curls splayed out on the pillow as a small smile tugged on his lips.

My eyes traveled down his body: a white tunic hung on his shoulders, drops of crimson painted the fabric. My dried blood colored his lips.

"You look like you just saw a ghost," Francis chuckled as he sat up on the bed. The sheet slid down his chest, revealing his torso.

"Moon save me." I rolled onto my back as the memories of last night rushed through my mind.

"I am afraid there is no salvation from me, Your Highness," Francis winked. "Would you—" His eyes narrowed. "Should I take my leave?"

"No!" I said a little too fast. "I mean, no, it's all right."

"All right then." A slow grin spread across Francis' face as he got comfortable between my sheets. His hands slowly wrapped around my waist, guiding me into a hug. My back was against his chest when he squeezed me so tight that it made me laugh. "So my Princess does know how to laugh, huh?" His breath tickled my ear before he planted a kiss on my temple.

Despite my best attempts at hiding the smile, it found its way onto my face when Francis kissed the corner of my lips.

His fingers traced along my neck, making their way down to my scar. They paused, feeling the rough skin. "Silver blade," Francis said as a matter of fact, studying the injury.

"He tried to cut my gown that night." The words escaped me for the first time. "He isn't very good with knives." I laughed, though my laughter fell short when Francis' hands tensed around me. "Sorry." I faced him. "I shouldn't have said that."

"No." Francis palmed my cheek, kissing the tip of my nose. "Don't apologize for that. If you ever want to talk about it," he met my gaze, "I will be right here."

I managed a weak nod in reply.

A corner of Francis' lips slightly rose. "Cannot wait to dry him empty." His gaze darkened.

"You will not." I shook my head, hating the words—I wished Timothy nothing but a long, painful death, but too much was at risk. "You can't kill him," I sounded like Mother.

"Is that so?" Francis chuckled, his brows flew up.

"I am being serious," my voice dropped a few octaves. "You can't. We need his father's support." My brows furrowed. "It will ruin everything—"

"All right, all right." His kiss stopped me from saying anything else.

Hours later Francis had left me to the privacy of my room. A foolish smile could not leave my face as I studied myself in the mirror. Shadows of his lips covered my skin; freshly healed bites bruised my flesh.

The bath grew red when I washed myself, forcing the flowers to bloom. My skin smelled like jasmine as I closed my eyes for his touches echoed down my body. I brushed through my raven hair, and for the first time in—what seemed to be—forever, I left it down.

The quiet castle welcomed me into its embrace as I made my way down the stairs into the common room. My steps bounced off the walls, echoing through the corridors.

"Where is everyone?" I made my way through the room towards Florence who sat on a cushion before the fire.

She peeked out from her book, smiling at me. "Francis went to the human village just beyond Faris. We are running low on blood; it seems we must host a ball next week." Florence offered me her untouched glass of crimson.

"Thank you." I took the glass, taking a seat beside her. The liquid reminded me of Francis' mouth on my neck, my cheeks flushed. "How are you feeling?" I pointed at Florence's stomach, ignoring my aflame body. "Can I bring you anything?"

"No, Cordelia." She caught my hand when I tried to get up. "Please don't coddle me," Florence smiled. "I get enough of that from Roxanne. And I am feeling well," she nodded, her lips turned into a thin line. "Actually, I was wondering if you would go down to Faris with me to spread the word about the ball."

"Of course," I said, taking the first sip of my drink.

"We'll leave in an hour then." She offered me a smile that did not reach her eyes as she went back to her book.

My hand rested on the hilt of the sword at my waist as we stood inside of Simon's tavern. The other brushed over the dagger Francis had left me earlier as he promised he would.

Florence was awfully quiet the whole trip to Faris. Every time she'd caught my worrisome gaze she had gifted me with a small smile as though nothing was out of the ordinary.

"Listen up, everyone!" Simon banged against the table; every head in the tavern turned his direction. "There will be a ball at the Bloodlake Castle—" He turned to Florence, asking, "When?"

"Same time next week," Florence said loudly for the whole tavern to hear.

Everyone cheered as we walked out of the establishment. "Bloodlake Castle?" I asked.

Florence nodded, turning onto the main street of Faris. "There is a legend that when our castle was built, the owner, who was sent there as a punishment, vowed to kill everyone who had wronged him: he vowed to fill the nearby lake with their blood."

"Who was the owner?" I asked, following Florence down the cobblestone road.

The streets of Faris were still destroyed: most of the buildings missed their windows. Yet it did not stop the shops from welcoming guests, nor did it stop the musicians from playing down the street.

"No one knows," Florence shrugged. "Some say the owner died a long time ago, some believe he is still among us."

An old woman sent me a curt nod when our gazes met. She sat behind the counter overflowed with jewelry—I had no doubt—she crafted herself. Her wrinkled hands gestured for me to take a look.

"A woman like you must know the value of a powerful amulet," she murmured when I studied the emerald stone she offered me.

It shone in my hands no matter the darkness of the night; its sharp edges dug into my palm. "It's beautiful," I whispered, handing it back to her.

"Keep it," the woman's voice lowered as her hands wrapped around my own, squeezing them until they hurt. "You'll need its protection."

Goosebumps traveled down my body at her touch. The hair on my neck rose from the urgency in her voice. "I have nothing to exchange," I smiled, trying to free myself of her embrace.

"No need." A smile made it onto her face, her blue as the ocean eyes saddened. "Don't let the sorrow stop you from what fate has in store for you." She turned me around. "No matter the pain you must endure, you shall finish what was not started by you." Her fingers tightened the ends of the string at the back of my neck; a shiver went through me at her cold touch, or perhaps it was her riddle that chilled my bones. "You are our salvation."

"What does that mean?" My brows furrowed when I turned back at her, yet she had already disappeared behind the wooden door that led to the depths of her shop. My fingers touched the emerald on my chest, trying to make any sense of this interaction.

I shook my head as I turned back towards Florence.

She stood in the middle of the road; her empty eyes glared into the distance. I traced her gaze: a big rainbow castle now was covered in shadows, children's laughter was replaced by the croaking of ravens that sat atop its roof.

A silent tear fell down Florence's cheek when my hands wrapped around her shoulders.

Slowly, she returned the gesture. Her hands held onto me as a drowning person would to a straw.

We did not speak, just held onto this embrace for a while, right in the middle of the street.

I didn't notice them at first—didn't notice the screams until Florence broke our hug, her eyes widened.

Chaos fell upon Faris as everyone flew in one direction. "You should go home, Cordelia." Florence took a slow step towards the crowd.

"What?" I followed after her. "What is going on?"

"Go back." She met my gaze before breaking into a run.

"Where are you going?" I rushed after her. "What is going on?"

Florence's lips turned into a thin line when she stopped before our horses. "To the human village." She untightened the reins off the tree. "The children have attacked the humans."

Chapter 33
Lost Princess

My hands trembled as I undid Annabelle's reins. The lump in my throat grew bigger, yet my mind was terrifyingly calm: it shoved me under the water where all the screams turned into no more than a muffled noise.

"You should really go back, Cordelia." Florence mounted her horse, shattering my pretend peace.

"No," I shook my head as I mounted Annabelle. "I am not leaving you." I ordered my horse to follow dozens of others—straight into the insanity that overflowed the main street of Faris.

"Francis is going to murder me," Florence mumbled under her breath, catching up to me.

The further we got, the more red painted the snow: drops of crimson covered every inch of the ground underneath the hooves. A chill went through me, yet it was not the winter that crushed upon us with its full glory. My grip on the reins tightened.

Excruciating screams broke through the air when the first houses of the human village entered my view. The children's cries froze my heart in place.

"Do not kill them!" someone yelled ahead of us. "Do not kill the orphans!"

My eyes widened as I traced the empty of blood bodies resting on the beaten roads. The snowflakes circled around them, hiding their flesh under a white blanket. Nausea made its way up my throat.

"Henry?" Florence jumped off her horse, tightening its reins to a nearby tree. "Henry!" she yelled, running after a little boy whose face was covered in blood. "Henry, stop!" She dragged the boy off a young woman's body resting on the ground. The women's empty eyes stared at the moon that was now crimson too.

More screams broke through the air as I tightened Annabelle's reins to the tree. My trembling legs carried me to Florence who held the crimson boy as he wailed, kicking her. "It's all right," she told him, bringing him closer.

"What are you two doing here?" Francis took the boy off Florence's hands. "Go home!" he yelled at her. "Now!"

"Not in eternity!" Florence yelled back, rushing towards the screams once again.

Francis caught her by her wrist. "There is enough help without you! Leave!"

"I will leave when I know that all thirty of the children are safe and back home!" Florence twisted her arm in an attempt to free herself.

"Florence!" Francis hissed at her; the boy's teeth dug into Francis' arm though it did not seem to bother him. "Wurdulacs are just waiting for us all to be in one place. You must leave!"

An excruciating wail swept through the ground as the sound of banging metal interrupted it. "Get the orphans into the carriages!" Someone ran past us. "They are taking them back to Faris."

"If Wurdulacs are coming, we won't be safe anywhere." Florence jerked herself out of Francis' grasp, rushing towards the chaos.

Francis swore before meeting my gaze. "Don't leave my side," he threw at me as he charged towards the carriages.

Crimson snow crushed under our steps; the sound brought an odd comfort to my ears as I followed after Francis. Three wooden carriages stood by the line of dense spruce. Its walls barely kept the mad children within.

The children thrashed against the wood, their hands stretched out from the tiny window, grabbing onto everything they could reach.

"Thirteen!" A blonde woman by the carriage shouted, taking the child off Francis' hands. She nudged the boy into the carriage, locking the door as though they were no more than wild animals.

My gaze widened as a paralyzing chill traveled through me.

"Stay here," Francis shoved a small black blade into my palm, wrapping my fingers around its hilt. "When the carriage is ready to depart, go with them and stay at the orphanage until I come back for you." His hands wrapped around my face; his eyes desperately searched mine, yet I could not will my gaze to leave the horrific scene playing out before me. "Cordelia!" Francis shook my shoulders. "Promise me, you will do as I said."

"I will," I whispered, swallowing the lump that grew in my throat.

Francis nodded once. His mouth opened and closed as though wanting to say more, yet when I finally moved my gaze to him he'd already left me by the three big carriages that overflowed with whining children.

"Is there any way to calm them?" A man whose eyes shone emerald green put another child inside: a girl who didn't look a day past three. "We won't make it far if they turn the carriage upside down."

The blonde woman shook her head, locking the door. "Only human blood will calm them," she replied. "We will have to bring them as they are."

"How many children left?" Florence asked, carrying a child in her arms.

"Fifteen."

A sharp pain went through my arm as a gasp escaped me. Small teeth pierced my wrist; glowing brown—full of tears—eyes met mine. The teeth left me just a moment later, realizing my blood wouldn't suffice.

"The first carriage is full!" someone yelled, just before the horses neighed, setting the carriage into movement.

"Wurdulacs!" someone cried. "Wur—"

"Help!" A child's voice traveled through the forest, breaking my trance. My head flew in that direction. "Help!" the child cried.

Before I could think better of it, my legs carried me towards two figures on the crimson snow.

"Stop it—" the child screamed, fighting against the figure laying atop him. "Stop! Ah—"

My hands wrapped around the girl atop him. Her teeth dug deep into the boy's shoulder.

"Charlotte?" I dragged her off the child's body. "Charlotte, it's me, Cordelia." I held her close as she thrashed against me, fighting for freedom. "Charlotte!"

"Let me go!" She bit my hands that wrapped around her waist, knocking me to the ground.

My small black blade vanished into the crimson snow.

"Let me go!" Charlotte roared.

"It's all right." I held her tighter. "You will be all right."

My muscles screamed in protest when Charlotte's teeth punctured my flesh. I would not be able to carry her by myself—not when she fought me as though her life depended on it. Another bite disabled my wrist—

"Take the child." Heavy boots crunched the crimson snow when a pair of hands reached for Charlotte.

"I won't go back!" she yelled when the hands ripped her out of my grasp. "Let me go!" She wailed against a redheaded man in a dark blue cloak.

The blood drained from my face when I met his dark as night eyes. A cruel smirk made its way onto his face as he eyed me with curiosity.

"Let her go," my voice sounded barely more than a whisper. "She is just a chi—" I tried to get to my feet but his boot pressed against my chest, depriving me of air.

"Isn't it the lost princess?" The other man in a blue cloak smirked. His blue as ice eyes shone bright. "We've been looking for you, you know." He forced me to my feet; his hands locked mine in place. "Kane will be ecstatic when we return with you." They both laughed.

"Let her go!" I screamed at the man, trying to free myself, yet his grip just hardened. "I will do whatever you want me to, just let the child go!" I looked around, searching for any familiar face. "Help!" I yelled towards the departing carriages—

The pain across my cheek stung my skin as my vision blurred into dozens of stars when my capturer's hand met my flesh in a loud thud. The corner of my eyes darkened, drowning me into oblivion.

The men laughed as they dragged me and Charlotte deep into the woods.

Chapter 34
Crimson Snow

"Let me go!" Charlotte's scream dragged me out of the darkness. "I won't go back!" She roared against the redheaded man's hand; her teeth pierced through the fabric of his cloak.

He struck her across her face, knocking the air out of her. She quieted.

"Don't touch her!" I screamed; my wrists wailed from the burning pain when I jerked them against the blue-eyed man's grasp. Panic pierced my whole body as I desperately listened for Charlotte's breathing. Her, full of tears, eyes met mine when she gasped for air.

The man ignored my weak attempts at freeing myself as he dragged me down the glistening snow.

My eyes watched the disappearing village behind me; the weak flashes of candlelight within the human houses were now barely visible. No one would hear my screams.

My breathing hilted as my boots dug into the ground, trying to create some friction.

I had to do something.

A pair of horses entered my view as a new wave of panic stroked my chest. If they got us onto those horses we would be as good as dead.

My heart dropped to my heels. I had to do something. I had to do something right now!

I filled my lungs before letting an ear-piercing scream out. One second. That was all the distraction I needed to free my burning wrist—my teeth dug into the man's hand, forcing his hold to open.

My hand found the hilt, dragging the sword out of its scabbard when he jerked me by my hair: but it was too late.

His grip on my hair tightened, my scalp screamed in protest, yet I paid it no attention—not right now.

The blade shimmered under the moonlight as I swung it towards him. The man laughed at my weak attempt at fighting, yet his laughter fell short when he traced a thin line of red on his arm.

"You bitch!" He threw me onto the ground, knocking the air out of me.

"Cordelia!" Charlotte cried.

Gasping for air, I put all of my energy into holding the hilt even when his boot found a firm place on my wrist. An excruciating scream broke through me as I heard my bone snap into two.

My vision darkened, my hold on the hilt loosened.

"Take the child back to the mansion, I will take care of our princess." He spat to the man, pointing my own sword at my neck.

I will die. My blood will paint the snow crimson. My last scream will forever flow in the air above my lifeless body. I will die.

"Cordelia!" Charlotte shrieked as the man carried her to the horses. "Cordelia!"

I drew a small breath in against the blade. Everything in my body stilled as I watched the man's face above mine. *Is this the last thing my eyes will ever witness? Is this the face I will carry to the Moon with my soul?*

"So beautiful, but so stupid," the man spat out, moving the sword to my lips.

I wished to close my eyes to not witness my end, to not know when it was coming, yet I could not. My vision blurred under the drops of tears.

"Surely, Kane wouldn't mind if we altered your appearance just slightly." The blade scratched along my lips, though there was no blood. Not yet.

The cold snow burned the uncovered skin of my neck. Snowflakes fell onto my cheeks, melting into tears.

I moved my gaze to the Moon that waited to witness my end and begged her for mercy.

"You might want to check on your cut," the voice echoed through the woods. I closed my eyes in pure relief, drawing another small breath. "Royal steel works quite fast." Caleb walked toward us.

The sword left my flesh as the man pointed it at Caleb. "You!" He smirked when Caleb unsheathed his own weapon.

I drew a long breath, crawling away from my attacker. The banging metal rang in my ears as I ran toward Charlotte.

The redheaded man threw her on the horse like a bag of hay when my silver dagger Francis had gifted me met his back.

My hands trembled as I retreated a step. His blood dripped down my cloak; my stomach turned upside down when my eyes fell onto the dagger burrowed in his flesh.

The man staggered backwards before he tried to reach me, yet I'd already mounted the horse Charlotte's unconscious body laid upon and ordered it to run.

Excruciating pain in my wrist traveled across my body as I squeezed the reins, holding onto Charlotte as though my life depended on it. I managed a glance at my injury: the bone was twisted in an unnatural angle, my skin turned dark blue from the assault of the blue-eyed man's boot.

My body shook when the sound of the horse's heavy gallop followed from behind. The redheaded man fled after us as though the injury I'd given him was no more than a papercut.

Charlotte's eyes fluttered as the panic creeped deep within them; a loud wail broke through the air when she held onto me tightly.

"You are safe," I told her, glancing at the man behind us. His cloak fluttered in the wind. "Everything will be all right." I willed our horse faster.

Charlotte's cries grew louder when the woods slowly thinned, welcoming the small houses of the human village. The snow slowly turned bright crimson the more steps we took. "Almost there." I held her closer against my chest.

"I won't go back!" Charlotte screamed in hysteria.

"It's all right." My eyes scanned the crimson village, desperately searching for a pair of familiar eyes. "It's all right."

Lifeless bodies covered the crimson ground—

A blade sliced through the air, flying past me with a terrifying whistle, landing right in the center of our follower's chest. His lips parted in a gasp as the blood dripped down from his injury. Relief washed over me as he forced his horse around, disappearing in the depths of the forest.

I traced the direction the knife flew out of when my eyes landed on Francis.

"Cordelia?" He unsheathed another dagger as he ran towards us, panic shone bright in his eyes.

"Caleb!" I screamed, glancing back at the woods. "Caleb is still there," I told him, helping Charlotte down.

Francis caught Charlotte, putting her feet on the ground. His eyes scanned me. "Are you hurt—" Francis' fingers brushed along the side of my cheek that still burned; his eyes fell onto my injured wrist.

"Help Caleb!" I interrupted him, shaking my head. "I am fine. Caleb is still there," I pointed in the direction we fled out of.

"Rox!" Francis called out. "Take them home," he told her as he glanced at me and Charlotte. "I will be right behind you."

Chapter 35
Royals Are No
Help

Charlotte's even breathing echoed through the room as she laid upon my bed. She'd refused to sleep anywhere else when we'd gotten back a few hours ago. Her face was still red from all the tears she'd spilled tonight.

Silver curled up against her shoulder as though protecting her sleep from nightmares.

My swollen wrist wailed in pain as I fixed the blanket around her small body. Every slight movement burned, filling my veins with agony. I certainly had a fever.

"Guard her," I whispered to the cat, silently closing the door to my room behind me.

I rushed down to the common room, my heartbeat quickened when I entered and didn't see his face.

"Is Francis back yet?" My voice cracked when I met Roxanne's and Florence's gazes. Nausea spun my head as my fingers slowly lost sensation.

"He just got back," Roxanne answered. "He couldn't find Caleb," she whispered. "Charlotte?"

My heart squeezed tight. Caleb had saved me and it might have cost him his life.

"She has finally fallen asleep." I closed my eyes as a new wave of pain swept over me.

"How many men were there?" Florence walked towards me. "Oh, dear Gods, Cordelia, your hand—"

"There were two," I croaked, cringing as I tried to move my fingers. I drew a deep breath as my wrist caught aflame.

"We need to treat your hand." Florence caught my shoulders when I wobbled to the side.

"Is it broken?" Roxanne frowned as they both walked me down the hall into—what appeared to be—some sort of study. Every shelf in the room overflowed with dozens of vials and differently colored glass bottles of medicine. "What happened?" Roxanne took a good look at my wrist before rushing towards the shelves.

"I am so sorry, Cordelia," Florence muttered, sitting me down on the chair when Roxanne searched for something in the drawers. "If I didn't insist on going—"

My head spun from the pain with every breath I took. "I'm all right." I shook my head which only made me dizzier. "The man stepped on my wrist when he realized I cut him with Royal steel," I mumbled.

"Take this," Roxanne gave me several berries I recognized as the vasyalisk berries. The healers in the palace used them to numb pain before an operation.

I put them in my mouth, my eyes watered as the bitter taste pierced my tongue.

"One of them still got my sword," I suddenly realized. "He fought Caleb with it." My stomach turned at the idea of Caleb being injured by Royal steel.

"I got her." Francis walked into the study. His black cloak was covered in blood. "We must straighten the bone before it starts to heal, Princess." He crouched before me as he doubled in my vision.

"All right," I whispered, leaning back in the chair. My eyes closed.

Florence got a hold of my other hand, squeezing it tightly. "I'm sorry, Cordelia." Her thumb rubbed against my skin.

Before I could reassure her it was not her fault, Francis' fingers brushed over my injured flesh. Dozens of needles pierced my skin under his touch—

"It's going to hurt," he said and before I was able to process the meaning of his words, his hands wrapped around my wrist as he pulled on it.

A cry escaped me when the bone popped against Francis' cold touch. My teeth punctured the inside of my cheek when Francis squeezed my wrist, pushing the bone back into its place.

Another cry pushed through my lips as the cold sweat broke through my skin despite the numbness of the berries. My lungs expanded taking in all the air they could fit; blood spilled in my mouth.

"That's it." Francis wrapped the tight fabric around my wrist as my head spun. "It will be perfectly fine by tomorrow." he said, tying the ends of the bandage.

Florence's hand wrapped around my shoulders when my mind threatened to pull me under.

"Caleb saved my life," I managed to say in between my rapid breaths.

"He is alive." Francis put a wet cloth onto my forehead that immediately made the pain more bearable. "If he was of no use to them, I would have at least found a dead body." He sat on the chair across from mine. "They captured him."

"What do we do now?" Roxanne asked, pouring the crimson liquid into a goblet.

"Get me a meeting with the Queen," my weak voice exclaimed.

The room quieted; three pairs of glowing eyes stared at me as though I had lost my mind.

"Get me a meeting with the Queen," I put all of my remaining energy into sounding confident.

"We tried several months ago; the royal council denied every letter," Roxanne replied. "She does not want to meet us."

"She will talk to me," I argued, as Florence changed the cloth on my forehead. The cold calmed my flaming skin, easing the pain that now traveled up my shoulder.

"It's dangerous," Francis chimed in, his hands fell onto my knees. "What if they harm you? What if she orders them to kill you?"

"Then make sure they don't." I met his gaze before facing Roxanne once again. "I will write a letter to her. Will you send it?"

Roxanne's eyes jumped between me and Francis before she finally replied, "Sure."

"Cordelia—" Francis sighed; a sad smile made it onto his face.

"It's the only way to actually do something and you know it," I interrupted him, blinking the fog out of my vision.

"Perhaps you could meet on neutral territory," Florence suggested. "She won't be able to bring a whole army with her."

"There is a hunting lodge near the palace," I nodded. "I could suggest that location in the letter."

"This is madness." Francis shook his head as he jumped to his feet. "Royals are no help." He faced Roxanne. "We stay away from them, remember?"

My eyebrows shot up.

"That's not what I meant—" Francis shook his head, looking at me as regret filled his eyes.

"Who did you meet in the Royal garden during the Crimson War celebration?" I argued, remembering the events from months ago. "Wasn't it one of the Queen's councils?"

Francis' lips turned into a thin line. "They denied us, Cordelia. That is exactly why we stay away from them from now on—before they get a chance to spread the word filled with lies about what we are trying to do."

"This is different," I persisted, getting up from the chair. My feet swayed to the side as Francis caught me by my waist. "The Queen will want to hear *my* judgment." I stared into amber eyes.

"Aye, because she took you seriously before?" Francis' voice was ice cold. "Or perhaps because she would hear your cries and still do as she pleases."

As if a dull dagger found its place in my chest, I staggered backwards: though not from the pain in my wrist this time. My mouth fell open before the mask of indifference made it onto my face.

"I am sorry," Francis closed his eyes. "I did not mean what I said."

I ignored his outstretched hands when I faced Roxanne. "I will write the letter tonight." I told her before storming out of the study.

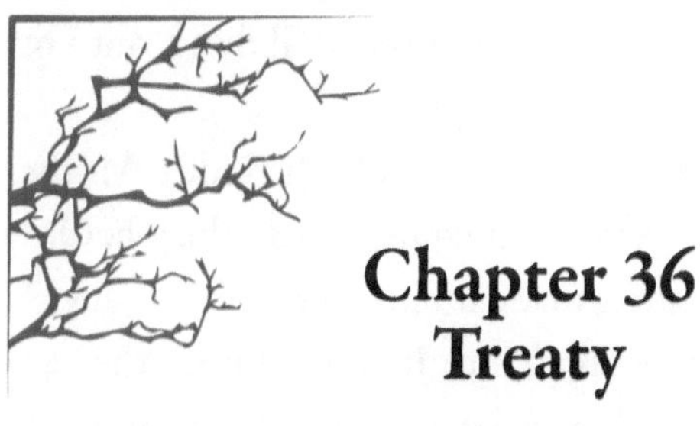

Chapter 36
Treaty

Francis' words crowded my mind like a shadow.

Of course I understood the risks of talking to Mother. What were the odds she would make us walk straight into a trap: too afraid of people finding out the truth about the attacks.

But she was no fool.

Unlike William Barren, she knew the seriousness of the situation. She knew she could not hide the situation for long nor could she stop the Wurdulacs solely with a human army.

Soon enough her people would find out one way or another, and then her authority would be no more than a jest.

She knew that, and I could only hope it was a good enough reason for her to hear me: allow us to work together.

My wrist ached uncomfortably as I held the quill. It had only been a few hours since Francis had put my bone into its place, yet the healing had already started. The numbness slowly disappeared.

I stared at the empty parchment before me and the words escaped my mind in an instant. What would I even say? *Good evening, Mother, the daughter you buried a few months ago is writing to you. Wurdulacs are planning a war: perhaps we could discuss it.*

A groan escaped my lips as I put the quill down onto my dressing table.

Perhaps Francis was right: it was a foolish idea. Mother never read her letters, leaving her council to do the job. Only important documentation made it onto her table.

I spun the stamp in my hand; it shone under the candlelight. Would the royal mark be enough for the council to deem it worthy of their Queen's attention?

"Cordelia?" A small voice called from the bed.

My eyes met Charlotte's as she moved the blanket to the side.

"Are you feeling any better?" I rushed towards her, dropping the stamp on the table.

Charlotte's hands wrapped around my neck when I sat beside her.

My hands held her tight. "You are safe here," I whispered. A pair of green eyes studied me as though desperately wanting to believe my words yet couldn't. "You are safe here, Charlotte." I moved a strand of matted hair out of her face.

She slowly nodded. "I am safe here," she repeated as though only saying it out loud would make it true. "Can I braid your hair?" Charlotte swallowed as her fingers brushed through my waves.

A small smile made it onto my face. "Of course," I whispered back, settling down on the floor for Charlotte to reach.

She did not speak of what had happened last night nor did she speak of what had happened when she had been captured.

Everyone else must have gone to rest, for not even whispers accompanied me as I sat at the table in the library.

It had taken a lot of convincing to manage Charlotte back in bed after she had braided my hair. She'd held Silver against her chest when the first rays of sunshine had appeared from behind black curtains as she'd slowly drifted to sleep.

Silver hadn't seemed to mind the embrace, his purrs had echoed through the quiet room when I'd closed the door behind me.

Candlelight illuminated the endless rows of bookshelves with dozens of sacred tomes and wicked novels settling down on the wood.

My eyes wandered through the titles when I couldn't force my mind to focus on yet another empty piece of parchment before me.

My back wailed in protest when I tried to adjust my position on the chair I'd spent Moon knew how long on. My eyelids grew heavier with every passing moment against my wishes, yet the words still would not come.

"How is the letter?" Francis' voice came from behind me.

"Not well," I fought through a yawn.

"Have you slept at all?" He frowned.

"I'm all right." I shook my head, my eyelids fluttered, fighting with the sleep that threatened to steal me at any moment.

"The letter can wait, Cordelia," Francis said, his hands stretched out towards me.

"I'm fine," I protested, yet my treasonous eyes wouldn't stay open.

"Come now, Princess." His hands wrapped around my waist, pulling me into his arms before I had a chance to counter. "You need rest." He carried me out of the library. "I will write the letter. You can sign it when you wake."

"What? No—" I tried to shake my head, but the warmth of his embrace welcomed the sleep to creep in from the darkness. Sweet dreams flowed through my mind, pulling me under.

"I am very sorry about what I said earlier," Francis told me, carrying me down the hall.

"It's all right," I mumbled, resting my head on his shoulder. "It's been a long night."

"It has been indeed." He opened the door to his room, navigating it in complete darkness.

"We will find Caleb," I whispered when the soft blankets covered my skin.

The sleep corrupted my mind before I was able to tell Francis I had my own bed to sleep in.

Lighting the candles in the ballroom, Florence and I barely spoke—deep in our own thoughts. No matter how hard I tried to focus on the task at hand, my mind spiraled through all the happenings of the previous days.

Francis had laughed hard when I'd read the first draft of the letter I'd written. "Good thing I intervened," He'd chuckled, though I couldn't have even found it in me to roll my eyes at his rudeness as I'd watched him fix the bed I'd fallen asleep in that night.

But the letter had been written, signed, and sent a few nights ago; all we could do then was wait.

Florence and I had walked Charlotte back home when she had started feeling better. All these passing days she'd refused to leave my side, following after me like a shadow.

It had broken my heart to leave her at the orphanage, but we might have to leave any day for the meeting, and only the Moon knew what awaited us on the Royal grounds.

I'd promised Charlotte, when her eyes had filled with tears, I would visit her the moment we were back. She'd refused to let go of our embrace as she'd hugged me tight, whispering into my ear, "If you don't come back in a week, I will walk to your castle myself. I memorized the way."

"Could you pass me that?" Florence pulled me out of my hurricane of thoughts.

"I cannot believe we are still having a ball after what happened." I offered her the silverware that she carefully put down on the table.

We had been setting up tables all evening in complete silence. I knew no one felt like having a ball right now—especially not the humans who would walk through these very doors—and I could not hide my disgust.

"We have to, Cordelia." A note of annoyance shone through Florence's voice as she explained for the tenth time,

"If we don't feed Faris they will go after humans on their own accord. They will have no other choice."

"I know," I said quietly, hating to admit the rationale of her words. "If I were a human, I would steer clear from this place after Wurdulacs butchered my people." I passed her another set.

"They know it is safer this way." Florence's lips turned into a thin line as though she wasn't exactly fond of the idea either. "We were the ones to stop the attack. We have a treaty: we did our part by protecting them, it is their turn to feed us."

"It sounds cruel," I muttered, walking towards the next table.

"War is never kind," Florence sighed. "And we—"

"They accepted." Roxanne's steps pounded on the marble floor as she ran into the ballroom; papers fluttered in her hands as she made her way towards us. She offered me the letter with a neat handwriting I immediately recognized as my mother's. A wicked smile made it onto Roxanne's face when she met my gaze, "Your mother agreed to meet us at the full moon."

Chapter 37
Repellent Messenger

The crisp snow reflected the moonlight, crunching under our horses' hooves. The four of us traveled through the dark forest for hours, slowly making our way to Francis' cabin.

"So," Roxanne turned in her saddle to look at me. "What is our plan exactly?" She moved a stray strand of hair behind her ear.

"Cordelia isn't much of a planner," Francis winked at me, grinning.

I glared at Francis before moving my gaze to Roxanne. "Speak of only what you know for a fact," I told my company. "Lying will only worsen our case. She knows everything that is happening beyond the palace but she and her council will play ignorance."

Florence's hands squeezed the reins when her, full of worry, eyes met mine.

"Her council will try to sabotage you at any given opportunity, ignore them. Don't say more than you need to." I sighed, "And let me take the lead. I know how to convince her."

Francis' lips turned into a thin line, though he refrained from contradicting my words—out loud at least.

"She will listen to me," I argued with his silence. "She has to. The Queen never agrees to meetings she deems worthless."

"Perhaps I should stay at the cabin," Florence muttered, her horse slightly slowed in front of me.

"No," Roxanne shook her head. "We don't separate when Wurdulacs are so close. Not when they already took Caleb." She stretched out her hand to the side, towards Florence who gratefully took it. "And I cannot stay with you," a sad smile spread across Roxanne's face. "Two of us are not nearly enough to face the Royal guards and the Queen."

"Everything will be all right," I reassured Florence. "They know they need us, nothing bad is going to happen."

"I envy your confidence, Princess," Francis muttered. "But Roxanne is right: we all have to go." He sighed before locking his gaze with mine. "If something goes wrong, we leave immediately."

"Moon help us," Florence shook her head, ordering her horse faster.

Flowers bloomed deep in my stomach remembering my teeth on Francis' flesh the last time I occupied this room. I undressed to my undergarments, ignoring my foolish body's reaction.

"May I come in?" Francis' voice traveled through the closed door as I crawled into bed.

"Yes." I pulled the sheets to my collarbone, staring up at the ceiling as though it had all the answers.

Roxanne and Florence had disappeared upstairs after we had a few glasses of crimson, leaving me and Francis to this tiny, crowded room.

"Are you all right?" Francis walked in.

"Fine." My heart banged against my rib cage with mad strength. "She won't kill me," I shook my head, unsure if I was trying to convince myself or Francis.

"She will not." Francis spread out a thick woolen blanket on the floor.

My brows furrowed as I propped myself on one elbow. "What are you doing?"

"Getting ready to sleep." He crooked one brow, laying down on the blanket. "We must leave the moment the sun goes down."

"On the floor?"

Francis smirked, "Why, Princess, are you inviting me into your bed?"

I shrugged as the heat swept through me, "Unless you prefer the floor." I crawled under the sheets, facing the wall.

An awkward silence fell upon the room: though it was loud all the same. I didn't dare to face him.

A whole minute had passed—or perhaps it had been eternity—before Francis' careful steps shortened the distance between us. "Thank you," he whispered, moving the sheet aside as he laid beside me.

My treasonous body caught aflame, yet I could not pay it any attention.

A hurricane of thoughts destroyed everything in its path when my mind wandered around the daunting events of tomorrow.

"Sleep, Princess. Everything will be well," Francis said as though reading my thoughts.

Sleep didn't come for a long while as dozens of questions spiraled in my mind.

What would my mother say when she saw me in my new being? Would she order her guards to kill us the moment we took a step in the lodge? Or perhaps she would see reason in my proposal?

Was I inviting my friends into jeopardy, blinded by my own naivety?

Would Sandra be there to witness my end?

My legs trembled as the hunting lodge—Father, Brian, Sandra, and I used to spend a week at every summer—entered my view. Five guards assessed us from a distance before one of them disappeared behind the wooden doors—announcing our presence to the Queen no doubt. None of them bowed.

The guards took a step forward when I attempted to walk past them. "You will be invited," he glared at me. "Disarm."

Despite the fact I was incapable of hurting anyone within the walls of the lodge, nor could I even use a dagger properly, his order made my hands turn into fist as I handed him the only weapon I possessed.

Roxanne followed my lead, handing over her bow and a quiver filled with arrows, rolling her eyes. Florence offered a small knife from her boot I had no idea she bore.

Francis hadn't moved a muscle.

"Disarm," the guard repeated himself, glaring down at him.

Francis shrugged, "As you wish." He slowly unsheathed the blade from his belt.

None of us needed weapons to protect ourselves, yet no one said that out loud.

The guard knocked on the wooden door; his eyes never left Francis.

Breathe. I ordered myself, putting on my mask of indifference.

A chill went through me as the door yanked open, welcoming us in. My heart finally escaped my chest as I stepped into the house.

Same stone walls I remembered from my childhood, same dining table right in the center of the spacious room. Same green eyes staring at me as the tears filled them.

"Cordelia," Sandra whispered, getting up from her chair.

Ignoring the withering glare our mother bestowed her with, my sister took a few slow steps toward me before her hands clutched around me in an embrace.

My fingers felt her long blonde hair as my eyes closed. My troubled mind calmed at the smell of home and caramel.

"I missed you," I whispered when Sandra's silent tears spilled onto my shoulder.

"I knew you were alive," she searched my eyes. "I felt it."

"This is a council meeting, daughter," the Queen bit out. Her pointed gaze fell onto Sandra. "Act like it or I will order you out."

Sandra reluctantly let go of my shoulders, nodding, breaking the short-lived peace within me.

I scanned the table my mother sat at the head of. The familiar eyes of Mother's council were filled with distrust as they glared down at me, including William Barren and his son.

Timothy's eyes darted from mine to Francis' as the blood drained from his face, though he quickly masked it with a disgusting smirk when Sandra took a seat beside him, noticeably moving the chair as far as possible from my former betrothed.

"Shall we?" Francis moved out chairs for me and Roxanne to sit across from my mother.

Florence chose to stand near the exit.

"I understand from your letter you have a proposition for me, Cordelia." The Queen exclaimed; the crown, she rarely wore, sparkled with her every slight move. "I am listening."

I swallowed the lump in my throat, meeting her gaze. "We propose combining our forces: we are ready to protect your people as our own if you supply us with Royal steel weaponry and soldiers that are ready to put our differences aside and fight as one united army." I glanced at Martin—the commander of my mother's army—as he broke into laughter.

The man with a scar across his face, I had never met before, carried the laugh along with William and Timothy. Only Sandra, Mother, and Athena—an old woman with dark brown skin, whom my mother always went to for advice—stayed quiet.

"They want our army," William Barren said through his laughter, yet it fell short when the Queen raised her hand, silencing the room.

"And what makes you think we need your help?" The Queen crooked her head so slightly.

"I am sure you are aware Wurdulacs attacked a village near Silverstone just a week ago." I glanced at William Barren who now seemed to avoid my gaze at all cost. "It took dozens of our kind to stop that attack, and they've already taken so many lives."

I studied my mother's features, yet couldn't find even a trace of concern in her eyes.

When the Queen hadn't replied I continued, "Their goal during the attack was not to destroy the village, but to weaken our forces. It is just the beginning." I paused, swallowing the lump that grew bigger. "Wurdulacs' goal has always been to rule, it won't be long until they come to the palace."

I glanced at Sandra as my chest ached from the idea of her and the twins getting hurt.

"We protected the palace just fine the last time," Timothy scoffed, placing his hand onto Sandra's lap.

My breathing hilted; my stomach turned inside out. Timothy crooked his head, staring at me; a cruel smile spread across his face.

"With the help of our people," Roxanne spat out, glaring at Timothy.

His brows furrowed when Roxanne's words settled in before he looked at the council for confirmation.

"No matter how hard you try to ignore the fact, it is still a fact," Francis chimed in. "The only thing that stopped Wurdulacs last time was the army of vampires that fought alongside humans."

Sandra carefully moved Timothy's hand away when our eyes locked. Her lips trembled when she forced a small smile. I gripped onto my chair to stop myself from strangling Timothy right here, in front of everyone.

"Wurdulacs are coming here, Mother." I moved my gaze to her.

"Hm," the Queen leaned to the side, listening to Athena's whisper.

I fought back the urge to roll my eyes at such unnecessary theatrics. The meeting would already be over were we to have a normal conversation.

"We are proposing a temporary treaty that would allow us to work together against what we know will be another war." Francis leaned on the back of my chair as though he couldn't be bothered to partake in this nonsense of a meeting.

"And what makes you a trustworthy candidate to propose such an agreement?" Martin narrowed his eyes, his voice finally reminded me of the silhouette I caught Francis and Roxanne talking to all those months ago.

"I have my own people to protect," Francis shrugged. "And I will do so with or without your help." He addressed the Queen, "It is your choice to allow our companionship, but make no mistake, if we aren't bonded by an agreement I will not be bothered with any aid that might be needed on your side."

"What are you? The savior of savages?" Timothy laughed, noting Francis' hand on the back of my chair.

"We actually aren't interested in saving *you*," Roxanne's eyes shot fire at Timothy.

"Enough," the Queen raised her hand, silencing the room. "How do we know you will carry out your part of the deal?" She directed the question at me, ignoring my company altogether. "So far your kind has brought nothing but disarray into our lives, and need I remind you of your own slanderous actions given the royal mark on the letter?"

"Your Majesty," Roxanne leaned in on her chair. "We had been trying to bring this matter to your table for months, but your trusted council has denied us every single time." Her gaze swept over Martin. "Given the extremity of the situation we had to resort to rather desperate actions."

"Hm." My mother met my gaze once again. "Perhaps you were driven by desperation, or perhaps you are scheming for the Royal family to fall: as your kind often wishes."

The mask of indifference slipped from my face as I couldn't resist the urge to roll my eyes. "Mother, you needn't play in whatever *scheme* you think necessary. We both know we need each other to prevent people *and* innocent vampires from dying at the hands of those who killed Brian and Father."

Silence fell onto the room, even Timothy froze in place at my boldness.

Mother bestowed me with the glare I'd always tried to avoid at all cost.

I glared back.

"I would like a word with Cordelia," the Queen said at last, her eyes never left mine. "Privately." She gestured for everyone out, including her guards.

"Your Majesty—" One of the guards started.

"Now!" Mother's voice sliced through the room.

The council and the guards reluctantly departed with calculating stares addressed to me.

I nodded at my company when they hadn't moved at the Queen's demands.

Florence's worried eyes met mine before she shut the door behind her.

"You would like to talk openly?" Mother asked me though I knew the question did not require my reply. "Very well then." She got up from the table. "You are right, we do need each other to survive whatever is to come. But," she crooked her head. "The agreement will not come without a valuable exchange of trust."

"As Francis has already said—"

"You made a great mistake associating with those thieves," she interrupted me. When my brows frowned, unable to hide my surprise, she continued. "Yes, I know very well of them; it is my Kingdom, Cordelia, do not make the mistake of ever forgetting that." Mother walked towards the window, studying the frozen patterns of ice. "They will bring no more than disaster into your now immortal being," she choked on the last two words, meeting my gaze. "I did not raise a thief."

"You did not raise me at all, Mother." I leaned back on the chair. "Need I remind you, you only took interest in my life when it suited your future political proposals?"

Her features hardened, yet I spotted a trace of hurt in her eyes. It disappeared as fast as it came. "It does not change the fact that you are walking a dangerous path that will get you killed."

"Since when do you worry yourself with my survival?" My brows shot up. "Can we get back to the matter at hand?"

The Queen sighed. "I am ready to accept your proposition if you present to me an army of your own ready to defend my people. I will give you half of the supplies at the next full moon and the rest when you come to our aid when we need it. If you fail to arrive in our time of need, the deal will be considered void and the exchange of weaponry will cease."

I nodded. "I would like a written agreement."

"Obviously." She studied me for a moment before sighing. "I knew it was you, back in the study with the orphan boy," she shook her head so slightly.

"He is a grown man, Mother, not a boy." I bit out.

Mother eyed me for a moment before a sad smile made it onto her face. "I knew it was a mistake to let you leave, to let you steal the documents, though my foolish heart did not allow me the words. So I just let you go."

"Do you regret it now?"

"No," she shook her head. "I do not. Although there were better ways of doing this, daughter."

"I will write to you," I told Sandra when we hugged goodbye. The snow fell onto her pink cheeks and her long lashes. "I will find a way to keep you far from him," I added quietly.

Recognition filled her eyes when our mother ordered her to follow. "I love you, Lia," Sandra quickly whispered before rushing into the carriage after the Queen.

"Will you write to me?" Timothy appeared from my right, snatching my hand before I had time to move away. He squeezed it tight when I tried to break free, bringing it to his lips. "I will miss you."

As I was about to jerk my hand from his forceful grasp, a piece of parchment scratched against my palm. My body stilled, my lungs froze in place.

A sneer made its way onto Timothy's face when our gazes locked.

"Get away from her," Francis sidestepped in front of me, forcing himself in between us.

Timothy retreated, "I must follow etiquette, orphan boy." He glared at Francis yet a trace of fear shone brightly within his eyes. "Then again, I doubt you know anything about manners." He turned to mount his horse alongside the council.

I squeezed the paper in my fist; my heart banged against my chest, threatening to explode.

I drew a long breath when Timothy ordered his horse into motion.

The council followed his lead, ushering after the Royal carriage, leaving the four of us by the entrance of the lodge.

"Let's get out of here," Roxanne's hand wrapped around Florence's who'd been quiet the whole time.

"Are you all right?" I asked her, ignoring Francis' burning gaze on my back as we walked to our horses.

"I'm not one for meetings," Florence simply said, sighing. "Especially ones with humans."

Chapter 38
Lovely
Conversation

Meet me at the meadow behind the palace at dawn if you want your sister alive. We need to talk. Come alone.

I studied the parchment for the hundredth time since we got back to Francis' cabin. My fingers brushed over the letter; my heart banged, desperate to escape my chest as I sat upon the bed Francis peacefully slept in.

His sharp features were now soft, the smirk abandoned him as though it never belonged on his face at all. I grabbed my boots, quietly closing the door behind me and wondered how livid he would be when he would wake without me by his side.

But that would be a problem for tomorrow.

The cabin was silent as everyone had gone to rest early: I only had a few hours to make it back before the sun would burn my flesh into ash.

My trembling hands laced my boots in the tiny kitchenette, my heart finally escaped. *Will there even be tomorrow?*

Surely Timothy wasn't foolish enough to hurt me when I could easily end his life in an instant. *Is he?*

Would I truly be able to protect myself if it meant taking someone's life?

I reached out for the handle of the main door—

"Don't you think it's a little late for a run?" Francis' low voice swept through the darkness behind me.

My eyes closed as my grip on the handle tightened. *Damnation.*

"Cordelia," he whispered, taking a step towards me. "Whatever you are thinking—stop."

"I am not going anywhere," I shook my head as I faced him. "I just would like some air."

"Why, don't offend me by lying. I am no fool. I saw the paper he slipped into your hand." His voice dropped a few octaves as he reached for my shoulder.

Of course he'd seen it.

"What does he want?" Francis persisted.

My lips turned into a thin line as I stared into his eyes.

"Cordelia!" Francis hissed when I didn't reply. "What does he want?"

"To talk," I hissed back, jerking my shoulder from his grasp. "He just wants to talk." I reached for the door as Francis' hand blocked my path. "Let me go, Francis." I glared into his glowing eyes.

"Not a chance in hell," Francis scoffed. "You are not going anywhere where that man is involved. He should be grateful I did not slaughter him at the meeting."

"I have to!" I tried to push Francis out the way. "For Sandra's sake, I have to go."

"Are you out of your mind?" Francis caught my hands on his chest; his fingers wrapped around my wrists, holding them hostage. "These are the royal grounds, Cordelia. It's a trap, and you know it," he whispered. "Cease letting your heart rule you."

My hands turned into fists as I fought his firm grasp. "I am not a fool either, and I am not a child who needs protection!" I seethed through clenched teeth.

"I never said you were," Francis sighed, closing his eyes. "I know it's hard to think rationally when the ones we love are involved," he added softly. "At least let me help."

"He told me to come alone," I shook my head. "I can do this," my words were barely a whisper.

"Of course you can." A sad smile made its way onto Francis' face as he cupped my cheeks. "But I am coming with you." He reached for the dagger on the small stool in the corner.

"No! I must—"

"We either go together," Francis interrupted; his voice was as rough as briar. "Or I will chain you to myself until we leave, it is your choice."

"Francis!" Disbelief washed over me.

"Which one is it, Princess?" He crooked his head, studying me. "I will not intervene unless absolutely necessary," Francis promised. "You won't even remember I am there."

"I highly doubt that," I rolled my eyes.

"Well?" His eyebrows shot up.

"Fine!" I bit out. "We can go together if you promise not to intervene," I demanded, though no part of me believed he would act upon his promise.

"Splendid." A smirk spread across Francis' face as he pushed the door open. "Let's be on our way then."

The snow reflected the moonlight, crunching under our steps as we walked toward our horses.

"Where does the bastard want to meet you?" Francis asked me quietly, not letting go of my hand for even a moment.

"Outside of the Royal cemetery," I replied.

The snowflakes fell onto my eyelashes as my unresting heart beat a little slower.

"Odd location for talking, don't you think?" Francis mocked me. "Such a lovely conversation it must be."

"Enough!" I freed myself of his grasp, mounting Annabelle. "I understand you are angry, but you have no right to be cruel to me! Not right now."

"I am not angry with you, Cordelia." Francis reached for my hand, soothing the back of my palm as to reassure me of the sincerity of his words. "I am angry at the fact that you keep putting yourself in such danger."

I took a deep breath, meeting his eyes. Now was not the time to fight. "We should go," I sighed. "The sun will rise soon."

Dawn crept in when we reached the small meadow behind the cemetery. The forest slowly awoke; the early morning birds quieted around us as though not wishing to miss the disarray that was about to fall upon the meadow. Francis' hand fell onto the small of my back when we abandoned the safety of the dense spruce trees.

The man stood in the center of the clearing; a sneer spread across his face. "I see you brought your new lover with you, *Your Highness,*" Timothy's voice carried, a note of fear shone through his words despite how hard he tried to hide it. "I thought I was clear about coming alone, or you still can't follow the simplest directions?" He flashed his teeth. "Perhaps he can join us, I don't mind," Timothy shrugged, taking one step forward.

"What do you want?" I spat out, glaring into the eyes I once loved.

"How disrespectful..." Timothy shook his head. "I thought you were adamant we refer to each other by our proper titles," he tsked. "Or how does that work exactly?" His brows furrowed when he pointed at me. "Do you still carry your title? Or perhaps I am finally above you?"

"What in the hell do you want?" I raised my voice, my hands turned into fists.

Timothy's laugh spread through the forest when he said, "Never in twenty years have I thought I would hear you speak such language." A gruesome smile tugged on his lips. "Isn't it obvious?" He crooked his head. "I want the bite. I will exchange it for Sandra."

A chill swept through me from my sister's name on his lips.

"You see, your sister went mad after your *disappearance,*" Timothy scoffed. "Never thought I would say this, but fucking you was more plesant."

My stomach turned inside out as the unwelcome nausea made its way up my throat.

Francis' body tensed beside me before he took two furious steps toward the man. Grabbing him by his collar, Francis put a dagger against his neck. "I have a better idea," he said, smirking as he moved the dagger to Timothy's abdomen. "How about I turn you into an eunuch before I behead you?"

Timothy returned the smile as he unleashed a dagger of his own. "Are you even capable of it, orphan boy?" The blade reflected the shimmering white snow; the handle wore a Royal mark.

Royal steel.

My breathing hilted, depriving me of any logical thought. I had seen Francis behead two guards with one swing of his weapon, yet the fright squeezed my throat shut.

"Would you like to see?" Francis replied with a sweet smile on his face, cutting the first layer of Timothy's clothes.

Timothy returned the gesture, pressing his royal dagger against Francis' chest.

"Stop!" I yelled as my legs carried me towards the men.

"Do listen to your spoiled sweetheart," Timothy murmured.

In a blink of an eye Francis spun out of the threat, putting himself against Timothy's back; his fingers wrapped around the Royal dagger, knocking it from Timothy's grasp.

Fright settled in the man's eyes as he was shoved onto his knees. Timothy twisted in Francis' grasp, desperate to free himself from the vulnerable position, just when Francis got a hold of his hair.

"Beg for Cordelia's forgiveness." Francis jerked Timothy's head upward; the Royal blade now met the neck of a man for whom I wished nothing but a dreadful end.

"I—" Timothy's face cringed when Francis pushed on the blade. "I'm sorry," he mumbled through his trembling lips.

The blade pressed deeper into his skin, spilling a few drops of crimson onto Timothy's tunic—

"Don't," my voice, as sharp as the tip of the dagger, carried through the meadow as I took a step forward. "Release him," I ordered Francis without sparing him a glance; my menacing glare burned into Timothy's eyes.

The blade left his uncovered skin in an instant; short-lived relief sparkled in Timothy's eyes as he stumbled onto his feet.

"No other soul shall ever be harmed by you," my voice sliced through the air as my hands grasped onto Timothy's tunic, yanking him forward until my teeth met his flesh.

My teeth cut through the skin on his neck, cut through his veins. I locked my jaw shut as his satisfying bellow reached my ears.

My mind swam in the delightful sound of his agony; my throat welcomed the warmth of his blood despite the bitter taste that tingled my tongue.

I savored every drop that spilled into my mouth until his legs gave out, his limp body dropped on the ground.

The silent scream painted his face as his empty, lifeless eyes watched the first rays of sunlight appear from the horizon.

The blood still flowed from his neck, painting the snow around his dead body crimson.

I killed a man.

My paralyzed body dropped to my knees beside the body.

I killed a man.

My skirt absorbed the crimson snow.

I killed a man.

Francis' hands wrapped around my waist, pulling me into his arms. "It's all right. You're all right. It's over, Princess," his whisper broke through the wall in my mind.

I killed a man.

Francis wiped the blood from my lips with his thumb, gently stroking my cheek. "Although I am upset you deprived me of the ability to make his death slow and miserable, I am glad he will never take another breath."

"I killed a man."

"It's over." Francis held me against his chest in a tight embrace. I counted every beat of his heart, staring straight past him: at Timothy's dead body in a pool of blood.

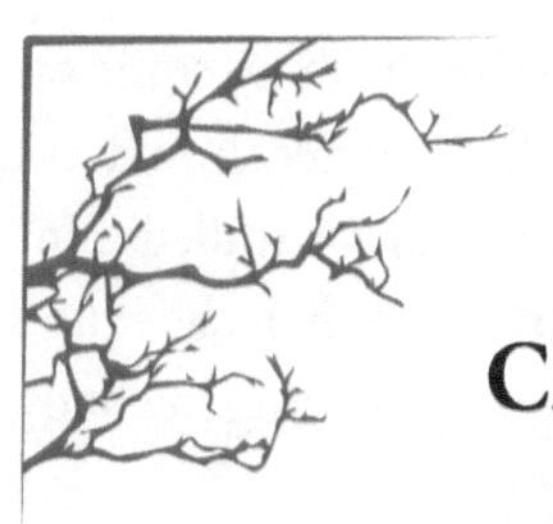

Chapter 39
Liar

Happiness.

Despite all of the troubles and danger that await-ed us, I felt happiness.

What a fragile state, that grew wings onto our backs. Wings that could disappear any moment, yet we still trusted them to carry us far, far away.

The scenario I feared most brought a forbidden relief to my aching heart. I had killed a man—a human being—yet all I had felt was happiness.

Sandra would never fear his touch again. I would never see his shadows in the dark corners of my room. He was gone and only Moon knew the fate of his soul—if he even had one.

"Aren't you handsome?" Florence chuckled when Silver rubbed himself against her leg.

She stood at the open door of my room, watching me arrange my hair for the ball.

We had barely any time to rest after our trip back home before the residents of Faris would have arrived at our doorsteps.

"Where did you find him?" Florence crouched, rubbing Silver's chin.

Her glorious gold dress matched the sunshine smile on her face; her divine curls graciously fell down her shoulders.

"I'm not sure I was the one to find him," I smiled, pinning up the front strands of hair off my face when the music reached us all the way from the ballroom, charging my body with a foreign excitement.

"Oh! I almost forgot!" Florence exclaimed, tracing the movement of my hands. "I have something for you." She smiled mischievously as she handed me a small pouch attached to her belt.

"For me?" My brows furrowed when I carefully pulled on the ribbon of the pouch, taking the mysterious item out.

A bronze brooch of a moth with dozens of dark green and brown beads sewed onto its wings.

"I thought you might like it," Florence shrugged.

"It's beautiful," I nodded; my fingers brushed over the tracery of the brooch.

"It was my sister's." Florence attached the brooch to my dress next to the emerald amulet on my chest. "I want you to have it."

"Are you certain?" I searched her eyes that shimmered from the candlelight.

"Absolutely," Florence smiled. "Ready?"

I took a long breath in. "Ready."

The music vibrated through my bones as I leaned on the wall in the corner of the glorious room that was now overflowing with dozens of candles and glasses of wine.

No matter the smiles on our guests' faces, the room was filled with gloominess: the events of the last month flowed overhead like a rainy cloud. The laughter felt forced, the dances less passionate.

Simon nodded once at me when our gazes met before he returned to his drink. Florence and Roxanne were nowhere to be seen.

Caleb was still missing.

"May I ask for a dance?" Francis stretched out his hand as he walked towards me.

"No bargaining tonight?" I frowned theatrically. "Why, Francis, are you ill?"

"I am afraid I have nothing else to offer." A small smile tugged on his lips, yet his eyes filled with a longing I had yet to witness him bear.

"Is everything all right?" I whispered.

"Please dance with me, Princess." Nothing of the playful, arrogant man I'd come to trust was left in his voice.

"All right," I nodded as my fingers brushed over his, accepting the request.

His hand gently fell around my waist; his fingers brushed along my skin as he spun us into a lazy dance. My eyelids closed in the embrace, letting the music sweep over me. As though an invisible strand pulled me closer to the man before me, I could never wish for our dance to end.

The music blurred into a frenzied resonance as my soul sung a song of her own: a song in a language I was yet to understand.

I cared not to think of my steps, leaving Francis as my only guide when the music seemed to stop completely. The ballroom blurred around us as I searched his hypnotizing eyes.

He did not smile as he bestowed me with the most heartbroken look I could not make sense of. He studied me as if I was a puzzle he'd been trying to solve for centuries. Admiring his features, I stared back.

"Walk with me?" Francis whispered into my ear before searching my eyes.

I nodded as he weaved his fingers through mine, guiding me away from the ballroom.

The muffled music stilled when Francis closed the door to his study behind us. An odd knot tightened around my heart as he stood before me: plea in his eyes.

"Could we talk?" Francis whispered.

"Is everything all right?" My hands fell onto his shoulders. "What is the matter?"

Francis nodded as his lips turned into a thin line. His eyes filled with regret.

"Francis?" My heart raced, skipping a few beats.

"I lied to you," he said slowly, as though each word pained him.

"Lied to me?" I repeated just as slowly, each word scratched my throat. "What about?" I slowly let go of his shoulders, forcing a small distance between us.

"Before I tell you, could you promise me you will listen to my explanation before coming to a conclusion?" he said quietly.

I nodded, though I was uncertain I could act upon such a promise. *Lied to me.*

"I—" he trailed off, exhaling. "When you were bitten—"

"No," I whispered, moving farther away from him. No, that couldn't be right.

"No! No!" Francis shook his head, taking a step toward me. "I wasn't the one who bit you. I swear to the Moon."

"What is it then?" My heart banged against my rib cage: ready to flee.

"I know who bit you, Cordelia," Francis told me carefully. "And that was the reason I brought you here." He took a deep breath before telling me the words that burned my heart like a sunray. "I brought you here in the hope to catch your creator, to catch the leader of the Wurdulacs."

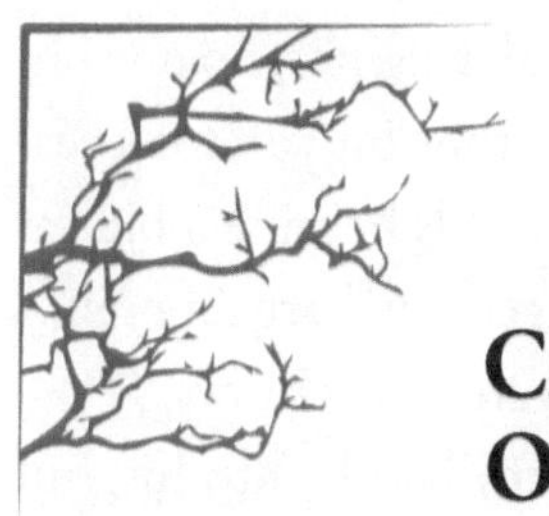

Chapter 40
Old Friend

Empty.

The world broke into pieces, leaving me for last. Standing in the middle of the disaster—right in the center of the hurricane—my mind was empty, my mind was silent: waiting for its last beat, for its last blow.

A small smile made its way onto my face, though my heart was in pieces. "You used me as bait," I said so calmly, I wasn't sure the voice belonged to me.

"Let me explain." He urged toward me. Suddenly the room felt ten times smaller. "You promised you would listen to my explanation."

"What is there to explain?" I shrugged. "I only have myself to blame. I was foolish enough to trust you, to think you truly cared. I thought—" my lips trembled. "Don't worry," I said at last, meeting his gaze. "You're not first to use me for your own gain."

"I do care for you, Cordelia!" Francis' voice broke. "I care for you. I truly do. I would never let anything harm you. I would never—"

Tears formed in my eyes. "It's all right," I whispered when my vision became a blur.

"No one would dare to turn a royal daughter, no one but a Wurdulac leader. Whoever they are, they bit you for a reason. I know it," Francis said, yet his words became a blur as well. "I thought they would come to get you, bargain even."

I closed my eyes, embracing the hurricane's blows.

"I would never—" Francis took my hands into his, but they were not strong enough to pull me out of the storm. "I would never let them take you, Cordelia," Francis said slowly. "I was going to kill the Wurdulac leader the moment he took a step toward you." He squeezed my hands. "When I created this plan, I didn't know you. I—" Francis swallowed hard. "I wasn't in love with you, Cordelia."

"Don't—" I whispered; a silent tear fell down my face after all. "You let me believe you, you let me kiss you," I said, smiling. "You let me trust you, knowing I was nothing more than a piece of your plan. Do not say you are in love with me."

"It's not like that, Cordelia." He let out a shaky breath. "I should have told you earlier, I know: I made a mistake. I tried to tell you, but—" Francis trailed off. "I could never find the courage to get the words out." His thumb wiped the tear off my face. "When I created this plan, all I cared about was to stop the Wurdulacs no matter the price. I am sorry."

You used me. I wanted to say, yet the hurricane had swallowed my voice. *You used me just like everyone else in my life.*

"Please say something." Francis' hands brushed over my face, and I could not even find it in me to move away. "Hit me, shout at me, say something, please!" he begged.

"You should have just asked me," I whispered. "I would have helped." I smiled at him through my tears, freeing myself from his embrace. "I need some air." I turned away, leaving the hurricane behind.

In the hallway I still heard the orchestra playing, yet could not enjoy the music. Streams of tears fell down my cheeks freely as my legs carried me away.

The main door entered my vision when the voices of two women froze me in place. Florence and Roxanne could not see me from this angle, engaged in their own conversation. My soul abandoned me when I walked toward the pair as the tears fell with new power.

"What happened this time?" Roxanne noticed me first. She crooked one brow at me as though my tears could never be worthy of her time.

"You knew," I bit out to Florence.

"Cordelia?" She stretched out her hand in an attempt to comfort me, yet I moved from her reach. "What's the matter?"

"You knew that he's been using me," my voice shook. "You all have."

"Cordelia..." She closed her eyes, shaking her head so slightly.

"I trusted you, Florence," I whispered. "I do not trust anyone, but I trusted you."

"Cordelia—" Her eyes turned into glass as she tried to take my hand into hers once again. "I am so very sorry."

I shook my head as I turned away from them, rushing through the main door.

Someone called after me when I slammed the door behind me.

The snow storm hit my face, forcing me to sober up. The cold froze my tears in place; the wind rushed down my skin in dozens of tiny cuts. Though I did not feel pain, I did not feel the cold as I walked out of the courtyard towards the woods, away from here.

The gloomy woods met me with outstretched hands, enveloping me in a tight hug. The sun would make its appearance soon, though I couldn't find it in me to care.

Despite my urge to leave this castle for good, I did not walk far. I had nowhere else to go, nor did I wish to actually leave despite my heart's painful wails. I just needed time. Perhaps an hour, perhaps a few. I needed time away from this disaster, from Roxanne, from Florence, from Francis.

I leaned on the giant oak just a mile away from the castle, staring at the lonely—like me—moon.

Of course I understood his motives; the hard decision Francis had to make, yet my heart refused me any logic. Now, away from everyone, I even understood Roxanne's annoyance towards my tears: there were bigger problems than my own. People were missing, Caleb was gone and we did not know where he was.

The war was knocking on our doors.

My own tears seemed foolish given the circumstance, but I could not rule my heart, therefore I had to deal with its storms. For it was my heart that whined so loudly in my chest; for it was my heart that broke into dozens of small snowflake-like pieces, making me feel all the pain and grief I wished to bury deep inside of me and never see again. For it was my heart that bled bright crimson.

A deprecating laugh escaped my lips. Of course he had used me.

Perhaps he was not even responsible for my pain, for it was my poor judgment that got me here. I'd been the one to allow any proximity between us, I'd been the one to be foolish enough to allow his charms to blind me, make me forget the true nature of life. I let the naivety speak for me: so desperate for affection I let my guards down.

I was to blame for it.

I didn't know you. I wasn't in love with you, Cordelia.

The wind blew at me, making my hair fly in every direction. I stared at the bright full moon, and asked her what to do now. The moon did not reply, hiding behind the cloud.

A raven flew past me, settling on the nearby branch it stretched out its wings. It let out a gurgling croak when its eyes met mine. I studied its feathers when the snow behind me crunched under someone's steps.

"I am not ready to talk," I said without even looking at my new company.

"Good thing I am not here to talk," the voice exclaimed, forcing my eye onto the owner.

"Caleb?" I yelped in disbelief. "Dear Gods, I thought I would never see you again." I walked towards him as a small smile covered my face. "We thought the Wurdulacs captured you."

Caleb smiled. "Who said they didn't?" He chuckled, hitting me across my face, making my world go black.

Chapter 41
Glass of Water

My lungs expanded taking in the mold and coldness of my surroundings. I counted every drop of water that hit the cold stone floor in a loud splash, trying to concentrate on anything but the pain that rang through my body.

As though church bells settled down in my head, the ringing did not stop, turning every noise into excruciating pain.

Nausea made its way up my throat, locking my jaw numb and I forced my body to turn to the side, emptying my stomach.

My heart raced, my lungs were desperate for fresh air, yet all I got was this cold, raw smell of dirt. I closed my eyes, laying back down on the cold stone, counting the water drops once again.

Will Francis notice my absence? Will he even care to search for me? Where am I?

Panic made its way through my mind, yet the pain shut it down immediately, refusing me the ability to think clearly.

I had to figure out where I was, I had to find my way out, I had to stay awake. "Awake," I mumbled, as my consciousness slowly left me.

I woke from the feeling of dozens of creatures crawling down my flesh. My hands flew toward my skin, brushing off the spiders that were making their way around my unconscious body. A nervous gasp escaped my lips.

The spiders rushed toward the tiny drain hole in the middle of the—where was I? My gaze fell down onto the metal bars that went from one wall to the other. Panic rushed through my veins, flashing into my mind. *My dear Gods.*

My eyes flew through the cell, trying to make any sense of my thoughts, until something shimmering caught my gaze. I made my way toward the bars; my hands grabbing the object.

"No," I gasped, dropping the hair pin as though it was hot metal. Sandra's hair pin. "No, no, no."

The sound of a creaking pair of heavy boots made its way toward me. I crawled away from the bars until my back hit the stone wall.

Unable to blink, I stared into the space behind the bars, waiting for whatever was coming next. A pair of brown eyes met mine.

A heavy silence fell upon us, depriving me of the ability to take a breath, as though the air was sucked out of the cell the moment Caleb made his presence known. He sighed, offering me a glass of clear liquid.

"What is this?" I heard my own voice, yet did not recognize it one bit.

"Water."

"Water?" I wanted to scream in disbelief. "Where am I?" I asked, already guessing the answer.

"Drink the water, Cordelia." His head fell as though he was ashamed of the offer.

"Where am I?" I demanded; my voice was as sharp as briar.

"Home."

I shook my head. "What have you done?"

Caleb sighed, "I am doing what is best for you. Please drink the water before you lose consciousness again."

My blood was on fire when I made my way toward the man. Grabbing the glass of water from his hands, I emptied it on his head.

My fingers toyed with the hair pin, studying its every curve. My heart whined and wailed, mourning my loss, yet the tears did not come. As though someone ripped my heart out of my chest, I stared at it in disgust, unable to feel its loud screams.

Perhaps she is alive. Perhaps the Royal family was notified of the attack and hid. Perhaps my siblings were safe. My mind tried to argue, yet my heart knew the gruesome fate I was unable to prevent.

My heart knew the gruesome fate awaiting me as well and I had already accepted it. I had accepted my coming end, and was grateful for such an outcome, for it would be my greatest punishment and my only salvation.

Perhaps an hour, perhaps a week had passed: I had no way of knowing. The cell did not have a window, not even a small crack to the outside world.

Whenever I woke there was a glass of water waiting for me on the floor by the bars. I poured the water out every single time.

Every single time except now.

I cared not if there was poison in the glass, I cared not if it was going to kill me. I emptied out the glass, satisfying my thirst. The thirst that had started to make me see the spiders crawling down my hands, yet when I tried to brush them off, my hands were met with nothingness.

The thirst that made me hear the orchestra playing loud and clear, yet I knew I was far from any life: deep down in the ground, in a Royal dungeon. It must have been at least a few nights I spent in the cell then.

Water satisfied my mind, yet it did nothing to the aching pain I felt in my throat. I needed blood.

My trembling hands stretched out toward the empty glass. My breathing quickened in anticipation. I hit the glass against the bars, breaking it into small pieces. The prickling in my throat hardened.

A broken piece of glass slid across my wrist, leaving a road of crimson behind it. My lips desperately covered my own flesh.

I sucked on the wound, yet the pain in my throat just increased. I drank and drank, but my own blood was no better than water.

"It won't work," the voice came from behind me, freezing me in place. "Although, I have to say, it was a clever idea."

I turned to look at my intruder. "What are you doing, Caleb?" I sent him an accusatory look. "What happened to my family?"

"I am just following my orders." He sat across from me. "From night one I was just following my orders. You don't understand it yet, Cordelia, but this is for your own good."

"What do you mean *from night one*?" I ignored his remark about how being locked in a cell was for my own good.

Caleb let out an exhausted sigh before replying, "I am your creator, Cordelia."

Chapter 42
For Your Own
Good

The blood from my long forgotten wound slid down my wrist, dripping down onto the floor with a loud splash. I moved away from the bars until my back hit the wall.

"Mories asked my father to turn you before we took the throne." Caleb's gaze bore into me.

"Where is my family?" I whispered. My mind traveled through every possibility of finding my way out, yet found none. The panic pierced my skin, making my lungs bleed in helplessness.

"My grandmother—my father's mother—Mories loves you like her own child, Cordelia." Caleb did not seem to care for my distress, continued his story. "She never wished you any harm," he added.

"I don't believe you," my voice broke. "She is not one of you!" I screamed. "She is kind!" My whole body shook, refusing to believe a word from this man's mouth. "She would never allow you to kill me! She would never allow you to kill innocent humans!"

"It is not for her to decide!" he screamed back, his eyes shooting fire.

I took a deep breath, choosing my words carefully. In a whisper I finally said, "Is she—she is—" I shook my head in disbelief.

"She is a human," Caleb finished my sentence for me.

"Then why..." My brows furrowed. "Why did you bring me here, Caleb? Where is my family?" I said as calmly as possible.

"I lied to you then." He sent me a sad smile. "In the training room when you asked about my family." Caleb sighed. "My mother never died, but she abandoned us at birth," he paused, searching my eyes. "She was young, sixteen years of age, when they had me. My mother's family did not approve of my father's social status, so after my birth they kicked him out: all by himself with a child in his arms to care for. They gifted him with a castle far away from here. The castle I call home." His gaze fell upon my bleeding wound. "My father was banished from returning." Caleb's voice became harsh, "After my mother married a *proper* man, she secretly gave my father a job as a smith." Caleb's jaw tensed. "My father accepted the offer, leaving me behind, with Mories to care for me."

"I do not care for your family, Caleb!" I interrupted him, despite my best attempts at not angering my capturer.

Caleb sent me a smile that covered my skin in goosebumps. "As you know, many royal marriages are arranged. Your parents were no exception. You see, your mother already had a suitor. They loved each other." I shook my head but Caleb continued, ignoring my reaction. "They kept it a secret from everyone, even your father. Until people started to talk about how two of the royal children did not look anything like the King."

"Stop!" I screamed, unable to hear anymore of his nonsense. "Stop it!"

"You have to know the truth, Cordelia," Caleb ignored my pleas. "Our mother had an affair with the smith. Our dead, useless King found out after seeing your—black as night—hair, but since he did not carry royal blood, he could not do much about it," he scowled. "Instead he began tormenting my father at every opportunity. He cut off my father's fingers for trying to recreate Royal steel, he ordered the guards to torture my father for months."

"Where is my family!" I shouted at him. "Tell me!"

"Right in front of you!" he yelled back at me, as though annoyed at my naivety. "You should worry about yourself right now, Cordelia." He grasped onto the bars until his knuckles were white.

"Where is my family?" I replied weakly.

"After the torture our father had to endure, our Queen finally gave him the order to leave and never come back for his own safety, leaving two of his children—you and Brian—to grow up without him." Caleb stared me straight in the eyes. "The King promised to raise you both as his own, if our mother promised to never see our father ever again. Father asked for one last favor from the Queen in return: to let Mories work here at the palace, to watch after her grandchildren," he said slowly, as though making sure I understood his words. "The Queen agreed. Our father left for good.

"After the torture Father barely survived, his health had failed him. He could barely stand on his own. I was thirteen when I had to take care of him all by myself. I thought he was going to die, part of me accepted it even, but Father was not ready to give up." Caleb's expression changed from sadness to pure rage. "He sought revenge for his troubles. He found a vampire that gifted him with a bite. *A medicine,* he told me." He let out a small laugh. "That is when he started planning revenge against the King, against all humans.

"He went mad." Caleb paused, as though waiting for me to say something; when he realized I wouldn't, he sighed. "Father wanted to kill the whole Royal family, his own children included, though Mories convinced him you—" he met my gaze, "you were nothing like them." Caleb laughed, shaking his head. "She told Father that you are like us. That's why he decided to spare you. To give you the bite," Caleb scoffed.

I swallowed a lump in my throat, waiting for Caleb's next words. He did not say anything for a long while, deep in his thoughts. I started to think he wasn't going to continue at all until he cleared his throat before speaking once again. "I was the one to bite you, for our father could not risk being seen on Royal grounds. I failed him and paid for my mistake." He looked at the scar across his hand. As though in a snowstorm, my heart froze in place. "You see, you were my first creation, Cordelia. I had never done it before, and quite frankly was terrified of the assignment," he scoffed. "I wasn't sure what to do: I panicked, and let you get away. I wanted to go after you, but I heard Francis nearby. I could not let him see me there. He would figure it out." Caleb paused before adding quietly, "He is like a brother to me. A brother I never got to meet."

My frozen heart suddenly set ablaze. Bitter words itched my tongue to let them free.

"All this time—" my voice shook. "All this time you stood by Francis who put his life at risk to save us from your father!" I shouted. "To save *you* from your father! And you, all this time—" I shook my head. "You destroyed the documents," I suddenly realized.

"You don't understand, Cordelia!" Caleb shouted. "*Our* father might be mad for starting this war, but he has the right to take what is his. The crown ruined everyone's life. It took everything from Father!" His words turned into a scream. "It took his only love, it took his children, it took his life!" Caleb's body visibly shook. "It is safer for us to be by his side; why don't you understand?" He got on his feet, leaning on the bars. For the first time, I was glad the bars were in place, for it was the only barrier from whatever madness Caleb wished upon me. "I saved your life by bringing you here!" He hit the bars. "You are lucky *our* father is giving you a chance to prove you are not like them! *Our* father chose to spare you, to keep you safe!" A tear fell down his cheek. "As long as you do as he wishes, you will never know trouble."

"Am I supposed to thank you?" I yelled. "You are a coward, Caleb." A sad smile spreads across my face. "You are a coward for choosing your own safety over doing what is right. You are weak," I spat out.

"You—" Caleb shouted, pointing at me. "You lived in luxury your whole life, ignoring those in need. Don't you dare call me a coward! You had everything, Cordelia, you never knew struggle. You had a mother." His shoulders jerked with rapid breaths. "I am merely being loyal to my family."

"Francis, Florence, and Roxanne are your family too," I said, shocked by my own calmness.

As though an inner battle was happening behind this shell of madness, a silent, helpless tear escaped Caleb's eye.

"Why did you save me from the Wurdulacs that night if you were just going to bring me to him anyway?" I asked him quietly.

He stared at me, as though seeing me for the first time, his face wrinkled in confliction. Perhaps he heard the sanity in my words, perhaps part of him wished to put this non-sense to an end. Part of me—deep down, behind all the anger and terror I felt toward the man before me—part of me felt sorry for him.

Nothing could justify the choice he had made, but who was I to talk about what was right. I understood. I under-stood the need to do what was asked of you, what went against all of your beliefs and wishes. The need to feel loved and needed by someone—anyone—even someone as evil as his father no matter the price. I understood.

Our gazes collided when Caleb finally broke the silence, "Our father will be here tomorrow at midnight. If you want to stay alive, do as he says." With that Caleb left the dungeon.

Sleep did not come, did not take me away from the horrors of this place. Francis did not come either.

"Let me out!" I roared into nothingness for hours after all of my efforts at breaking the bars had failed. "Let me out, you bastard!" I kicked the metal. "I will kill you with my bare hands! Do you hear me? I will fucking kill you!"

"I hear you, daughter." A low chuckle finally replied to my threats.

I traced the source of the voice and my eyes landed on Brian. I had gone mad.

"Daughter," an ugly smile spread across his face. "You have grown since the last time I saw you. Of course I do not expect you to call me Father, you may refer to me as Kane."

I glared at the man who stood a few feet away from me. His freshly trimmed beard could not hide his scarred face, shoulder length hair was tight in a low bun.

I blinked several times before realizing it was not Brian standing before me, though the similarities made me sick to my stomach.

"Sorry for such formalities," Kane gestured around the cage I was in. "You have my word that you will be free soon. We just have one last matter to attend to."

"Where are my siblings?" I spat out.

"The King's offspring are not your concern, daughter." He crooked his head, studying me.

"I am not your daughter," I seethed.

"You got your mother's tongue, but my hair," the man hummed. "Raven," he stretched out his hands towards my strands.

"Do not fucking touch me," I bit out, taking a step back.

"Raven is what I wished to name you, daughter, but your mother insisted it was not a Royal name." His lips curled.

"Interesting creatures they are, don't you think? So intelligent, so loyal, yet most dislike them for their cleverness."

My heart banged into my rib cage, my teeth ached for this man's neck. "Let me out!" My voice carried through the dungeon.

"Soon," the man nodded. "We must take care of an inconvenience first."

"What do you want from me?"

Laughter broke through the walls when Kane looked at me. "It's been brought to my attention you aren't what I expected you to be."

"What do you want from me!" I took a step forward.

"I see you inherited your patience from your mother as well. No doubt you would make a great Queen," Kane smiled. "A little test, if you will. Should you pass, I will personally ensure your safety, but you must first prove your worth to me, daughter." He narrowed his eyes on me. "Bring her in," Kane ordered the guards, taking a step back from the bars.

A golden haired woman was dragged into the dungeon and my heart stopped. I took a step back, wishing an unknown force would end me right here, right now.

Oh, how I wished Caleb had indeed poisoned my water, or perhaps the fire in my throat would have finally come into reality, taking my body with it, burning my flesh until nothing but ash was left of me.

How I wished a silver arrow was shot through my heart, stopping it forever.

How I wished I could take my own life to spare hers.

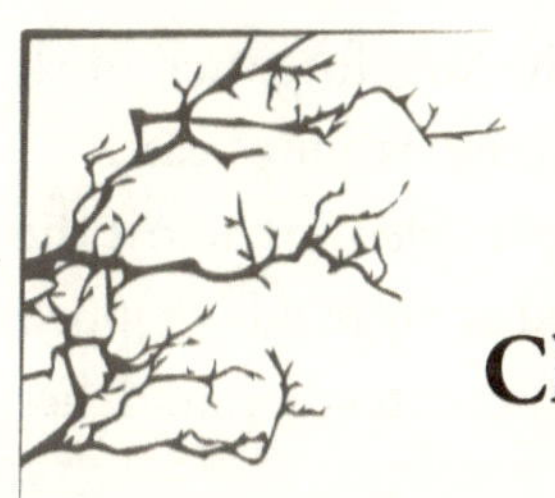

Chapter 43
A Gift

Sandra stood before me.

Her hands were locked in a tight rope in front of her. Her terrified gaze met my own.

Silent tears slid down my cheeks.

Through the fear that shone bright in her eyes, Sandra whispered, "I love you."

The bars of my cell slid open as my hands held onto the wall behind me, refusing to let go. I closed my eyes, willing my mind to wake up. I was asleep. This was just a nightmare.

Several heavy steps rushed out of the dungeon, leaving silence to take their place. I did not breathe, did not move—

A terrifying bellow echoed through the dungeon.

My eyes flew open, traveling down the traces of crimson on Sandra's wrists. Kane dropped the piece of crimson covered glass I had broken earlier as he walked out of the dungeon, leaving me and Sandra alone.

Crimson flowed down her fingers, dripping onto the stone floor. "It's all right, it's all right," she kept whispering as dozens of tears fell from her eyes.

Sandra collapsed onto her knees as the floor turned crimson in mere seconds. The crimson escaped her body in a strong wave.

Blood. My head spun drunk as the long forgotten smell burned my nostrils, daring me to feed the starving beast.

The world stopped when my legs carried me across the cell despite my pleas. The world ended as my hands wrapped around her wrists when my treasonous teeth found her wounds.

"It's all right," her voice vibrated through my mind, as a cry escaped my lips.

Stop! Stop!

Her blood traveled down my throat, easing the pain and fire. Her blood traveled down my throat, breaking my bones in half.

Stop!

My muscles didn't obey me, my jaw was locked on her wrist, despite the screams, despite the pleas. A roar escaped me, yet it did not scare away the beast that willed me.

Let go! My hands squeezed even tighter. I fell down on my knees, drying her empty.

Stop!

Every drop of her blood erased any clear thoughts, every cry that escaped my lips made my heart beat slower.

"Cordelia!" A scream broke through the walls of my mind. "Stop!" Someone's strong hands dragged me off of my sister.

"Cordelia!" Caleb's hand struck across my face, bringing me back to reality.

My foggy vision cleared. "Sandra?" I dropped onto the stone floor before my sister who kneeled in a pool of blood.

"It's all right," she nodded.

"Help her!" I screamed at Caleb as he ripped the ends of his tunic, tying them around Sandra's wrists. "Help her!"

The blood painted the white tunic in mere seconds as I held her wrists willing the blood to stop escaping.

"It's all right," Sandra shook her head. "It's a gift."

"Sandra—"

"It is not your fault." She smiled through the tears. "I do not wish to stay here without Frederick and Eleanor. This is a gift." She gasped.

"She is dying!" I screamed to Caleb who now stared at Sandra in horror. "Help her!"

Sandra's eyes fluttered. "I love you," Sandra's pale lips trembled. "Goodbye, Lia."

"Sandra!" A scream ripped through my throat. "Sandra!"

My trembling hands felt her pulse. A weak heartbeat reached my fingers. "Help her!" I screamed at Caleb, yet my eyes did not leave my sister. "Help her! Her heart is still beating, help her!"

"Cordelia," his voice was barely a whisper.

"Just help her, please." A choked sob left my lips. "I will do whatever you want. Anything."

"Cordelia, I can't," Caleb shook his head so slightly. His eyes slowly closed.

"Help her, you bastard!" I shouted. "Do it!"

"She is human. There is nothing I can do."

"Then turn her!" I hit his chest. "Tell me how to turn her!"

"It won't work, her body is too weak," he shook his head. "She won't survive it," Caleb whispered, looking me straight in the eyes. "I am sorry."

Sorry? No! No, no, no! I brought Sandra's wrist to my lips. It's just a bite, just a bite.

A bite should be presented as a gift: nothing should be taken in return.

My teeth pierced her flesh, careful not to let a drop of blood spill into my mouth.

I put my ear to her chest.

There was no movement, no sign of life.

I heard my heart beating in my ears, I heard the sound of water dripping down on the stone. Yet the sound I longed for most did not make an appearance. Silence.

"I love you, Sandra," I whispered as my tears fell onto her smooth skin. "I love you."

I'd killed my little sister. My sister who had always been by my side. The only person I'd truly loved in this life.

"I am sorry," Caleb's hand touched my shoulder as he whispered.

"How dare you!" I shoved his hand away. "How dare you say that to me!" I hit his chest. "Burn in hell! I hope you burn in hell!"

Caleb staggered backward as I kept hitting his chest.

"I wish you burn in hell." I met his eyes. "I wish you burn in hell for eternity."

I dropped to my knees as a scream tore my throat; my lungs burned.

I held my sister close to my chest, brushing her hair with my palm. "I am sorry," I whispered. Her golden strands were now red, her full pink lips were now pale. Her empty green eyes stared into nothingness behind me. "I am so sorry."

Several steps rushed into the room as my hands tightened around Sandra's shoulders. I could not let them take her from me. I would not let them separate us.

"Cordelia?" A familiar voice broke through the walls in my mind. The voice sounded so real, so close. "Cordelia."

I shook my head, not letting go of Sandra's body in my arms. "Don't take her," I whispered. "Please don't take her."

"Oh, dear Gods," another familiar voice joined in. Florence.

"Please don't take her," I pleaded.

"Francis, the guards are coming this way, we have to hurry," Roxanne said.

"We must go." Two pairs of hands pulled me from Sandra. "I'm so sorry."

My vision blurred when Roxanne and Florence dragged me out of the dungeon. "No!"

"Get her out of here," Caleb instructed. "There is a passage in the back, get away as far as possible." He handed Francis his sword, "You know what you need to do, brother."

Francis took the sword from Caleb's hands, squeezing the handle. "Don't ever call me that again," he said, putting the sword straight through Caleb's stomach. "If I see you near her again, the blade will be royal steel."

Chapter 44
Goodbye, Lia

My eyes fluttered open when her excruciating scream forced my mind to wake. Pushing the sheets aside, I rushed to the bathing chamber in my room as my stomach emptied itself out.

Tears escaped my eyes, burning my cheeks as I washed my face with cold water. My lungs exploded with every breath I took, though it might have been my heart.

Sandra's screams never quieted, her blood never washed off my hands.

I stared at my reflection, not recognizing the person I saw and yet recognized her all too well.

I'd killed my sister.

Kane had killed my little Frederick and Eleanor.

I stared at my reflection and swore to the Moon that I will find every being responsible.

And I shall kill them one by one.

Acknowledgments

Wow. I never thought I would be writing acknowledgments, but here we are.

First and foremost, I want to thank every single one of you who made it this far. This means so much to me, and I still can't wrap my head around the fact that someone did indeed read my madness. I hope you enjoyed reading it as much as I enjoyed writing it!

Thank you to my partner in crime (and life), Bradley, who has been by my side throughout this journey! Thank you for listening to my daily yaps about my characters and brainstorming different ideas with me! And thank you for spending a whole month of your life helping me edit the disaster this book was when "Cordelia started the music."

Thank you to you, Lennon, for being the best friend possible. I will never be able to express how grateful I am to have you in my life! Thank you for adding all the missing commas and leaving me the funniest comments ever!

Thank you to my editor, Ambria, for helping me to bring my dream to life and catching every time I misspelled the word 'hoarse'!

Thank you to my cat, Silver, for graciously allowing me to use your persona in my book! I wouldn't be able to finish this book if it wasn't for your constant help in terms of laying on my keyboard.

And lastly, thank you to everyone who didn't believe in me! Every time I doubted myself it was your words that pushed me to keep going.

About the Author

Arya was born in the middle of a horrific snowstorm on a dark, gloomy night in Siberia; scientists claim it was merely a coincidence, yet there hasn't been another snowstorm of that scale, in her hometown, since she moved to the States.

Her whole life Arya used writing to process and express her feelings in the form of poetry and short stories. She's had a passion for literature ever since she was young; there was nothing she dreamed of more than becoming an author one day.

Even after completing a degree in Mathematics, Arya couldn't help but to return to her peculiar worlds.

When not writing, Arya spends most of her time figure skating, reading spooky books, and collecting dry flowers!

Learn more on:
Instagram @aryasloaneauthor
TikTok @aryasloaneauthor

9 798218 558666